Finding Faith

Seduced in Scotland
Book 2

Matilda Madison

I0778720

Dragonblade Publishing, Inc. is an imprint of Kathryn Le Veque Novels, Inc.
P.O. Box 23
Moreno Valley, CA 92556
ceo@dragonbladepublishing.com

Produced in the United States of America

First Edition April 2025
Trade Paperback Edition

ARE YOU SIGNED UP FOR DRAGONBLADE'S BLOG?

You'll get the latest news and information on exclusive giveaways, exclusive excerpts, coming releases, sales, free books, cover reveals and more.

Check out our complete list of authors, too!

No spam, no junk. That's a promise!

Sign Up Here

www.dragonbladepublishing.com

Dearest Reader;

Thank you for your support of a small press. At Dragonblade Publishing, we strive to bring you the highest quality Historical Romance from some of the best authors in the business. Without your support, there is no 'us', so we sincerely hope you adore these stories and find some new favorite authors along the way.

Happy Reading!

CEO, Dragonblade Publishing

Additional Dragonblade books by
Author Matilda Madison

Seduced in Scotland Series
Hope in the Highlands (Book 1)
Finding Faith (Book 2)

Gambling Peers Series
A Duke Makes a Deal (Book 1)
The Baron Takes a Bet (Book 2)
The Earl Breaks Even (Book 3)

Chapter One

Dearest Faith,

I am writing to inform you that the painting, Odalisque Reclined, has been sold to a private collector. I am aware of the promise I made to you, but the stipend was too grand to ignore, especially if I'm to ever live beyond my commissions. Please accept my apologies and this monetary gift, as I believe it is what you are due.

I hope you will forgive me.

Sincerely,

Donovan

Faith Sharpe stared at the letter in her hand, mouth agape, as a tremor went through her. This could not be happening. It was a jest, surely. A poorly conceived joke of some sort. Donovan had promised never to sell that particular piece, and she had believed him. He had sworn that it would only ever be used to illustrate his talent to prospective clients and that he would keep it in his possession forever. *Cherish it for a lifetime.* Those were the exact words he had used.

He couldn't have sold it.

Faith crushed the letter in her fist and brought it to her pursed lips without thinking. This was, without a doubt, the worst thing that could ever happen to her. Particularly during breakfast.

"Faith?"

Looking up, she quickly remembered that she wasn't alone. She was, in fact, completely surrounded by her family. Her elder sister, Hope, sat across the dining room table, her brow pinched together with concern. Faith dropped her hand to the edge of the timeworn wooden table. Everything in Lismore Hall was timeworn. It had been the generational home of the MacKinnon family for hundreds of years. That is, until Aunt Belle won it in a card game.

"Yes?" Faith croaked.

"Are you all right?"

Three other pairs of eyes landed on Faith. Her younger sister, Grace, their great-aunt, Lady Belle Smyth, and Hope's husband, Graham MacKinnon, all stared at Faith with curiosity.

"Your cheeks are rather pale," Grace said with a slight frown. "Has something happened?"

For a moment, Faith didn't know how to answer. Of course she wasn't all right, but she wasn't about to admit it. She had always been a very private person, and she had never told anyone about the painting. Especially not her sisters.

Glancing around the table ladened with apple-and-honey tarts, sausages, puddings, and jams, she wondered what she could say that would distract everyone. Her brother-in-law shared the same concerned look as her sisters, but Aunt Belle gaze appeared keenly interested in the letter she was holding.

She could not tell them the truth. As much as she loved her family, Faith was not the kind of woman to reveal such personal things, even to those who were closest to her. Nor was she the type to panic. And even if she were, she certainly wouldn't do so in a room full of people.

She needed to leave immediately.

Swallowing, she dropped her hand into her lap.

"Nothing has happened. I am quite well," she lied as she stood up. "May I be excused?"

"My dear, what news have you received?" her aunt asked. Belle's bejeweled hand rose and pointed to Faith's fist. "Who has written you?"

Faith quickly tucked the crumpled letter into the folds of her canary-colored skirt.

"Ah, well, it's from…" Faith stalled before spitting out the first name that came to mind. "Renee. It's a letter from Renee Delaney."

"Renee?" Grace repeated, her frown deepening. "Didn't you just receive a letter from her yesterday?"

"Yes, I did, but this one is about a different matter," Faith said quickly. "Renee's brother is engaged." A servant came up to push her chair in as she moved around it. "Evidently, the wedding is to take place this July."

"Oh no," Hope said, going to stand as well. "I'm so sorry, Faith. Are you sure you are all right?"

Guilt washed over Faith, hearing the concern in Hope's voice. It wasn't a lie, technically. Faith *had* learned that her former beau had proposed to Miss Molly Sheffield in yesterday's letter, but she perhaps being a tiny bit manipulative when she framed it as the reason she was upset. She knew that her sisters still believed her to be infatuated with Mr. Delaney, but the truth was that at present, she couldn't care less about him. Still, it was an acceptable excuse to try and be alone. Otherwise, she'd have to explain why there was a very large, very revealing painting of her being shipped to a private collector.

Heaven above, let it be on a ship to Australia.

Swallowing her embarrassment, she shook her head.

"I'm quite all right," Faith said with a nod. "I just wish to be excused."

"Shall I go with you?" Grace asked, coming to stand, but Faith held out her hand to stay her.

"No. No, I would just like a bit of time. Please," Faith said, noting the pity in the collective faces that stared at her.

"Of course, dear," Belle said, nodding as she looked around the company. "Take all the time you need. We shan't bother you."

"Thank you."

Turning on her heel, Faith exited the ancient dining room, her leather boots clicking loudly against the flagstone floor of Lismore Hall. She couldn't bear the idea of being cornered by one or both of her sisters who would try and force her into talking about things she could not speak of. She needed to escape, to leave the hall for a bit to sort all this out.

Oh, why had she ever posed for that painting?

As a footman opened the front door for her, Faith nodded her thanks and hurried down the stone steps. She, of course, knew the answer to her question. She had fancied herself in love with Donovan and would have done anything to please him.

The long-forgotten humiliation of their relationship resurfaced in her mind. The memories of all their encounters spilled over her as she headed for the forest path that lay to the west of Lismore Hall. Donovan had always been so warm and kind, yet he'd held her at arm's length always, insisting that anticipation of their love would shine through his work. Faith had believed him. She had believed Donovan to be a worldly, poetic soul whose talent far surpassed that of anyone Faith had ever met, and though he'd never so much as kissed her, she had believed that they had shared a genuine and honest love.

Faith had trusted him completely. She had been nervous when he asked to paint her, but had consented when he'd promised never to sell it, explaining that he only wanted a piece of her that he could keep forever. Faith had thought the entire thing terribly romantic. Yet their brief time together, while exceptional, had amounted to little. And when it had ended—abruptly and with no notice—Faith had been left shamed and brokenhearted, while Donovan had packed up his entire life in London and snuck away to Paris.

A gentle thunder rumbled overhead, and Faith's gaze rose to the sky. It was overcast, and the faint gray hue promised rain. *Fitting*, she thought as her feet left the crushed stone drive that veered off onto a wooden path around the walled garden.

She tucked her hands into the pockets of her gown, only to feel the envelope stuffed full of banknotes that Donovan had sent with his letter. A heartless gesture, even though she supposed it was his way of apologizing. For a poor painter to part from any money was at least some sort of sign—

No! No. She wouldn't make excuses for him. It had been difficult enough suffering in silence for months after his unannounced departure. She had barely begun to recover from her heartbreak before she and her sisters had become embroiled in the scandal that had brought them to Scotland last year. Now, twelve months later, her life was completely different from what she had always expected it would be like, but even so, Faith had always slept soundly, believing that Donovan wouldn't break his promise.

She kicked a stone on the path before her. What a fool she had been to trust him and all his flowery, pretty words. He had said that she was the loveliest creature he had ever seen, and what a shame it would be to hide such beauty from the rest of the world.

Vanity, thy name is Faith.

Perhaps she could write him and ask who had purchased the painting? Or ask Aunt Belle for a loan to try and repurchase it? But no. No, she wouldn't be able to bear to tell anyone how stupid she had been. She could threaten legal action perhaps, but then she'd have to confess to things she would never willingly admit to—and anyway, she didn't know any solicitors.

Faith kicked the stone again as she walked between the tall pines, the scents of heather and impending rain in the air. It was useless. Even if she could find the new owner of her painting, she wouldn't ever have the funds to buy it. And beyond that, she wouldn't have the backbone to meet the owner, knowing they would probably instantly recognize her as the model in the portrait.

She sighed, concluding that she simply had to pray that she wouldn't see recognition in the eyes of every new person she met.

Oh, good Lord, it was going to be a long life.

A cool breeze blew across the grassy meadow that opened up beyond the scope of pines, shaking her from her internal suffering. Faith looked up and caught sight of Loch Fyne stretched out beneath the rolling mountains of the Highlands. Grace had come to this spot weekly to gather bog myrtle and tormentil, medicinal herbs that Dr. Barkley paid her to collect. Gazing across the choppy water, she tilted her head back as her eyes lifted. Rough rock sheared through the green ground further up the slope, and she was briefly taken away from her misery as she stared in awe at the harsh yet stunning landscape.

At least she would never run into that horrible painting out here in the wilds of Scotland.

"Blasted hell!" a man's voice suddenly called out, startling her.

Faith glanced around but saw no one. Her brow pinched together as a smattering of curses continued to echo around her. She knew that voice, was certain she had heard it plenty of times before, but she couldn't quite place it.

Peering down by the loch's edge where a large, partially flat boulder the size of four men stood, she heard a scuffle of what sounded like a stick hitting the ground. Picking up her yellow skirt, she moved a few paces to the left to peer around the rock, only to frown at who she saw.

Logan Harris stood on the bank of the loch, apparently beating the ground with a long stick. A tall, blackish-gray dog sat near his feet, short, stumpy tail wagging in the dirt as he watched his master.

Instantly displeased, Faith sent up a silent curse herself. Was this to be a day with uncomfortable shocks at every turn? Logan Harris was one of her least favorite people, as he had made her and her sisters' arrival in the Highlands anything but pleasant. Not only was he unbearably rude, but Faith had never met someone so argumentative in her entire life. And if he wasn't arguing with her, he ignored her, which only added to her dislike of him.

Unfortunately, Logan Harris was Graham McKinnon's oldest and dearest friend, and he was a frequent guest at Lismore Hall, though Faith had done her best to avoid him during his visits.

She watched him for another moment as he fought with what looked like a fishing rod and a wicker basket slung around his chest. She smirked, enjoying the sight of this usually self-possessed man letting his frustration get the better of him. She was convinced that she was witnessing all she needed to know about him at that moment. He often demonstrated a calm, cool, and collected exterior to everyone, but Faith knew he had a simmering temper bubbling just below the surface. This simply proved it.

Having seen enough, she was about to turn back, hoping to avoid him altogether without her presence being discovered, when he suddenly stopped flailing about and stilled, causing her to pause.

His chest expanded and contracted quickly, almost unnaturally. Even from a distance, Faith could see his eyes were shut tightly, and his mouth was closed, his entire face pained. Was he ill? His hair, which wasn't dark enough to be considered brown nor light enough to be called blond, was tousled by the wind as his tall form seemed to rattle with ragged breath.

Tilting her head with curiosity, Faith watched, waiting for him to settle. It was clear he was trying to calm himself down from whatever annoyance he had been struggling with, but the longer she watched him, the more his face scrunched up, almost as if he was fighting some internal battle.

A small part of her worried that he might be seriously ill or hurt. While Faith wasn't particularly interested in Mr. Harris's well-being, a small, decent part of her told her that if a person were in distress, she should try to help him. By the look on his face, she could see that he wasn't doing well, and as much as it grated her to consider helping him, something propelled her forward.

Faith took a step forward without looking down and stepped on a stick.

SNAP!

The massive, blackish-gray dog turned his head instantly. *Shoot.*

Now it would undoubtedly appear as though she had been spying on him. Sure enough, when she glanced back up, Logan stared in her direction as the large animal began sauntering toward her, growling with its teeth bared.

Dread splinted within Faith's chest. She didn't like big dogs. She'd had the misfortune of being bitten by a neighbor's dog in her youth and had tried to avoid them ever since. She strained to recall what Grace had told her about dogs. They could sense fear, supposedly, and responded aggressively if they felt you were closing in on them. If she remained still, she should be fine.

Squaring her shoulders, she spoke loudly.

"M-Mr. Harris," she called out. "Please restrain your animal. I've no wish to be mauled this morning."

For a moment, she worried that he might not have heard her, for the dog continued to amble toward her in a predatory way. Surely he wouldn't let the dog attack, would he?

"Heel, Jaco," he said after a moment, and the dog instantly sat, though he kept his eyes on Faith.

Faith took a bracing breath and walked straight ahead, though she kept a fair distance between herself and the animal. Coming to a stop only a few feet away from the water's edge, she nodded politely, noting that his breathing had returned to normal. Since he clearly did not need assistance, she saw no reason to mention his earlier state.

"I'm sorry to have interrupted your fishing expedition," she said. "May I ask what you are doing on this side of the loch?"

"No, you may not," he said stiffly as he stared back at her, his hazel eyes locked on her face.

She glared at him. What an awful man, indeed.

Well, that's what she got for trying to be neighborly. Her mouth set in a hard line as she gazed into his oval-shaped face. His straight, thick eyebrows were darker than the rest of his hair, making it easy to spot even from a distance when his perpetual scowl deepened. Faith had often noted that his evenly proportioned mouth was usually pointed down when they met, as if he couldn't help but frown whenever he saw her.

He was attractive in a classical way, which made Faith's dislike for him all the more potent. If he had been ugly or scarred, she might have forgiven his poor manners and ill temper, but to be handsome in the most apparent way left little charity in her opinion of him. Still, she had to remind herself she wasn't attracted to the discourteous Scotsman.

"Very well then," she said as she gathered her skirts to move around him. She would continue her walk north around the eastern shore of the loch and wait somewhere until he left before making her way back home. "If you'll excuse me."

"What are you doing out here so early? And alone?" he asked, causing her to stop.

"It's no concern of yours," she said, giving him a taste of his own medicine.

He took a step toward her.

"A lady, however imprudent," he said, "shouldn't be walking around alone at this hour of the day."

"Why? Will one of your kelpies steal me away?" she asked sarcastically, referring to the local legend. Though her sisters had found the locals' folk stories charming, Faith did not. "Keep your fairytales to yourself, Mr. Harris. I have a practical mind."

"And yet you wear no overcoat or wrap during a storm."

"What storm?"

As if by divine intervention, the skies above opened up as a torrential downpour opened over them. The self-satisfied smirk on the man's face made her want to stomp her foot, but instead, she stuck out her chin.

"A light drizzle will not deter me," she said as a crack of

thunder sounded in the distance.

Amusement flashed in his eyes, and Faith had to fight off the irrational bemusement she felt as he gazed at her.

"Come," he said, walking toward her. "I'll see you back to Lismore."

"No," she said, holding her hand up, stopping him. "I do not need an escort."

"It's raining."

"Yes, I'm aware." She stood on her tippy toes to look around one of his large shoulders. "And considering you've a very long boat ride home, I would think you'd like to start on your own way back to your side of the loch."

Logan glanced over his shoulder before looking back at her.

"Graham would not like it if I saw you out here in this weather and didn't see you safely home."

"My brother-in-law need not know we even met."

"*I* would know."

"Then do your best to forget it," she quipped, turning around.

Faith took a step, unaware of how slick the rocks on this portion of the shore could be particularly in the rain. Her foot slipped off the moss-covered rock. Bracing herself by bringing her hands up, she was holding her breath, waiting to see if her balance would hold, when a sudden strong arm wrapped around her chest, hoisting her backward.

Spooked by the sudden grab, Faith spun herself around in his arms and pushed at Logan's chest, throwing him off balance as they both fell into the shallow waters of the loch.

SPLASH!

The dog, Jaco, began barking and leaping from side to side on the shore.

"Augh!" Logan bellowed as he tried to push Faith up. "What the bloody hell do you think you're doing?"

"Me?" she said as the icy waters soaked into her gown. "You're the one who grabbed me!"

"To stop you from falling!" he snapped, turning to the dog. "Jaco, stop."

The dog instantly stopped barking.

"Well, how was I supposed to know that?" Faith asked, her hands clawing at his chest as she tried to stabilize herself.

"Because I'd sooner marry an eel then try anything with you."

"Believe me, an eel would be a welcomed companion if I could trade him for you," Faith said as she struggled to stand.

Logan got to his feet, hauling her out of the water within seconds. Faith began to shake. Spring weather in the Highlands was unpredictable, and the waters this far north were still frigid. Logan held her close to his chest, and Faith could feel a heat emanating from him even though he was soaked. She looked up and stared into his face.

His nose was large and straight, and to her surprise, she saw several flecks of peculiarly white skin on the underside of his chin, almost as if he had been burned. She frowned. What had caused that?

As her breathing steadied, her eyes lifted to his mouth, where his bottom lip hung slightly open. Further up, her eyes met his and she saw an intensity in his glare that she had never witnessed before. She shivered then, which seemed to knock him out of a trance. He pulled her roughly toward the shore.

"You'll catch your death," Logan said gruffly. "Come on, get your feet out of the water."

He tried to help her by holding her hand, but she snatched it out of his grip.

"I can fare just fine without you."

He glowered at her, his gaze dark.

"Fine then, go."

Holding her chin up, Faith tried her best to walk out of the water without tripping. Unfortunately, the rocks in the water were just as dangerous as those on the shore. She would have toppled over again, except that Logan's hands landed on her waist, steadying her from behind.

Though it irritated her greatly, she allowed him to steer her out of the water, stomping away from him once she was beyond the rocks. Jaco approached her, sniffing at her water-logged skirts as she backed away from him.

"Stop that. Shoo. Go away."

"Jaco, sit," Logan said in a firm voice, and the dog sat. Logan turned to Faith, his hazel eyes shining with some sort of bemusement. "What is it? You don't like dogs?"

"I don't like big dogs," she corrected him, eyeing the animal. "Particularly ones who look like they bite."

"Jaco doesn't bite."

"Then why did he bare his teeth at me before?"

"He probably thought you were someone dangerous," he said before adding, "and as he's a poor judge of character, he doesn't find you all that threatening."

She narrowed her eyes at him.

"It's a wonder he remains your pet then, considering your character."

Faith had once overheard Logan and Graham discussing a plot to marry her sister Hope so that Graham could regain ownership of Lismore Hall. It had been a wicked plan and though everything eventually worked out in the end, and she knew that Graham truly loved Hope for herself and not merely her inheritance, Faith had never quite forgiven Logan for his involvement.

It seemed he hadn't forgotten either.

"I will not apologize for trying to help Graham," he said. "And from what I understand, you've forgiven him for it."

"Yes, because he is family now. But that doesn't negate your involvement."

"I was merely supporting a friend. Besides, they are happily married now, are they not?"

"Only because they fell in love," Faith said, before adding under her breath, "impractical as that is."

"Indeed."

Her gaze met his and she cocked her head.

"See? We can agree on at least one thing, Mr. Harris. Now, if you'll excuse me, I need to return to Lismore Hall. I can't carry on in these wet clothes."

"I will escort you—"

"No. No, I think I've suffered enough of your company for one day."

To her surprise, he let out a snicker as she turned away to trudge back the way she'd come. The rain began to come down even harder. If she hadn't already been drenched, Faith would have guessed that the walk home would have been enough to soak her. When she finally reached the garden wall of Lismore, she glanced over her shoulder to see that Logan hadn't followed her. But Jaco had. The dog paused upon seeing her stop.

"Go away. Shoo." But he didn't move. She let out a breath. "Foolish dog. Jaco. Go."

The dog's ears perked up at his name, and at the command, he turned, trotting off down the path that he had followed her down.

What a terrible day, indeed.

Chapter Two

L OGAN LEANED AGAINST a large boulder as he began to shiver from the cold. His eyes focused on the path that led to Lismore, waiting for Jaco to return. The dog had followed Faith back, and he was once again grateful for having been talked into getting the dog by his sister, Arabella, last fall. Jaco was some sort of German/Scottish mutt of no great pedigree, but he was exceedingly intelligent, not to mention useful—particularly in this circumstance, as Logan himself didn't want to accompany Faith back home, but he couldn't let her go alone.

It wasn't because he didn't like her—although it was very true that he didn't. Faith Sharpe was one of the most annoying women he had ever had the displeasure of knowing. She was constantly giving her opinion when no one asked for it, and when, rather than upbraiding her as she deserved, he would ignore her, the end result was to be seethed at by her for any number of hours. She was prickly and haughty, as any granddaughter of an earl would be. Not to mention that she was beautiful, and it grated Logan's nerves that he found her so attractive.

But having held her, wet and shivering in his arms, just moments after experiencing the beginning of one of his episodes, his emotions were a bit jumbled. Logan shifted his weight against the boulder, wondering why he felt so out of sorts.

Ever since returning home from the Second Burmese War, he had suffered bouts of crippling anxiety. It would manifest after becoming frustrated, which was why he had been prompted to take up fishing in the first place. Except that the sport only seemed to cause him more grief, particularly on mornings such as this one when his mood was already low from another restless night.

Sleep had long since evaded Logan. When the sun went down, his nerves would fire, and he would become more awake than he was during the day. It didn't help that he lived with his father and sister, who were aware of his midnight wanderings. They always tried to soothe him with suggestions and new crackpot ideas on how to sleep when what he really needed was to be left alone. His sister had even suggested sleeping with certain gemstones beneath his pillow, to supposedly sooth away his insomnia.

Which was ridiculous, to say the least.

It was why Logan had left Harris House so early. Pretending that fishing brought him joy and required an ungodly number of hours gave him some distance from his family. So, every morning, he would leave before the sun rose, head down to the loch just over the hill from his home, and paddle out into the water with only Jaco for company.

The rain was still pouring down, and Logan folded his arms across his chest. His clothes were already soaked, and the wind that came along with the rain chilled him. He whistled for Jaco, hoping the dog would return soon.

The wind had been fiercer that morning than usual, which was why Logan and Jaco had ended up on this side of the loch. The fishing gear had gotten tangled after only a few casts, and as the clouds rolled over, threatening his already dark mood with rain, he had gotten lost in a fit of frustration.

Only to be brought out of it by a woman who set his teeth on edge.

Just thinking about Faith made him irrationally irritated. Her personality was her greatest fault, but being English didn't help either. Thanks to his English mother who abandoned him and his family shortly after his sister's birth, he detested the English. And Faith was the definition of an English lady. Self-important, self-righteous, with a conceit that tried his nerves. He had disliked her from the moment he first laid eyes on her.

Or at least, he *should* have disliked her at first glance. The truth was rather more uncomfortable to admit. The very first time he saw Faith had been at a clan banquet. She stood out from her sisters, dressed in a silver gown that had so much beadwork she practically shined like a hundred stars. Her curly hair was only a shade or two lighter than her sisters', but her green eyes and arched brows had caused an unwelcome stirring in his stomach. She was pretty, far prettier than any woman he had ever seen before—but then she spoke, and the fact that she was English had promptly turned him sour against her. The beauty that had charmed him a moment ago only repelled him after that. He was sure she was proud of her beauty, and that that pride fed her arrogance.

Just then, Jaco's bark echoed through the rain and in the next instant, he appeared beneath the crest of the hill let led into a pine tree grove. He stalled a moment before spotting his master, after which he ran straight to Logan. Jumping up, he searched for affection as his reward for a job well done. Logan grinned in spite of himself and tussled his head back and forth.

"Yes, yes. Good boy. And I know. She's not the nicest person, is she?"

The dog whimpered and dropped back to his hind legs. He tilted his head as if questioning Logan.

"Do you disagree? Surely not."

The dog whimpered again.

"Look here, I'm not having another conversation with you. I'll be sent off to the city's Parrish Asylum."

Jaco barked twice and then moved around Logan down to the boat.

"Oh no. It's too dangerous to row back in this weather. We'll have to walk."

Feeling confident that the long walk home would aid in his sleep that evening, Logan left his fishing supplies in the dingy and began walking along the southwestern shore. The rain had let up somewhat, coming down in a drizzle. As he walked, his mind began to wander. Had Faith seen him during his bout of anxiety? He hoped not. No doubt in her dislike for him, she would tell everyone she met what she'd seen.

The whole English lot wasn't to be trusted.

But then he knew he wasn't to be trusted either.

No. No, he didn't need to let his thoughts turn down that dark path. Instead, he tried to focus on anything else. His drenched clothes, for one. That should have been distraction enough, except that he could still feel the weight of Faith's body pressed against his. As he'd guided her out of the frigid waters, the softness of her waist and the flare of her hips beneath his hands had caused him to consider what the rest of her body might feel like under his hands.

Logan stopped and shook his head.

What the devil was wrong with him? He didn't even like the sharp-tongued woman. He certainly wouldn't entertain fantasies about her.

Deciding to hum a Bothy ballad to keep his mind from wandering, he continued his walk, whistling the high parts loudly as he went. Soon, he was in his familiar part of the world, where he had played as a child and where he had built his home not five years ago.

Harris House had been built in a Gothic Revival style, with Scottish red granite; it had four turrets, large oval peaked windows, and a three-story, blackwood greenhouse built on the right side of the house. A peculiar feature but one his sister had asked for when he had first been gifted the land by the Crown in return for services during the war. He had shied away from the spoils granted to him for some time, mainly because he felt like he hadn't earned them, but his father had convinced him that it wouldn't do anyone any good if Logan turned his back on his fortune out of spite. The war was over and there was no changing the past. It still took Logan some time to accept that—especially since he hadn't been able to bring every soldier home.

Duncan's bloody face flashed in his mind, causing him to stall. Logan took a deep breath and forced the memory away. *Not today.* Not again.

Sighing, he continued walking up the slight incline of the hill that overlooked the loch. Harris House stood nearly a field back, flanked by pines. To Logan's surprise, a carriage stood before the front entrance of his home, and several servants seemed to be struggling with a large, square package wrapped in brown paper and twine. His sister stood off to the side dressed in a heavy cloak. Upon seeing Logan, she waved her hand. He waved back, grinning his first genuine grin all morning.

It seemed his painting had finally arrived from Paris.

Long strides carried him across the lawn as his sister came forward.

"There you are," Arabella said, her blonde hair covered with a lace cap. "I was wondering what took you so long."

"The rain made it unsafe to cross in the boat. I had to walk," he said, coming forward. "Is this what I think it is?"

"Another one of your paintings?" she mused. "I suppose. It's quite large though, isn't it?"

"It is."

"What's the subject of this one? Another equine?"

Logan smirked at her sarcastic tone. He had quite an extensive art collection, having decided to become a collector in recent years. He had started off with landscapes and moved on to horses and animals, only recently becoming transfixed with portraits. This particular piece had been suggested to him by none other than Lady Belle Smyth when she had overheard his desire to purchase a pair of Marchelies. She had advised him that Marchelies was overpriced and not a good investment, while a new and upcoming artist out of Paris, a man known as Donovan, had recently begun making a name for himself in the art world.

He was a portraitist and was rumored to have painted the most stunning courtesan, though it had been announced that that particular painting was not for sale.

Intrigued and eager, Logan had offered him a king's ransom for the piece, taking Belle's word to not be dissuaded. Eventually, the young artist had been persuaded to sell the piece after all, and now the portrait was his.

"It's a woman," he said, nodding to the house as the servants moved the piece up the front steps.

A short man with a prominent bald spot and a thin, brown mustache bowed. Evans, the butler, had come from an aristocratic household in Fife. He had been let go when the earl had suffered some poor investments. Logan hadn't even wanted to hire him, particularly because he was so stringent, but he had proven to be a loyal servant.

"Where would you like it, sir?" he asked.

"Bring it to my bedchambers, Evans," Logan answered before returning to Arabella.

"A woman?" she asked. "Who?"

"Well, that's the interesting part," Logan said as he waited for his sister to enter the house, followed by Jaco. "Rumor has it that the model for this piece is some member from the ton."

"Really?"

"Yes. Possibly a member of the royal family, but who knows if that rumor is to be believed."

"Is that why you bought it?"

"Partly. And Lady Belle suggested this up-and-coming artist as a good investment."

"What's his name?"

"Donovan."

Arabella made a face.

"I've never heard of him."

"He's still rather new to the art world, but his talent has been discussed at length in the periodicals. He's a strange artist, however."

"Aren't they all?"

Logan smirked.

"I suppose so. But he is even more so. Apparently, he only works on commissioned pieces. When his clients wanted evidence of his talent before hiring him, they would be invited to his studio where he would reveal one painting."

"Only one?"

"Yes, but apparently this painting was so beautiful that it was enough to secure ten years' worth of commissions."

Arabella's eyes widened.

"Goodness! That's rather impressive, I suppose."

"That's what I thought," Logan said. "So, I bought it."

She gave him a look, as a maid helped remove her cloak. A golden teardrop-shaped stone hung from a pendant around her neck, giving him pause. Many years ago, Arabella had given Logan a circular piece of amber stone, with a hole drilled through it. It was a small custom in their area, to give stones to people for protection. As a child, Arabella had been convinced that amber was lucky. She had been sad when he'd returned from Burma without her good luck charm, but she had held fast to the belief that it had saved his life.

"You're quite like a dragon, you know," Arabella said, shaking him from his thoughts. "Piling up your coffers with treasures."

"And you read too many fairytales," he said as he followed her into the parlor where their father sat in the corner, sleeping in an oversized, overstuffed chair. "You should try being more practical."

She rolled her eyes as she sat across from their father.

"And become boring and disillusioned with life? No thank you."

Just then, the old man woke, startled by the noises.

"Eh? Helen?" he said before his eyes opened, causing the siblings to pause.

Helen had been their mother's name, and though she had

abandoned them fifteen years prior, their father had never stopped loving her. It was rare for him to say her name, though it did happen, particularly when he was tired.

"No, Father," Logan said, his voice somewhat strained. "It's just us."

"Hmm? Oh yes. Ah," he said, rubbing one eye. "Late morning today. Did you catch anything?"

Their father had suffered a nearly fatal bout of typhoid several years earlier while Logan had been away. Arabella miraculously hadn't become sick, but their father had suffered greatly. Ever since, his health had been delicate, and he was prone to taking long naps with occasional bouts of bedrest during the cooler months. He was a far cry from the robust man they remembered from their childhoods, and they had fallen into a tentative relationship with him.

"No," Logan said, reaching for a newspaper one of the servants brought in. "No fish today."

"Ah, well, you were always terrible at it. I remember I used to take you when you were younger. Never had the patience for it."

"You should go with him one morning, Father," Arabella tried, earning her a pointed look from Logan. "Perhaps you could teach him."

"No, no," he said, shaking his head. "My fishing days have long since passed."

"I don't know about that," Logan said, reading the newspaper. "Fishing is an old man's sport. I'd say you've just come into your prime."

"Well," the old man said, struggling to stand. He shooed away the butler. "I'm fine. No, I think... I think this cold weather is best to stay out of."

"Oh, but it's only a little storm."

"Don't worry, my dear," he said, bending down to kiss his daughter's forehead. "I shall be up and at it when the weather turns."

He left the room. Logan could feel his sister's eyes on him, and when he looked up, sure enough, she was staring at him.

"What?"

"Why don't you try and take him with you?"

"You heard him—he isn't interested. And quite frankly, I don't think I'd be able to keep my temper if I took him out."

"He's withering away. If he doesn't go out and get some sort of exercise, he'll likely…"

Though she didn't say it, Logan knew she was worried about their father's health. He had deteriorated rapidly the past year. Perhaps it *would* do him good to go out fishing, but Logan wasn't interested in hearing his father lament about his mother for hours at a time. As far as he was concerned, she had forgotten about them, and it was only fair that he had done the same.

Folding the paper and placing it on the end table, he stood.

"Excuse me."

His sister opened her mouth to argue, but he was quickly away and out of the room, eager to visit his bedchamber and admire his newly acquired piece.

Climbing the stairs, he wondered what sort of a fool would be so taken with someone that they would neglect every other aspect of their lives the way their father had done since his wife had left him. Logan had long ago sworn never to love someone so desperately, and thankfully, he had avoided such a tragic relationship thus far.

Entering his room, Logan peeled off his coat and untucked his still-damp shirt. The painting had been leaned against the far wall for his inspection, and deciding not to delay it any longer, he removed the brown paper.

Untying the twine, the paper fell away, and he was left staring at a painting that struck him with astonishment.

A woman lay on a bed of pillows, her form wrapped precariously around the waist by a stretch of yellow velvet. Her upper body was unclothed, though she was turned to the side, revealing only the side of her right breast. Her medium-dark, curly hair was pinned to the top of her head with a length of silk and a peacock feather, which matched the small fan she held at her waist.

It was a stunning piece. Brushstrokes were nearly nonexistent, and the colors were vibrant. And the detail was outstanding. The shading and the light made it look like she might come to life in his room and step out of the canvas.

She was perfection. A vision beyond compare, and yet, Logan found himself both aroused and instantly annoyed. He knew this woman, had argued with her, and had fought with himself over the physical attraction for her that he couldn't repress.

He wanted to tell himself that he was seeing things, imagining a resemblance where none existed. Still, as he gazed into those sharp green eyes that stared back at him beneath a familiar arched brow, Logan could feel it, deep in his bones, that he knew exactly who this woman was.

"Blasted hell."

Chapter Three

F AITH SAT ON the back of a Connemara pony, one of two that had been bought specifically for her and Grace to learn how to ride on. Faith and her sisters hadn't been able to afford lessons after their parents passed away, when they went to go live with their grandmother Alice in London. For her part, Faith had been content not to learn in her younger years. At four and twenty, Faith felt unsure that she could still learn something that most people learned during their formative years.

Graham and Hope had insisted on the lessons, though. The Connemara was considered a gentle breed for novice riders. Faith's horse, a light palomino aptly named Sweetness, twitched its tail as they stood out before the stables of Lismore Hall the following day, waiting for Graham's cousin, Jeanne Carlyle.

"I'm not sure what the point to this is," Faith said nervously from her position atop Sweetness's back, glancing at Grace. "I'm perfectly happy not knowing how to ride."

"As am I, but it is what is expected of well-bred ladies," her younger sister said softly, her gaze on Hope and Graham as they moved about on their own horses several yards away.

"I'd rather be painting. I've just started a new work, a landscape of the loch."

"Oh?"

"Yes, and it would be far more enjoyable to me than traipsing about the Highlands on this tiny horse."

"Faith, it's a kind gesture by our brother-in-law to provide us with the horses and the lessons. Hope would be pleased to no end knowing that we enjoyed them."

"But we don't enjoy them."

"Hush, here they come," Grace said before looking up with a broad smile plastered on her face. "A fine day for a ride!"

"Yes, particularly since we were rained out yesterday," Graham said. "I'm still amazed you were so drenched, Faith."

Faith had left a track of wet footprints through the foyer and up the stairs yesterday after returning from her unexpected encounter with Logan. Evidently, Graham had nearly slipped. She gave him an apologetic look.

"I am sorry for the mess."

"It's of no matter," Graham said, turning his face to the sky. "But I believe the weather will hold out today."

"I think so as well," Hope said.

Faith sighed, noting Hope's happiness as she gazed at her husband's profile. The two were constantly doting on one another, which always made Faith uncomfortable to witness. In her experience, men were not to be trusted, and while Graham had thus far proved to be an excellent husband, save that whole nonsense about tricking Hope into marrying him, Faith couldn't help but remain skeptical.

"'Allo!" The sweet sound of Jeanne's voice carried on the wind.

Everyone turned to see a smartly dressed, coppered-headed woman riding quickly up the drive. Dressed in her favorite striped pattern, Jeanne Carlyle beamed as she reached them, riding upon a frightening black steed.

"My! What a darling pair of ponies, cousin," she said breathlessly, addressing Graham first. "They're as lovely as you described them, Hope."

"Aren't they?" She beamed. "Faith and Grace adore them."

"Is that so?" Jeanne said, her knowing observation landing on Faith, who nodded politely. Jeanne had the uncanny ability to see through people; to Faith's dismay, she winked. "Well, then. Shall we start?"

Turning her horse to the side, Jeanne reared back and let out a rough "Yah" as the black stallion neighed. She took off at a frightening speed.

Faith's heart fell into her stomach. No, this was not how she wished to spend her day. She'd much rather paint these beasts than ride them. She had a soft spot for equine artwork. But with Hope's encouraging smile, Faith forced herself to smile and fell into line behind Jeanne.

For nearly two hours, the company rode on grass roads and muddy paths, through fields and forests, up craigs, and down into valleys. It was a trying experience, and Faith was surprised by how much her entire body began to ache. Her sides, in particular, became more sore the longer they rode. It was truly a laborious experience.

After another hour or so, she trotted in tandem with Jeanne as they climbed a particularly uneven stretch of ground leading up to Stob Ridge, which overlooked the northern part of Loch Fyne.

Evidently, Faith's face showed her discomfort.

"Not your cup of tea, is it?" Jeanne asked as the two settled into the back of the line.

Faith gave her an apologetic look.

"I'm afraid not. I'm not very good at this."

"Ochs, you only need practice. Riding is really quite enjoyable once you've mastered it." Faith doubted it and grimaced, but Jeanne only laughed at her expression. "Very well. Graham is going to take Hope and Grace the long way down, over the other side of the ridge and back around. But you and I can go this way," she said, nodding to the west. "We should be able to come down around Harris House, to the main road."

Faith knew that Harris House belonged to Logan, and she did not wish to see him. But the steepness of their current path was too much for her, and she gave Jeanne a stiff nod.

"Very well."

Jeanne called out to Graham and told him their intended path. He appeared somewhat apprehensive, but Jeanne's skill as a horsewoman was without question, and eventually he waved his hand with a nod.

Jeanne cut in front of Faith's horse, and they steadily declined down the ridge. Though the morning sky promised a clear day, Faith could see far beyond the mountains. Dark clouds were rolling and billowing toward them.

Would there ever be any pleasant weather in this place?

After a half hour of silently steering their horses down the slope, grassy fields opened up before them. Faith continued on the well-worn path until she suddenly noticed Jeanne had stopped. Pulling her reins back, Faith followed her gaze to a little stone house built at the base of a mountain far in the distance.

It looked uninhabited, and Faith wasn't sure what was so fascinating about it.

"What is it?" she asked after a moment, coming up to Jeanne's side.

"Hm? Oh, 'tis nothing," Jeanne said, though a pained expression could be seen plainly across her face.

Faith frowned.

"Are you sure? You seem rather sad."

Jeanne's horse shook its mane, stepping sideways, but she kept her eyes on the tiny cottage.

"It's just... I used to come here. A long time ago, with my Duncan."

Faith glanced back at the pile of rubble. She had heard only snippets about Duncan Carlyle, a man who had supposedly been the heart of his friends and family, though he was rarely spoken about. He had died in the Second Burmese War some five years earlier. Faith presumed it was too painful for most to talk about him, particularly Jeanne, who had married him just before he left for his campaign.

Unsure of how to be a comfort, Faith said the only thing that came to her mind.

"It must be difficult," she began awkwardly. "To go on without him."

Jeanne nodded slowly before glancing at her.

"Aye, it is. It's been five years now and I've managed quite well. But, sometimes," she paused, looking back at the structure. "Sometimes, it's as if no time has passed. It's as if he never left."

Faith wasn't sure what she meant, but she had never had a husband pass away. A loud rumble from above jostled them from their thoughts, and Jeanne took a deep breath.

"Come. The storm won't wait for us."

Faith was sure that Jeanne could outrun the storm alone, but she was not so talented a horsewoman and kept her mare going only at a trot. When the thunder boomed again, the skies opened up, and cold, unforgiving rain beat down on them, pelting them like tiny stones.

For the second day in a row, Faith was soaked to the bone in a matter of minutes. It might not have been all that terrible if the wind were not so brutal. It whipped around them as the rain turned to icy pellets. Even though it was midday, the world around them had been covered in sheets of gray rain, and soon Faith was shaking to keep warm.

"There!" Jeanne shouted after a while, pointing to a vague group of yellow lights. "We can take shelter and try and wait the storm out!"

Grateful for any chance to get off her horse, Faith followed Jeanne as fast as she could. As they rode closer to the lights, Faith realized that it was a house. A rather grand house made of red granite. It looked like some sort of Gothic castle, with turrets and parapets, though the entire structure seemed far more modern than an ancient stronghold.

They rode straight up to the front steps. The front doors opened immediately, and two servants in oversized brown overcoats came hurrying out, helping them down, one taking the horses as the other escorted them inside.

Once the doors had closed behind them, Faith could barely

contain her shivering.

"Tell Sir Logan that we are here," Jeanne said.

"I'm sorry, ma'am, but Sir Logan in not in. Miss Harris is in the drawing room, however, with Mr. Harris."

Sir Logan? Faith didn't know that Logan's father had been knighted—or that the two men shared the same Christian name.

Jeanne moved passed the footman just as a short, blond-haired woman appeared in the hallway several yards away.

"Jeanne? Is that you?"

"Arabella, dear, we were caught in the storm and are soaked all the way through. Might we press upon you to borrow some clothes before we catch our deaths?"

"Oh, my goodness, of course. Of course," she said, coming forward. With a slight curtsy, she acknowledged Faith. "An unfortunate circumstance to meet under, I'm afraid. I'm Miss Arabella Harris."

"Miss Faith… Faith… Achoo!"

"Oh dear, there's no time for that. Follow me. Morgan?"

"Yes, my lady?"

"Tell the maids to come at once and have the footmen bring hot water to the floral guest rooms. Have them gather my warmest gowns and have cook prepare something warm for our guests. Follow me," she said as Jeanne came up to her side. "The floral guest rooms each have a standing bath, though I'm sure hot tub would be best for both of you."

Faith had never seen a standing bath but had heard about them.

"I'm sure I am… am…fine—Achoo!"

Jeanne peered over her shoulder.

"Oh yes, you sound quite well," she said sarcastically. "Graham is going to have me quartered if you come down with a cold."

Faith wanted to argue that there was no reason to worry, as she had a strong constitution, but fevers were not to be taken lightly, and the chill in her body seemed to emanate from within.

The sooner she was in a bath, the better.

The style of the home was rather fitting, considering its outward appearance. The second-floor hallways were painted emerald green and lined with dark-paneling chair rails. Faith followed the others as they took a left upon the landing and entered the second room on the right. White wallpaper adorned with dozens of types of blooms hung from the walls. Shiny, pale-wood furniture with white-and-green bedding gave the room a delicate springtime atmosphere, and though she was dripping wet, Faith felt instantly warmer.

"You undress here," Arabella said, turning. "Jeanne? Follow me."

Faith nodded as two maids came in to help her undress. Within minutes, a bath had been prepared in an adjoining room designed solely for bathing. Faith glanced around the tiled room, amazed. She had never seen a room like this, with copper pipes and ceramic knobs fitted over a white bathtub permanently fixed to the floor.

"In you go, miss," the maid said as Faith stepped into the nearly filled bath.

Hot water surrounded her, sinking deep into her soul as Faith closed her eyes. She dipped her head back and tried to shake all the cold from her. The maids left her with a sliver of soap, and she worked it into a lather. She scrubbed her body as best she could, hoping to remove any remnants of a chill. After nearly half an hour, she found that she still couldn't quite warm herself and decided to dress.

A pale-pink day gown, lined with gray trim had been laid out for her to borrow. She dressed slowly, with one of the maid's help. It was too short, as it showed her ankles, but Faith was grateful to be clad in something dry. Thankfully she had also been provided with thick wool stockings and a heavy gray-and-purple plaid shawl. Her hair was combed out, parted, and plaited, then wrapped around together to form an interlocking half circle at the back of her neck.

A gentle knock at the door revealed Arabella, followed by another maid who held a tray. The scent of beef and vegetable stew filled Faith's senses, and her mouth began to water. She hadn't realized just how hungry being cold had made her.

"How are you faring, Miss Sharpe?" she asked, motioning for the maid to place the tray on a small, bird's-eye maple table before a large window overlooking the northern woods.

"Very well, thank you," Faith said. "And please, call me Faith."

"Only if you call me Arabella," she said with a cheerful smile. "I must admit, I had hoped to meet you sooner. I have met one of your sisters, Hope. But I understand you were in Italy with your aunt for the past six months. Is that correct?"

That was true. Faith had just returned to Scotland a few weeks ago. She, Grace, and Aunt Belle had traveled to Rome to visit with famed Italian surgeon, Dr. Ramaglia, in an effort to address Belle's failing health. Thankfully, Dr. Ramaglia had some knowledge of what had ailed her and had saved Belle's life by performing a rather risky procedure. Grace had apprenticed with the doctor during their trip, which left Faith to care for Belle in her recovery.

"Yes. My younger sister Grace and I attended to Aunt Belle during her stay there. She had an operation."

"Did she?" Arabella asked, leaning forward. "How very interesting."

A pause followed. Faith wasn't sure why the young woman was staring at her so intently. She cleared her throat.

"Thank you so much for letting us invade your home," Faith said, hoping to break the tension.

"Oh, of course, of course," she said, shaking her head. "Goodness, you must think I have terrible manners. It's just... You're nothing like how I imagined you would be."

Faith blinked.

"I'm not?"

"No. My brother always said you were... Well... You're quite lovely is what I'm trying to say."

Faith stared momentarily, unsure how to reply, as her cheeks warmed.

"Oh, well. That's very kind of you. Although that leads me to believe that your brother's description of me has been less than flattering."

"Oh, you mustn't take anything he says at face value. Logan can be… harsh. Especially with the English. I'd blame it on his time as a solider, but he's always been rather, well, particular." Arabella motioned to the chair. "Please, sit and eat."

"Yes, something to do with our vitriolic histories, I assume," Faith said offhandedly as she sat down.

"Oh no, it's because of our mama."

Faith paused just as Arabella took a seat across from her.

"I beg your pardon?"

"Our mama was English. Or still is, rather," she said, shaking her head as she looked down. "I never met her—not that I can recall. She left when I was a bairn."

"Oh. I… I'm sorry."

Arabella waved her hand.

"I'm quite immune to it. Having never met her, I hold no expectations, but Papa and Logan, well, they tend to have varying thoughts on the matter."

"I see."

A pregnant pause followed, and Arabella stood up.

"I'll let you eat in peace then. This storm is a brutal one, I'm afraid," she said, glancing out the window. A strike of lightning lit up the sky. "It doesn't look like it will end soon."

"Well, I'm very grateful for your hospitality."

She waved her hand in the air once more as thunder rumbled.

"Think nothing of it. We are neighbors after all. And I dare say we may be friends before long." With a nod, she turned to leave before adding, "Jeanne and I will be downstairs in the parlor, should you like to join us."

"Thank you," Faith said as the young woman disappeared

behind the door.

Well, this was certainly not what she had expected. Arabella Harris was a kind, sweet-tempered young lady, not quite as old as Faith but seemingly more mature than most ladies her age. And she was very welcoming and friendly, as opposed to her brother.

Faith picked up her spoon and dipped it into the steaming, savory stew as Logan's face crossed her mind. Where was he? Not that she cared, but shouldn't the owner of the house like to make sure that those in his care were well? She supposed she couldn't expect a man like Logan to have any real manners, yet she wondered where he had gone through the rest of her meal.

Having finished her soup, Faith left her room and found herself alone in a long hallway. She was curious about the estate and debated wandering about for a bit before thinking better of it. It would not do to go snooping about this house. And she certainly didn't want to be caught in the act. So instead, she went to the staircase and walked down in search of the parlor.

Crossing the waxed parquet floor, Faith entered a stunning room. The walls were painted burnt orange and outlined with white-marble archways. Dozens of gold-leaf frames held paintings of various animals, from birds to hounds and, to her delight, horses. They were remarkable pieces, and Faith found herself studying one in particular, a dapple-gray steed atop a hill in a rearing position. The power of the animal had been conveyed so perfectly that she wouldn't have been surprised if it ran right off the canvas.

"Faith?" Jeanne's voice sounded, catching her attention.

Faith turned to see Jeanne and Arabella sitting across from one another before a grand fireplace with a roaring fire in it. In the corner of the room, in an overstuffed chair, sat an elderly man with a blanket draped over his lap. His eyes were closed and his upper lip twitched as he snored, in an almost comical way.

"Hello," Faith said, returning to the painting before approaching them. "That's a magnificent piece. It's a Gericault, if I'm not mistaken."

"I could not begin to pretend to know anything about it," Arabella said, stirring her tea. "Are you fan of art, Faith?"

"I am," she said, standing next to where her companions sat. "I have a great love for art. I even paint a little myself."

"Is that so?" Jeanne said.

"And you like that particular piece?" Arabella asked, nodding back at the horse painting.

"Yes," she replied, noting a small smile curve across Arabella's mouth. "Is that amusing?"

"No, of course not. It's just that that painting happens to be one of my brother's favorites."

Faith's smile vanished.

"Is it? I didn't know Mr. Harris enjoyed art."

"'Enjoy' is hardly the correct word. Logan is *obsessed*," Arabella said, leaning forward and wiggling her brows in an exaggerated way as Faith sat down. A flash of lightning followed by a crack of thunder echoed throughout the room. "This storm is relentless."

Faith glanced out of the cathedral windows, outlined in the same white marble as the arches.

"It does seem so. I hate to think how we will travel home."

"Oh, but you mustn't go," Arabella said, frowning. "The winds are too violent. It would be safer to stay the night."

"Oh no, I shouldn't want to impose."

"I insist."

"But—"

Just then, the old man twisted and snorted.

"Hmm?" he said loudly before his eyes opened.

A faint blush shone on the bridge of Arabella's nose as she stood up.

"Forgive my father. He's not been terribly well recently," she said quietly as she approached him. "Papa? Papa, we have guests."

"Hmm? Oh, beg pardon," he said, shifting in his chair.

He was a fair-haired man with sunken cheeks and dark eyes. There was a strange quality about him that Faith noticed immediately. He seemed far older than she would guess him to be, yet she couldn't say what it was about him that gave that impression.

His dark gaze landed on Faith, and his brows perked up as he wiggled himself to sit up straight.

"Come now, who is this?"

"This is Miss Faith Sharpe, Papa. Lady Belle's niece," Arabella said, looking at Faith. "She lives in Lismore Hall, across the loch."

"Is that so? Belle's niece?" he said, leaning forward. "Lady Belle Smyth?"

"Yes, Sir Logan," Faith said, dipping her chin. "A pleasure to meet you."

But the man smirked and looked at his daughter.

"Did she call me sir?"

Arabella's face became suddenly drawn.

"Oh, um, a misunderstanding, Papa."

Faith bit the inside of her cheek. Hadn't the servant called him Sir Logan?

"And English," he said, interrupting Faith's thoughts as his face lit up. "Well, what a lucky day indeed."

Faith smiled warily.

"We were having a riding lesson when we got caught in the storm," Jeanne said, sipping her tea. "It's dreadful outside and the rain will not stop."

"Ah, well, Scottish springs can be like that, I suppose," he said, motioning to a chair beside him. "Come, Miss Sharpe. It has been ages since I've met someone new. Tell me, how does your aunt fare? I've always enjoyed her visits."

Faith stood up and went to him.

"She's faring quite well, although I didn't know she visited here."

"Oh, only sparingly," he said with a cheerful grin, not unlike his daughter. "But then again, not recently either."

"We were away, I'm afraid. On an extended holiday in Italy."

"Italy? You don't say."

"Yes."

"Hmm," he said, leaning forward slightly. "I never much

cared for the Mediterranean. Much too warm for my liking. Now, tell me about this riding lesson. You were caught in this storm, were you?"

Jeanne spoke, giving Faith a reprieve as she watched the old man. Arabella was correct. He did not look particularly well and was dressed in clothing that had been out of style for nearly twenty years. But he was kindly, and he showed an earnest concern when he heard about their plight. He kept giving Faith curious glances, and though she was sure he didn't mean to make her uncomfortable, she felt somewhat uneasy beneath his inquisitive gaze.

"—which is why I insist that they stay the night," Arabella said as another roll of thunder bellowed around them.

"Absolutely, absolutely. I should hate to think what Lady Belle would do to me if I let one of her nieces go traipsing about the Highlands in a storm such as this."

Faith tried to smile. It seemed she would not be leaving, much to her discontent. And once again, her displeasure must have been displayed on her face, for a frowning Arabella leaned toward her.

"If it would please you, my brother has quite an extensive art gallery here. He's terribly proud of it and I'm sure he would be most eager to share it with you."

"I wouldn't want to impose on your brother."

"Oh, it would be no imposition. Logan is vastly proud of it. Why, in fact, just yesterday he acquired a piece—"

"Who in the world has come to visit on such a day?" Logan's deep voice echoed throughout the room, causing Faith to spin around.

There, beneath the marble archway, stood Logan, his body frozen at the sight of her. His solid form was tense and commanding, as if he were still serving in a regiment, flanked by his faithful mutt, Jaco. The dog's tail wagged happily at seeing them, but Logan's demeanor was the opposite. The recognition in his eyes sent Faith's heart aflutter. Though she tried to ignore such a foolish reaction, waiting for his impending frown, she was surprised to realize that he only stared at her with wide-eyed fascination, as if seeing something about her for the first time.

How curious.

"You," he said softly.

Swallowing hard at the low, accusatory whisper, Faith hoped against hope that he wouldn't begin sparring with her in front of the present company.

"I'm sorry to intrude," she said, stepping toward him. "But Jeanne and I were out riding and were caught in the storm. Your sister here has provided us with warm clothes and shelter, and if it pleases you, we shall be leaving shortly."

"No, you really mustn't," Arabella protested.

"I'm afraid she is correct, Faith," Jeanne said. "The storm is too boisterous."

Faith persisted.

"If Mr. Harris doesn't wish for us to be here—"

"Of course he doesn't mind," Arabella said, scowling at her brother. "Isn't that right, Logan?"

"—then we should leave."

"You will stay," Logan interrupted suddenly, causing the rest of them to stop talking. "The weather will not permit you to do otherwise."

Faith stared at him, sure that he was annoyed with the situation even if it was unavoidable. She nodded.

"Thank you, Mr. Harris," she said, only to see him turn his back on her as he left the room.

Was there a ruder man in all of Scotland? Surely not, and yet, the look he had given her was far from his usual glower. It had almost been one of, well, desire.

Faith blinked. Then she bit the inside of her cheek, trying to stop her train of thought. What a preposterous thing to think.

"Do not pay any attention to my son, Miss Sharpe," the elderly man said, causing her to turn around. "He's rarely in a good mood, but we won't let him dampen ours." He looked at his daughter. "Now, what will we be having for supper?"

Chapter Four

W HAT A DEVIL *of a thing to occur,* Logan thought as he stalked his way through Harris House. What were the chances of having Faith seek shelter at his home during a storm?

Well, the probability for that was somewhat high, actually. They were neighbors, after all, and to be caught in a spring storm wasn't unheard of in these parts. But seeing her again, after being tormented by his latest acquired painting? It was as if he were staring directly into the eyes of the subject painted in *Odalisque Reclined.*

Was it really her? Certainly, the resemblance was uncanny. But it didn't seem as if it could be possible. In her bearing and personality, Faith was so unlike the alluring lady in the portrait. Surely it must be a coincidence that she and the model looked so alike. Or did he simply wish to believe that because he did not care to admit that he found the piece—the piece that looked so very much like Faith—to be unbearably tempting? Looking at it made him question all of his beliefs about Faith and himself. He was not the sort to simply succumb to a beautiful woman, even if she was his ideal in every physical way. He was an intelligent man and required substance to his attraction. Layers of depth that would unfurl like a blooming rose, and he was certain Faith didn't possess any of that.

And beyond that, he couldn't bring himself to believe that she would sit for a portrait like that. It was scandalous. She was innocent, regardless of how blistering she might be. There was simply no way that someone as cold and snippety as Faith had sat for such a provocative piece.

Logan returned to his room, eager to remove the clothes that were soaked through from his trip to Glencoe that morning. Dr. James Hall had been visiting his country office as he did every first of the month when he would return from Glasgow to tend to his mother. Logan had a standing appointment with the doctor to document his dark spells and continuing insomnia. But it seemed there was nothing to be done for Logan's anxious occurrences besides living through them. Dr. Hall had suggested a dram of strong scotch at night, but alcohol was never a sure thing when it came to mitigating Logan's anxieties. Sometimes, it would be a comfort to fall into a drunken stupor, while other times, it would only enhance the feelings of powerless misery.

It was best to simply go on as he had. Silently and alone.

He kicked off his boots and eyed the painting leaning against the wall. The mischievous glint in the model's eye seemed to mock him as if she knew about his nervous bouts. He had stayed up late the night before, pacing the floor of his room as darkness descended around him, with only this painting as company, as Jaco preferred to sleep in the kitchens.

He took a step toward the painting and tilted his head. He wondered what she might say, having witnessed his restlessness.

"No doubt something scathing," he mumbled, aware that his fits of panic were the crux of failures. "Especially if it were her."

Her, of course, being Faith. The longer he gazed at the piece, the more it seemed she was smirking, as if this inanimate object could somehow acknowledge him. He wished that she would simply speak and confirm his suspicions.

Pulling a wooden chair directly before the painting, Logan sat, searching the artwork for any hint of confirmation. Her head was turned over her shoulder, showing three-quarters of her face. Though the green eyes were more flirtatious than he had ever witnessed in real life, the dark, arched brows really caught his attention. One brow was arched slightly higher than the other, just like Faith's. While it could be understood that the model had simply lifted one brow in a gesture of amusement or seduction, Logan couldn't shake that the artist had captured a genuine characteristic of his model. It had been one of the first things Logan had noticed about Faith, particularly because it gave off a superior air.

Sighing, he leaned back, folding his arms across his chest. How could this possibly be Faith? He frowned at the painting as his eyes traveled down the length of her curved back, the yellow velvet draped over her backside, and the long, shapely legs, one tucked under the other. Then his eye caught on something.

A spot, or rather, several spots, just between her ankle and her Achilles tendon. Squinting, Logan moved closer to the painting. Perhaps it was a speck of dirt that had managed to get on the canvas during its travel. He swiped gently with the pad of his thumb, but it would not be removed.

It was a small grouping of freckles. A birthmark.

He squinted at it as his mind began to work. Well, then. If this was an accurate depiction of the model's skin, all he needed to do was get a glimpse of Faith's bare ankles, and he would know for sure. But how would he do that?

Standing up, he began to ready himself for dinner. With the continuous booming of thunder overhead, he made his way down the stairs and into the dining hall, where an unlikely sight met him.

Faith and his father were dancing while his sister clapped in rhythm, grinning at the two of them. Jeanne was standing with her back toward Logan, blocking the view of the dancers as she clapped along too. It was hard to process, as he had never seen his father dance. Logan believed him too weak to even consider it. It wasn't pretty, as they both seemed unable to avoid missteps, but they moved about the room in a circle, smiling at one another as they went.

"You are a fine dancing partner, Miss Sharpe," his father said. "One of the best I've had the pleasure of knowing."

"Thank you, Mr. Harris," Faith said. "But I must admit, waltzes are my favorite."

"Bravo, Papa!" Arabella said joyously. She sat in a chair and turned around from the dining room table. "I did not know you could dance."

"Of course I can," he said, his breath strained, causing Logan an ounce of worry. "My dancing enticed many a lady in my day."

"Then you are woefully out of practice," Logan said, entering the room.

Faith's smile disappeared as her eyes met his. Jeanne turned around as his father and sister beamed.

"Isn't Papa impressive?" Arabella said, standing up and going to him. "I shouldn't have thought it possible."

"What little faith you have in me," her father said with a smile before looking back at his dance partner. "But how could I refuse Miss Sharpe's blatant challenge?"

That perpetual brow arched a touch higher, and a torrent of unwanted attraction washed over Logan. He tried to steel his nerves.

"I did no such thing," Faith said, a small smile on her lips. "I merely said that this country was lacking for gentlemen who are proficient dance partners. Why, I had to dance with Jeanne at a house party last summer because there were too few gentlemen."

"It's true," Jeanne said. "Of course, my brothers were away at the time on a hunting trip. But thankfully, Faith is tall like myself. We were quite compatible."

Faith smiled at her friend.

"No gentlemen? That's preposterous," Mr. Harris said, waving a hand at his son. "Surely my boy here has asked you to dance before?"

The joyful atmosphere dimmed slightly as Faith looked at Logan. A sense of yearning carved through him at the idea of dancing with Faith, but he ignored it.

"No," she said softly, causing his blood to pump harder through his veins. "I've not had the pleasure."

Her tone indicated that it would be anything but pleasurable to be held by Logan, and while logically he agreed, there was a part of him that wanted to prove her wrong.

"Logan doesn't like to dance, Papa," Arabella said. "Don't you remember?"

"Why ever not?"

All eyes turned to Logan. A small, anxious part of him began to beat to life, and he had to take a deep breath to move past it. Inhaling through his nose and exhaling through his mouth, he donned a laissez-faire attitude.

"Because there are far more interesting things to do," he said, moving around the table to sit.

The rest moved around the room to find their seats at his signal. Faith took the seat furthest from his left, next to his father, while Arabella and Jeanne sat on his right. Two servants came out of a door in the corner that led to the kitchen, holding silver-covered food trays.

"What could possibly be more interesting that dancing with a lovely lady?" his father asked as he leaned toward Faith. "I've not had that much fun in years."

"It is a miracle that you were able to do so," Logan said, unable to keep a condescending tone out of his voice as he spoke. "Considering you haven't stretched your legs properly all winter."

His father sneered at him.

"And you know everything I do in private?" he countered.

"Lord, do not tell me," Logan murmured.

"I wish you could have attended the McTavish banquet last year, Mr. Harris," Faith said, interrupting the two as she looked at the elderly man. A servant spooned a cream of asparagus soup into their bowls. "I should have very much enjoyed your company."

"Ah, I was under the weather last year, I'm afraid. My old bones will not hold me like they used to."

"That's only because you've not worked them for so long,"

Arabella said. "Perhaps if Miss Sharpe isn't too put out, she might come visit from time to time."

"I would enjoy that—"

"No."

The definitive tone of Logan's voice startled everyone into silence. *Damn.* He hadn't meant to say it out loud. Though he was often cutting to Faith, he knew he had crossed a line. Clearing his throat, he spoke.

"What I mean to say is, no doubt Miss Sharpe is very busy."

"Not at all," she said defiantly, her challenging emerald-eyed gaze locked on his face. "In fact, it would be my pleasure to visit Mr. Harris." She turned back to face him. "If you will have me."

"How could I say no to you?" he said charmingly, and Logan wished there was something more substantial on his plate to stab at, instead of soup.

Good lord. Were there ever two more annoying people? And his father should be ashamed, blatantly flirting with a woman young enough to be his daughter.

"I think it is a fine idea," Jeanne said, taking a spoonful of soup. "It's been so long since anyone has seen you out and about, Mr. Harris."

"Yes, well," he said, appearing suddenly flushed. "It cannot be helped. Age has not been kind to me, I'm afraid."

"Well, perhaps you could accompany me around the loch one afternoon?" Faith said. "Since moving to Scotland, I've become quite fond of walking the countryside."

"Oh, I don't know," Mr. Harris said, suddenly reserved. "I've not left the house in ages."

"Why not?"

Though it was an innocent enough question, Logan's steady gaze was on his father. He suspected the man was not long for this world. While it wasn't a nice thought, it was true. Though he had managed well enough in the first years after his wife left, his father's desire for a living seemed to diminish once Logan came of age. Arabella had said that he had been robust when Logan was away at war, but he doubted it. Ever since typhoid had nearly killed his father, it seemed the life had gone out of him.

Still, Logan didn't wish for him to have to lie to their guests, so he interrupted.

"Is it true Graham bought you a Connemara horse?" he asked, pulling Faith's focus to him. She nearly spoke, but he continued. "What a daft thing to do."

Faith's brow pinched.

"Excuse me?"

"You're too tall for a Connemara. I've no doubt you look as Arabella would look riding a donkey."

Faith glared at him.

"I'm very fond of Sweetness, thank you very much, and it was very generous of my brother-in-law to acquire her."

"Sweetness?" Logan repeated humor in his voice. "Is that what you named it?"

"It was already named."

"Ah, Faith, how is your brother-in-law's honey enterprise?" Arabella interrupted, shooting Logan a tense glare. "Logan here has mentioned something about a confectionary factory in Glasgow. Is that true?"

It was, and Arabella knew it. Logan had discussed it with her multiple times as he had invested in it, but he suspected she was trying to defuse the rising tension between himself and Faith.

"Yes. I believe Graham is doing quite well," she said as Jeanne and Arabella broke into a conversation about fashions.

"Quite well" didn't even begin to describe the progress of Graham's candy business. It was a blaring success so far, and Logan himself had bought into the enterprise that past winter, having a supposed talent with investments. That knack was why had had been able to afford Harris House. While the Crown had granted the land in recompense for his supposed heroics at war, he had also been given a small monetary gift. Logan had never felt right in accepting it, believing it to be blood money. He had tried to rid himself of it by investing it in several short-term loans that had miraculously all turned out to be profitable.

As dinner progressed, Logan decided to keep quiet, unable to add anything but a biting remark or saucy reply to almost everything Faith said. Why did she bother him so much? He had always told himself that his sharpness was justified by her blatant arrogance toward him, but as he watched her interact with his family and Jeanne, he wondered if he was the only one to suffer her haughtiness.

She was undoubtedly a headstrong woman with firm beliefs and a presence that demanded respect. It had grated on him at first, but upon observing her now, she seemed also charming and patient amongst his loved ones. She listened intently when another spoke, and her replies were firm and well thought out.

She seemed to know exactly who she was and what she was worth, and Logan was sure he had never met another woman like her. The ladies he had known in his youth were strong in many ways but they were also far more playful. Faith seemed almost rigid in comparison, probably due to her English upbringing, but then what about the painting? Didn't it convey a side of her that might be far more adventurous, wild, and free than what she exhibited socially?

That is to say, if the model was indeed Faith.

His eyes traveled down her face, long neck, chest, and waist to where the rest of her body disappeared beneath the dining table. He needed to see her ankle, but how? He could simply demand it, but as his gaze lifted, he saw her glaring eyes.

Evidently, she didn't like being looked at. Well, too bad.

"Logan," Arabella said, noting the glances between the two. "Faith here was very impressed with your horse painting, in the parlor. The gray one?"

"Oh?" he said without curiosity.

He didn't continue.

"Yes," Arabella said, her tone slightly terse as she continued to try and facilitate a conversation. "In fact, she knew who painted it straight away."

Now that was surprising. Only one other person had ever correctly named the artist of the particular piece. So, she was a student of the arts, was she? That certainly leaned in favor of the idea that the painting in his bedroom was of her. He observed Faith.

"And are you a fan of all art or just Gericault?"

"All art that is worthy," she said smartly. "I even studied a bit myself in London. Though that was years ago and I'm afraid I was not very good at it."

"Did you?" Jeanne asked. "What sort of things did you draw?"

"Oh, still life mostly. It's easy when the subject cannot move, although the light does change every hour or so, changing the entire feel of the theme," she said, a small smile coming to her lips. "Actually, I've just recently started a landscape of the loch that I'm rather excited about."

"What about portraits?" Logan asked, unable to stop himself.

Jeanne gave him a questioning look as his father spoke.

"Logan has become obsessed with portraits as of late. He can't seem to get enough of them in his collection."

"'Obsessed' isn't an accurate descriptor. I would say I've become *interested* in them. That's all."

"Oh," Faith said. "Well, I have done a few portraits, but I never was very good at capturing likenesses. I've only managed to do a few of my family members any justice. In fact, there was one particular piece that nearly caused my friend Renee to break down into tears. Thankfully, her brother explained that it simply wasn't my forte."

"Her brother?" Arabella said.

"Yes. He was my art instructor when I came back to painting."

"Came back?" Logan repeated. "Where did you go?"

The crest of Faith's cheeks suddenly became pink and a tiny crease formed between her brows. It was strange, but Logan was intrigued by the small line. He wasn't sure why or how, but he knew that whatever would next come out of her mouth would be a lie.

"Oh, I had taken a year off. To pursue other things."

"Such as?" he pressed.

Faith stared him directly in the eye.

"Piano."

"And did you have a proficiency for that?"

"No, so I came back to painting."

"I see."

"I'm glad," she said sarcastically.

After a moment, he realized that their back and forth had caused the others to glance between the two with concern.

"Well," Arabella began, unsure. "While you two are here, I insist that you see the greenhouse. It is my pride and joy. My brother very kindly commissioned it when he built this house. It spans three floors."

"Three floors?" Jeanne said, turning in her seat. "How peculiar."

"It is, and it holds the most amazing plants. I'm something of an amateur gardener."

"You are being too modest, sister," Logan said, looking around the table. "Arabella has a proverbial green thumb when it comes to exotic plants."

"How lovely," Faith said.

Arabella smiled.

"And as I told you before, Faith, Logan has an extensive art collection that you really must see to believe. You are welcome to view it. I would be glad to give you a tour of it, although I'm not as knowledgeable as my brother."

Faith gave his sister a pained smile, and Logan suddenly found himself wanting to annoy their guest.

"I'd be happy to show it to you myself," he smirked. "And Jeanne, of course, if she is interested."

"Oh, I don't know the difference between a Da Vinci and a, well, anything, really," Jeanne laughed. "I'm afraid a collection such as yours would be lost on me."

"How about you then, Miss Sharpe? What say you?"

It was a challenge, and Logan was discovering that Faith could be baited.

"Yes. Thank you, Mr. Harris."

"Evans?" The butler stepped forward from his position near the buffet table. "Would you light the gallery for our guest?"

"Yes sir," Evans replied, nodding to the underbutler across the room who left instantly.

Once dinner had finished, Arabella, their father, and Jeanne retired to the parlor as the storm continued to rage. Logan waited for Faith to join him at the base of the stairs as the others proceeded to their destination. To his equal amusement and annoyance, Faith took the stairs two at a time, seemingly unwilling to wait for him, even though she had no idea where she was going. In response, he took his time climbing the stairs, making her stay at the top.

However, just before he reached the landing, he stopped, his gaze fixated on the hem of her dress. Her skirts were several inches higher than the floor, and she only wore stockings to cover her legs. Frowning, he looked up to find her staring daggers at him.

"This is your sister's dress," she said, noting where his eyes had been. "My riding habit and shoes were soaked through. I had to borrow these."

"It's too short."

"My, aren't you're the observant one?" she said smartly, the charm she had displayed for the others vanishing.

This Faith he knew, all bristly and sharp. He nearly countered with a biting remark, but the nagging idea that she could be the lady from the painting gave him pause. Instead, he just stared at her momentarily, watching her defensive armor falter.

"What?"

"I did not say anything."

"No, but you're staring at me in a way that…"

He took the final step up the stairs and stood before her,

looking down into her eyes.

"In what way?" he asked, his tone more roguish than intended.

Faith took a step back, her throat bobbing like she was swallowing. Logan's gaze transfixed on her neck, and he had to bite his tongue to expel several outrageous fantasies.

What the devil was wrong with him?

Faith shook her head after a moment and turned.

"Which way is the gallery?" she asked over her shoulder.

"Left," he said, and she continued on her way, his eyes on her back.

Really, he didn't understand his reaction to her. He loathed this woman, yet outlandish images kept springing to mind whenever he stared too long at her. Faith, wrapped in that yellow velvet, laid out on his bed. Faith, standing in front of his fireplace wearing only a seductive grin. Yet then she'd open her mouth to speak and all sorts of conflicting thoughts would enter his mind.

As they reached the end of the hallway, a marble archway on the right led into a vast room with a vaulted ceiling that had been engineered to hold as many glass windows as possible between the beams so that the natural light could come in. Still, as only flashes of lightning currently lit up the evening sky, dozens of standing candelabras and oil lamps lit the room. At the opposite end of the gallery stood two large French doors that opened onto a half-circle balcony overlooking the gardens. Logan often found himself out there at night, gazing into the nothingness of space as he tried to quiet his anxious mind.

Where all the rest of the house had been painted or lined with colorful wallpapers, this gallery was left stark white, with light wooden floors to allow the hundreds of paintings that hung from the walls to shine without distraction or competition.

The audible gasp from Faith gave Logan a tremendous amount of satisfaction, and he watched as she moved slowly into the room, her captivated gaze lifting to the artwork. Her mouth fell open slightly, and he found himself frozen, staring at her profile. Though the painting showed a sensual, flirtatious woman, this sight of Faith, lost in her reaction, caught him off guard. She was well and truly amazed, and he was in awe of how much he enjoyed seeing the wonderment in her expression.

"There have to be hundreds," she whispered, more to herself than to him, but her words did shake him from his stupor, and he stepped forward.

"Eight hundred and seventy-two, in this room," he said, following her gaze up to a huge painting. "Do you recognize it?"

Faith shook her head slowly. He knew she couldn't believe what she saw.

"It can't be," she whispered, her hand reaching her chin.

Logan swallowed.

"It is."

She continued to shake her head, unwilling to believe her own eyes.

"But it's been in the Palace of Versailles since the eighteen thirties. It's well documented. I've seen it in a book."

"And art books are always correct?"

She swiveled around, her eyes wide.

"There is no feasible way you can have this. It must be a forgery."

"It is by Jacques-Louis David himself. You can see his signature in the corner. Right," he pointed to the bottom edge of the artwork, "there."

Faith turned back to face the enormous painting.

"How on earth did you come to own *The Coronation of Napoleon*? It's a French national treasure. It is impossible to have it."

Logan smirked, impressed by her knowledge, but he still wanted to test her more.

"Do you see Napoleon's sisters?" he asked as Faith turned back around to observe the work. "Particularly the second in from the left?"

"Yes. The one in pink?" Faith asked before frowning. "Wait. She is wearing a pink gown." Logan watched as Faith worked through it. She turned again. "All the sisters wore white in the original."

"They did."

"So, this is not the original?"

"It is not the first," Logan said, looking back at the painting. "In 1808, an American commissioned Jacques-Louis David to make another. He did, although it took him fourteen years to complete. By that time the original commissioner had died, leaving it to his family who stored it away in their London home. They are exact copies of one another, except for that dress," he nodded. "That was the only thing he changed."

"Why?"

"Rumor has it that when Jacques-Louis David became the official court painter, he was tasked with painting individual portraits of Napoleon's sisters. It's said that he fell in love with Princess Caroline. Since there was no conceivable way for him to even approach her, he kept it a secret. But when this painting was revealed, he supposedly told his assistant that he'd made Caroline's gown pink, so that she would stand out for everyone to see for all ages, just as she always had for him."

Silence fell over them as Logan stared up at the artwork. It was a romantic story he had heard when he had found the piece, and though he doubted its truth, he also couldn't deny it.

A slight sniffle emanated from his side. Turning, he saw Faith, her knuckles pressed against her forehead as she grimaced. He had never seen Faith so much as pout, let alone cry, and he wasn't exactly sure how to respond. Worried, he lifted a hand to her elbow, but she pulled away and spun around, causing him to still. After a moment, he spoke.

"I must admit, I underestimated your love for art."

"It's not that," she said softly. Lifting her head, she inhaled and exhaled deeply before turning back to face him. Her eyes were not red but watery, and he found it decidedly uncomfortable to witness her upset.

"What is it then?"

She shook her head, seeming unwilling to explain, but then she spoke.

"Painters. Artists. The whole lot of them. They're all so eager to show the world their passion and yet... They cannot bear to live those passions in real life. They're all cowards."

"Cowards?"

"Yes, the lot of them," she said, as her eyes lifted to gaze upon the painting. "They're too afraid to experience life and so they paint it instead. But this is not real. It cannot feel, it does not yearn." She let out a bitter huff of breath. "But supposedly he loved her?"

Logan nodded, unsure.

"It's what I've been told."

She nodded as well.

"But circumstance separated them. This," she said, lifting her hand, "is a love letter, to a woman who never knew and to a life never shared." She paused for a moment before dropping her hand and turning to him. "It would be heartbreaking, if it weren't so cowardly."

Logan watched her, astounded that she would speak so openly and eloquently about this piece. While he had never approached the matter from that point of view, he could understand her thought process.

Interpreting art was a joy of his, and neither his father nor sister ever cared to share their impressions. It was rather nice to have someone who had a different perspective.

"I never consider it before, but I suppose you're correct. Perhaps it was all he could do, though. To let the world know that at one point, he was a man who loved."

"Perhaps," Faith said. "But if it were I, I would want the love of a person instead of a constant reminder of what might have been. Even if the world never knew." She looked down, almost dejected. "But then, I am not an artist."

For some reason, Logan didn't like that. Nor did he appreciate how sad she seemed.

"Unfortunately, you are not able to determine that on your own," he said. "It is often noted that painters are their own worst critics. You must show your work to people, and let the majority speak on your talents."

Faith smiled ruefully after a moment, and Logan felt his heart expand. She had never before smiled because of something he said.

"Then I should burn all my works to avoid such criticisms. I do not paint for others. I paint for myself."

"I would like to see your paintings."

Faith let out an actual laugh, and Logan felt the wind go out of him.

"You, sir, will never see any of my work."

"Why not?"

"Because you've a houseful of masters whose talents far surpass my own," she said, waving her arm down the length of the gallery. "And I will not be compared."

"I would never compare you to anyone."

Though his words were innocent enough, Faith's smile faded. There was a heat between them, an energy that seemed to dance, not unlike the lightning that sparked outside.

"Thank you, for sharing your collection with me, Mr. Harris. But I think I should retire for the evening. It has been a trying day, and I worry that I've not had much rest."

Logan was surprised at how much he didn't like to hear that. Especially since he still hadn't figured out how he was going to see her bare ankle, but instead, he nodded.

"Of course. Good night, Miss Sharpe."

"Good night, Mr. Harris."

Faith moved past him, and for a moment, Logan was sure he would reach for her, but he didn't. He let her pass without obstruction and turned to watch her disappear into the hallway.

And now it was nighttime once more, and he was alone. Grasping his wrist with his hand behind his back, he began to walk the length of the gallery, just like he did most nights, as the storm raged on outside.

Chapter Five

THE EARLY MORNING light came all too soon into Faith's room, causing a wicked thumping feeling in her head before she even opened her eyes. The chill that had sunk into her bones the day before had grown into an unbearable heat that consumed her entire body. Her hands drifted up to her chest, but slowly, as if she were moving her arm through mud. Her fingers touched her throat, and she realized she was sweating profusely, so much so that her nightgown was nearly drenched. However, after only a few moments, she began to shake as a chill came over her.

She was sick. Properly sick. Faith's eyes barely opened as the glaring sunlight from the windows told her that the storm had finished. At least she could return to Lismore today. Struggling beneath the heavy blankets that lay on top of her, she fought to get up, rolling herself off the edge of the bed as the pounding in her head continued.

But Faith was barely across the room when a maid entered the room, carrying her cleaned and freshly pressed riding habit. Upon seeing Faith's hunched over form, she hurriedly came forward, tossing the dress onto a hope chest at the foot of the bed.

"My lady, what is wrong?" the maid asked.

"Nothing," she tried, but her scratchy voice betrayed her as the maid's arm wrapped around Faith's waist. "I'm just eager to dress."

The maid brought her hand to Faith's forehead.

"Oh no, my lady. You're as hot as a poker. You have to return to bed at once."

"I really must be going."

"You canne leave in this condition. You'd likely drop dead before you got out the threshold."

"I must."

"Sir Logan will not consent to it. He'll insist you stay, least your health be put into serious jeopardy and my lady, I would agree."

Faith was about to argue but didn't. She was distracted by the maid's use of that term again. She put her hand over the maid's to still her.

"Why do you call Mr. Harris, Sir Logan, as though he has been knighted?"

The maid gave her a strange expression as if she had just asked an absurd question, but Faith only stared. Evidently, the maid saw her chance to distract the patient, and she began to lead Faith back toward the bed. Weak and intrigued, Faith let her.

"Because he has been, my lady."

Faith's mouth dropped a little.

"He has?"

"Of course, my lady. He was knighted upon his return from Burma, by her majesty, for heroics in battle." Faith placed her hands on the mattress's edge and climbed back under the covers. "He saved an entire ship while fighting beneath Lord..." The maid looked around the room as her voice dipped. "Lord Dalhousie."

"Dalhousie?" Faith repeated, familiar with the name. "The one from the papers?"

She had read about him. Lord Dalhousie had led the campaign against the Burmese during the war but had been challenged in Parliament over his reasons. Apparently, Dalhousie was known as a combustible commodore. Though many saw his stance in Burma as one that demonstrated British excellence, some viewed his connection with the East India Company dubiously and held suspicions about his campaign overseas, to the point where many had come to view Dalhousie as a villain.

The maid's face scrunched up in worry, looking about the empty room once more as if someone might overhear her.

"Yes, my lady. Although, I pray you do not mention that man's name too loudly. Especially in Sir Logan's presence. He has forbidden it."

"Has he? Why?"

The maid shook her head.

"I did not ask, my lady. Nor should you," she said, standing up as she gave her a look over. "I'll inform Miss Arabella of your condition at once and have some beef tea brought straight away."

With a quick curtsey, the maid hurried from the room, leaving Faith alone with her thoughts. How odd that Logan had been knighted yet refused to go by his title. Faith had only met two knighted gentlemen previously, and both had been exceedingly proud of the honor. She wondered why Logan was so against it and if it had anything to do with his time in Burma. For the first time since knowing him, she wondered what it had been like for Logan during his military career.

Faith had been caught by surprise by her interaction with him last night. His usual arrogant attitude had vanished upon entering the art gallery, and she had sensed his deep appreciation for the pieces he kept. Almost as if by magic, she had noticed his entire person relax as he stared up at the artwork. It had been months since she had been able to discuss art with someone who truly appreciated it, as neither of her sisters had an eye for it. Aunt Belle had accompanied her in Italy to several museums, but while she enjoyed the arts, she was an admirer of sculpture, first and foremost. Faith could value it as a medium, but her true love was oil paintings, and so it seemed was Logan's.

She hadn't meant to reveal so much of herself while inspecting *The Coronation of Napoleon* painting, but then he hadn't balked or tried to lead her to a different understanding, as so many others had done before. Donovan had corrected her interpretations at least a dozen times during their relationship, which had constantly exasperated Faith. He was sure that his view was the only correct one, and she had agreed at first, but then his perspective always seemed to contrast with her own thoughts. Eventually, she had simply refrained from speaking to avoid being hushed.

But Logan hadn't done that. He had seemed genuinely intrigued by her opinion, which was certainly a first. Their usual sparring had been replaced by honesty, which had unnerved her. So much so that she had practically run away from him in the gallery.

Which was precisely what she intended to do now.

Faith threw off the covers again and swung her legs over the bed using all her strength. But before her feet could touch the ground, Arabella entered the room, followed by Jaco. Her sweet countenance was replaced with shock as she witnessed Faith's feeble attempt at escape. She gathered her pale-pink skirts in her hands and hurried to Faith's side.

"Oh, you mustn't get up," she said, approaching the bed's edge. "I knew this would happen. You were soaked to the bone when you arrived yesterday."

Faith didn't wish to reveal that she had also been soaked the day before last as well, during her morning outing, though she privately wondered if that had anything to do with her current state. Had Logan mentioned their meeting? Most likely not. She tried to sit up.

"It's really not terrible. I only have a chill," she said as the pounding sensation behind her eyes intensified. The heel of her palm came up to her brow, and she pressed slightly. "And a slight headache."

"You must stay in bed until you are well again. I shall call for a doctor."

"No, really, there is no need. If I can return to Lismore Hall, my sister Grace will be able to tend to me."

"Your sister?" Arabella said, surprised. "But how can she?"

"Grace has been apprenticing with Dr. Barkley in Glencoe

since we returned from Italy. She even attended with the doctor who treated Aunt Belle."

"Really?"

"Yes. Grace is quite knowledgeable when it comes to sickbeds."

Arabella gently moved Faith's feet beneath the covers, tucking her in like a frail child. She sat on the bed just as Jaco leaped up onto the mattress.

"Jaco! No. Get down."

"Oh, it's all right, I suppose," Faith said, though she inched away. "I don't mind."

"But Logan said you were terrified of dogs."

Faith looked at Arabella, somewhat surprised. Why would Logan tell her that?

"I'm not terrified of dogs," she began. "I just find that the larger the dog, the more frightening they are."

Jaco crossed his arms and laid his head down just below her hip. He nuzzled her slightly, but she didn't touch him. Nor did she move away.

"Jaco is nothing but a sweetheart," Arabella said, patting the reclining dog on the back. "But tell me more about your sister. That is fascinating that those doctors would let a woman practice medicine beneath them. Is it not a male profession? Wouldn't she find more success as a nurse?"

"It certainly would be easier for her, but Grace is determined. And she is quite proficient, I assure you. Which is why I really must return home."

She tried to hoist herself up but was too weak to do so. Arabella gave her a pleading look.

"Please, Faith. You must stay. I should hate to think that we weren't able to at least tend to you while you were sick. And I'm sure your sisters would want you to remain in comfort." She pressed the back of her hand to Faith's forehead. "You are burning up."

Faith knew that once her sisters were made aware of her

condition, they would likely become amused to learn that she was going to be staying at Harris House, with her comfort under the control of Logan—the very man Faith had often complained about.

But she was ill, and her headache seemed to double whenever she moved. She dreaded even the thought of taking a carriage ride home, but to stay here? Which would be worse?

"I don't wish to be a bother…"

Arabella smiled.

"No bother at all. You shall remain here until your fever subsides. In the meantime, we will keep you well fed and warm and in good company when you are able to have it."

Arabella's kindness seemed to be also prompted by an eagerness. Faith wondered if she had many friends but knew to ask would be rude.

"Thank you," she said quietly before adding. "Although, I don't think your brother will be much pleased."

"Logan would be far more upset to learn that you died on the way home than that you remained here, staying in bed," she said, but Faith doubted it. "Besides, he has just left and likely won't even be aware of your staying here."

Faith's gaze snapped to Arabella's face.

"Oh?"

"Yes, he had some sort of business in Glasgow that needed his attention. He will be gone for at least four days. And I'm sure you will be healthy by then."

"One hopes."

But as the day carried on, Faith only felt herself grow worse. It was outrageous that such a silly thing as a storm could cause her to be so unwell, and she was frustrated with herself for getting into such a situation. How had she allowed herself to become sick? She usually had such a strong constitution. And why did it have to be at Harris House? Even without Logan there, she felt his presence all around her. It was as if she could just close her eyes and imagine him standing beside her.

With eyes purposely open, Faith examined the painting that hung on the opposite wall, just above the fireplace. She knew Logan must have picked it out specifically for this room, as he likely had for all the artwork in the house. It was a river landscape painting by Theodore Rousseau, and it looked as though it was one of his earlier works. Faith had noted it the moment she had first entered the room yesterday. Rousseau was a realism painter from the Romantic movement, and while his talent could not be denied, Faith had always felt despondent when admiring his work.

Rousseau's pieces felt inherently sad to Faith and she wondered why Logan would display such a heavy piece in a guest room. Wouldn't a host want to convey a cheerful, peaceful kind of atmosphere? But perhaps Logan liked the work, even though the bleak skies seemed to hold a sense of dread about them. Or perhaps it merely seemed that way because she was feeling so ill.

She closed her eyes and tried to sleep through the fever, only to be awakened hours later, in the dark, to the cold touch of a feminine hand. Startled, she jumped, then groaned at the ache that had settled into her joints. She hurt all over.

"Shhh, easy there. It's me, Grace," her sister whispered in her gentlest tone.

"Hmm? Grace?" Faith rasped; her prickly voice was barely audible. "What are you doing here?"

"I've been here for a few hours," she said as Faith opened her eyes fully. The room was semidark, with only a few oil lamps lit, which gave the room an ominous glow. "But I'm afraid you've been in and out of consciousness. You are quite unwell."

"It's only a cold."

"I don't think so."

"It is. I'll be better in the morning. You needn't have troubled yourself in coming here."

For a moment, neither spoke. Faith glanced at her sister, whose mouth was pursed. Grace rarely, if ever, let her emotions show, but right now, they were displayed on her face. Faith began to worry. "What is it?"

"It seems your fever has come on rather quickly and your rest not been peaceful. I'm of the mind that you have pneumonia."

Faith closed her eyes, aware that pneumonia was a severe condition. Her sister had been particularly interested in the sickness several years ago while reading one of her books on illnesses. Grace had talked at length about it to anyone who was close enough to listen and Faith had often been the closest to her.

"Is that the one with the sickness in the lungs?" Faith asked.

"An infection, yes. It's most dangerous in weak children and the elderly, which I have advised Arabella to keep her father downstairs, lest he catches it. But I'm afraid you have to be on bedrest for at least a week, if not longer."

Faith closed her eyes tightly, trying to fight the desire to cough. She didn't want to be here when Logan returned.

"I can't stay here for that long. I don't wish to be here when Mr. Harris returns. You must take me home."

But Grace only shook her head.

"I'm afraid you have no choice. To move you would only distract your body from fighting off the infection. I'm sure Mr. Harris will not mind." Faith gave a little, unbelieving snort, but her sister continued. "Now Dr. Barkley will be here in the morning to reassess your condition. He will be able to diagnosis you properly, but I'm quite sure I've identified it."

Faith tried to raise her arm, to grip her sister's hand in a pleading way, but she found that her limbs were unbearably heavy, and the scratch in her throat would not desist. Tired from even their short conversation, Faith nodded and hoped that she might be able to sleep through the worst of it.

"Three days," she said as sleep overtook her. "I need to leave in three days."

But Grace merely shushed her and patted her clammy forehead as Faith fell into a dreamless sleep.

Faith was in and out of consciousness for the next three days, with her fever ebbing and flowing in the most uncomfortable ways. When she was hot, she was scorching, her body dripping in sweat. When she was cold, she was freezing, and no amount of blankets, furs, soups, or teas could make her comfortable. And perhaps she might have been able to handle that if not for the persistent cough that had come upon her suddenly.

Thankfully, Grace decided to stay at Harris House after Dr. Barkley confirmed her diagnosis. Grace had been diligent in her requests that no one enter Faith's room in an effort to sequester the illness. It was a rather radical method that Dr. Barkley believed was unnecessary. Still, Faith was glad that no one aside from her sister and a few of the maids would see her in the state she was in, so she entirely agreed with her sister's decision to keep everybody away.

Save Jaco, who had become something of a guard dog, occasionally frightening off even the staff with a deep growl whenever he sensed Faith's unease at being seen. It was remarkable that an animal could be so aware of her feelings. She hoped Logan wouldn't be annoyed with the dog for being so disloyal.

Not everyone was frightened off by the giant black dog, however. Late during the fifth night of her illness, Faith was awakened when she heard her door open. She was lying on her side, facing away from the door, and barely opened her eyes when Grace's harsh whisper sounded behind her.

"Sir, no one is permitted in here."

"I appreciate your professional opinion, Miss Sharpe," Logan's deep voice vibrated. Faith's heart beat erratically as she strained to hear him. "But I won't be dictated to in my own home."

"Then you must think of this room as not a part of your home, but as a sick room. Faith needs rest, and any interruption to that rest may interfere with her recovery."

Though she couldn't see him, Faith knew Logan was at odds with her sister. He disliked being ordered about, especially in his own home, and she waited to hear him argue. He would no doubt bicker with Grace.

"Very well," he said suddenly, causing Faith to frown. Why was he never so accommodating with her? She had half a mind to roll over when he spoke again. "How is she faring?"

"She is a little better today, though it was quite a nasty fever in the beginning. I'm sure she will make a full recovery, should she continue to improve."

"Had I known she was sick, I would have returned immediately."

A pause hung in the air.

"Whatever for, Mr. Harris?"

Faith strained to hear, curious why he would need to return home because of her.

"Only because she is under the care of my household—which makes seeing to her needs my responsibility," he said with some hesitation. "She should have all the comforts I can provide to aid in her recovery." When Grace didn't answer right away, he added hastily, "So that she might leave as soon as possible."

Faith's frown deepened, confused by his tone.

"Of course, Mr. Harris. But might we continue this conversation outside of her room? I should hate for her to wake up."

"Very well. Jaco?" he called, and to Faith's surprise, the dog whimpered instead of obeying Logan instantly. "Jaco. Come."

"I'm afraid your dog hasn't left her side since the sickness came over her," Grace said as Jaco remained on the bed.

"She doesn't like dogs," he said matter-of-factly.

"Well, she doesn't mind this one," Grace said. "Now, please. I don't want to wake her."

Without another word, Faith heard them leave as the door latch clicked behind them. Turning over, she stared at the door as her betraying, erratic heartbeat returned to a reasonable pace. He had wanted to check on her? To see that she had everything she needed?

Well, that was undoubtedly kind of him, though she was sure he'd meant the last words he said. He didn't want her in Harris House any more than she liked being there, but for some reason, that night, she slept as soundly as any of her sickness.

When Faith awoke the following day, she was surprised to find that her limbs were no longer heavy and that the painful, scratchy throat had subsided to a mild irritation. She hungrily ate her breakfast for the first time in days, though it was mostly sickbed fare of bone broth and mint tea, coupled with some plain toast.

"Can't I have more?" she asked Grace, who took the empty tray from her lap, to place it outside Faith's room. "I'm still hungry."

"You haven't had much to eat in a week. If you overdo it, you'll make yourself sick."

"I should think you'd want my appetite to return."

"I do, but overindulging it will only hinder your recovery."

"But I am recovered. And hungry."

"And luncheon will be served in a few hours."

Faith folded her arms across her chest and leaned back against the wooden headboard.

"I've come through a sickness only to be starved to death," she pouted as Grace rolled her eyes.

"I see you're feeling close to your old, churlish self."

Faith made a face before looking out the window. The skies were once again a dreary grayish white, and though it wasn't raining, she was sure it would eventually. It seemed she had been sick during a dry spell, only to recover just as the rains returned.

"This must be the wettest part of the world," she said as her hands came together over her lap. She glanced at her sister. "May I take a walk around the grounds?"

"Certainly not," Grace said as she sat at the bird's-eye maple table beneath the window. She opened a small leather booklet and picked up a writing utensil before marking a page. It had become a custom for Grace to record the family's health issues in detail, from onset to recovery. "You'll remain off your feet for at least today. Then tomorrow, you may have something more substantial to eat, and the following day you may try to walk."

"What a fearful doctor you are," Faith said teasingly, causing Grace to scowl as she wrote. "And I don't see why I can't walk today. I've been stuck in the bed for over a week and I'm sure to go mad if I can't at least dress."

Grace put her pen down and turned toward her.

"You really must regain your strength before you can leave."

"I won't leave the room then. Help me dress and I can walk in circles before the fireplace."

Grace shook her head in exasperation but stood up to help when she saw that Faith wouldn't be deterred. She had brought with her one of Faith's least restrictive gowns, a pale-blue-and-white gingham dress with buttons down the bodice. She pulled it out of the wardrobe, but Faith couldn't see any undergarments.

"Have you forgotten my corset?"

"Your lungs are weak and need no restriction. You shouldn't wear a corset for at least a month, so that your lungs might strengthen again."

Faith gave her an incredulous look.

"Have you lost your senses? I can't go about without a corset on."

"You absolutely can and will. You may wear dresses that tie in the back."

"And what of this one?"

Grace looked at it.

"We'll wrap you in a shawl."

Faith shook her head and got out of bed, only to look down at her chemise. Though she had been changed daily, she hadn't washed herself in some time and urgently desired to do so.

"Perhaps a bath first?"

Grace paused, then nodded.

"Yes, I think so."

It took over an hour to scrub, clean, and dress herself. The maid who had attended her when Faith first arrived, a girl known as Kassandra, helped to brush out and wrap her curls as Faith sat at the table.

A knock at the door caused her to panic slightly. But when Arabella's head popped through the crack of the door, Faith smiled.

"I heard you were up and about," she said, though her eyes went to Grace. "May I come in?"

"Yes," Grace said. "The maids took all the sheets and clothing and the windows have been open all morning. I don't see why not."

Arabella came in, carrying a flat, square wooden box. She beamed at the both of them.

"I brought you a chess board, to see if you were up to playing it?"

Faith smiled. She and Grace had become fans of the game during their time abroad.

"Yes. That would be lovely. Although, I must admit, I'm not very good. But I do enjoy it."

"Papa will be glad to hear it. He's been so worried that you might play just as well as your sister," she said, nodding toward Grace.

"Have you been playing Mr. Harris?" Faith asked.

"Yes. He's quite good."

"Not a good as you, though," Arabella said, causing the barest of pinks to color Grace's cheeks.

Faith smirked, enjoying her sister's discomfort. Grace wasn't often praised by people outside the family for her intellect. It had always been more of a hinderance to her to be so clever, and it was nice to see others take notice.

"Your father is a worthy opponent."

"I will tell him you said so. He will be very pleased to hear you think so."

"If he will listen to you, might I suggest trying to get him to see Dr. Barkley?" Grace said. "He's in need of a physical. I'm not particularly pleased with his gait when he walks, nor the inflammation around his neck. I've tried to diagnosis him several times during our evening chess matches, but he refuses to hear it."

"I hope you do not hold it against him. Papa is stubborn. Logan and I have tried to convince him to visit Dr. Hall for ages, but he refuses."

"Dr. Hall?" Grace said, her full attention to Arabella. "Aren't his practices a bit…contemporary for someone like your father? I should think you'd have more luck with Dr. Barkley, considering his age."

"Age isn't the issue. It wouldn't matter if Dr. Hall was older than Dr. Barkley. Papa refuses to see anyone, which is why I hope you were not offended by his dismissal when you tried to help him, although I'm sure he was baffled to learn about your studies. A female doctor is a rarity. He says you're by far the strictest practitioner he's ever encountered."

"I'm not a doctor yet," Grace said, though her cheeks turned a deeper shade of pink. "I haven't finished my apprenticeship, nor have I been accepted to any medical schools. But I hope one day to be."

"Do you have to go to school?" Arabella asked, causing a tense look to pass between the sisters.

No school in the entire United Kingdom had permitted Grace entry due to her being a woman. Yet, as frustrating as it was, Grace continued to apply to schools, even though she continued to be denied entry. Her only course of action was to apprentice with any doctor that would have her, and it had been difficult convincing even Dr. Barkley to do so.

"One day, perhaps," Grace said. "But until they permit women to go to school, I'll have to manage the old-fashioned way."

"Oh," Arabella said, somewhat dejected, before adding. "I believe Dr. Hall went to the University of Glasgow. Could you try there?"

"I have," Grace said, looking down at her notes. "Believe me."

It bothered Faith to no end that her sister, intelligent and determined as she was, could not pursue her passions. She was tenacious and brilliant, and simply because she was a woman, she was denied her life's desire. Still, Faith knew it bothered Grace to discuss it, so she decided to change the subject.

"I hope your brother was not too displeased with my still being here," she said as she set up the chess board. "I hate to think I've been a bother to him."

"Of course not," Arabella said. "On the contrary, he was quite eager to make sure you were well taken care of. Isn't that right, Grace?"

"Yes, but..." Grace said, looking at Faith. "How did you know Mr. Harris was returned?"

Faith stared at her sister, keeping her face purposefully blank. She didn't want to confess to overhearing their conversation the night before.

"I assumed. Arabella said he would be gone for three days. It has been almost a week."

Grace squinted at her sister but returned to her notes as Arabella made the first move. They played for an hour or so before breaking to take tea—a bland meal that mainly consisted of dry toast and a carrot soup that lacked any flavor, much to Faith's displeasure. She ate all of it, though, in an effort to get her sister to afford her more food. But after tea, Grace insisted that Faith needed to rest, and left with Arabella. They decided to take a tour of the grounds while Faith slept.

Only Faith couldn't sleep.

Bored and not tired in the least, she waited a half hour before going to the window. Peering down, she saw Grace and Arabella as they strolled the neatly kept hedgerow that outlined the gardens at the back of the house. Faith was sure she had plenty of time to tour the art gallery some more before they returned. She doubted Logan was in residence since he was often at Lismore Hall visiting with Graham, and as Mr. Harris couldn't come upstairs, she was sure she would be entirely alone.

Wrapping a shawl around her shoulders, Faith slid on a pair of slippers Grace had brought from home and crossed the room without making a noise. Jaco yawned and stretched his legs out before jumping off the bed. He landed on the floor with a soft thud, earning him a look from Faith.

Carefully, she turned back to the door and opened it. Peering through the crack, she saw no one and opened it further. Poking her entire head out, she looked back and forth just as she caught sight of Logan, reaching the top of the stairs. Desperate to not be caught and chastised, particularly by him, she turned and was trying to scramble back into the room when he called out to her.

"Faith?" he said, his tone worried.

Faith squeezed her eyes shut, cursing herself for leaving her room at that exact moment. Shaking her head, she donned a pleasant enough expression and turned to face him.

Logan was dressed in a brown tweed pair of pants and matching vest, his white shirtsleeves unadorned with a coat. He wore a thin, black-and-tan silk neck scarf pinned in place, and as he approached, Faith couldn't help but notice how complementary the color was, particularly in contrast with his hazel eyes.

His full mouth was quirked up, as if he was both partially amused and partially concerned. Faith had to ignore how pleasant she found the line of his jaw and to her humiliation, she visibly shook on her weakened legs.

"Are you well?" he asked.

"Yes, of course. Thank you," she said, trying to think of something to get him to leave. "I was just, um… well…"

"Escaping?" he said with a smirk.

Though she was resistant to explain herself to him, a part of her was hopeful that he might take pity on her plight. She smiled shyly.

"Honestly, yes. I can't abide staying in this room any longer and my sister has taken to a tyrannical bedside manner." Her gaze dropped to the floor. "I know she knows what's best in these circumstances, but I'm bored and so dreadfully hungry."

"Hungry?" he said with a frown. "Are you not being fed?"

"I am, but only sickroom foods. I've had nothing but broth

and toast for days."

"Well, then come on," he said, holding his arm to her. "I'll see you to the kitchens."

Faith stared at his arm for a moment, unsure. She knew she was weak, but she didn't like admitting it, and certainly not to a man she had considered an enemy for over a year.

Sensing her apprehension, he gave her a somewhat condescending stare.

"Unless you're too afraid to disobey your sister's orders."

Faith narrowed her eyes at him and took a step toward him.

"I am not afraid of anything," she said primly, resting her hand gently on his solid forearm.

"I am well aware of that," he said under his breath as he escorted her down the hall as Jaco followed.

Chapter Six

NEITHER OF THEM spoke as they made their way down the staircase, through the main hallway to a narrow door. It was strange, as most of their time in each other's company was comprised of snipping at one another, but at that moment, the sole focus of her attention was the heat that stemmed between her hand and his arm. Never in her life had she felt a forearm so large and rigid. It made her curious what his bicep felt like, and soon she wondered if his entire body was as firm and strong.

"I see you've stolen my dog's loyalty," he said, his tone neither accusatory nor mirthful. "I would have thought you'd prefer him to stay away."

She bent down slightly as they walked, patting Jaco on the head.

"He was a great comfort during my illness and Grace allowed him to stay in the room."

"So she tells me."

By the time they reached the kitchens, Faith was warm and flustered, though she assumed it was because she hadn't had any sort of exercise in days. Apparently, her appearance was altered enough for Logan to comment on it.

"Are you certain you are well enough for this?" he asked, his tone concerned. "Your cheeks are red."

"Are they?" she said, taking her hand away from him as they entered the doorway leading to a servants' dining room. She pressed her fingers to her cheek. He watched her closely as she sat on a long wooden bench beside a rough-cut table where the servants' meals took place. "You know, it isn't polite to point out someone's physical flaws."

"I didn't say your cheeks were flawed."

"No, but red cheeks are hardly considered pleasing."

"On the contrary, I quite enjoy seeing you flushed." Faith knew he was teasing her, but the heat in his eyes made her pulse flutter and she swallowed. Really, it was very impolite of him to make such comments, and she was appalled to find that she was flattered by them. "Now, what would you like to eat?" he asked, walking into the kitchen portion of the large room, where several cooks and maids were busy preparing dinner. Several servants paused in their work to see if he had any orders for them, but with a wave of his hand, Logan seemed to convey that their presence wasn't intended to disturb the servants' work. A number of large brass pots and pans hung from the opposite whitewashed stone wall while the clanging of metal utensils echoed throughout the open room. "Puddings? Meats? Cheeses? Or something sweet, like tarts or biscuits?"

Faith's stomach growled, and she put her hand to it.

"I'm nervous anything too rich would make me unwell. Perhaps a plate of biscuits?"

With a nod, Logan moved around the kitchen quickly as if he had spent much time there. That was absurd, of course, as men of position rarely ventured into the kitchens. They could simply request something, and a servant would bring it. But Logan seemed capable and soon procured a delicate blue-and-white plate piled ridiculously high with shortbread biscuits. The cook, a stout older woman named Mrs. MacGregor, brought a pot of strong black tea, cream, and sugar and set it before them without a secondary glance. It seemed she was used to Logan being in her kitchen. But not Jaco.

"Come along, you mangy mutt," Mrs. MacGregor said, holding a piece of overcooked meat above the dog's head. He followed her instantly as she led him away from the table. "Out of my kitchen."

The dog followed her to the door, which she opened before tossing the meat out. Jaco ran after it.

"He's as faithful as a snake," Faith mused, taking up one of the buttery shortbread biscuits.

"Aye, he is," Logan said with a smirk as his voice dipped. "But he's far better at retrieving sticks."

Faith felt a giggle bubble up as she bit into the delicious pastry. Whether it was because she hadn't had anything sweet in days or because the cook was an accomplished baker, Faith didn't know. All she knew was they were the most excellent biscuits she had ever tasted.

She might have restricted herself slightly if she had been at a formal dining table or been in the company of someone whose good opinion she sought, but that wasn't the case here, and she was well and truly hungry. She ate three circular biscuits before even looking up, only to find Logan watching her with his brows slightly raised and a faint smile on his lips, seemingly entertained by her famishment.

Taking a sip of her tea, Faith swallowed the delightful treats, noting a surprising lack of aftertaste that she was used to.

"These are delicious. You have a very talented cook," she said, loud enough for Mrs. MacGregor to hear. Faith could see the old woman's profile pull up into a smirk as she tended to her steaming pots over the stove. "But they're different than the ones at Lismore Hall." Faith picked up another one. "What is the difference?"

"That's because Graham has long since convinced Lady Belle to use honey in nearly every recipe. When he started his honey business, he had his cook whip up a shortbread recipe using honey as the sweetener, and he gave them to Lady Belle to try. Whether she genuinely enjoyed them or not, who knows, but she told the cook to begin using that recipe forthwith," Logan said, adding loudly over his shoulder, "However, Mrs. MacGregor would sooner shoot me the take any requests to change her recipes. Isn't that right, Mrs. MacGregor?"

"There's no use fooling with a good and proper recipe," she answered from her post.

Logan smiled and faced Faith. She took another bite of a biscuit, delighted to discover the relaxed rapport Logan shared with his staff. For some reason, she had always assumed that he would be an arrogant master, but he seemed to be on a more familiar level with his staff.

Seemingly aware that he had surprised her, he tilted his head. "What is it?"

"I always assumed that you would be an overbearing employer," she said, dipping her chin. "Someone who barked orders or even belittled those who worked for you."

"Why is that?"

"From all our interactions, I suppose."

Faith knew he knew what she meant, so he exhaled slowly.

"We did manage to make some pretty severe impressions on one another, didn't we?"

"Yes."

"It seems rather a ridiculous thing to occur now, looking back."

"Well, it wasn't me who started it," Faith started, lifting her chin. "You were rather rude from the time we first met at the MacTavish house."

The crease between Logan's brow deepened.

"If I was, it was only in response to you."

She frowned back at him.

"How so?"

"It was evident you didn't want to be there. When Graham told the story of Tam Lin to you and your sisters, you were uninterested. I'm sure you may have even rolled your eyes during his telling."

"I did not."

"Oh, you most certainly did."

"Were you watching me?"

"No," he said quickly. "But your indifference was evident."

"If that's true, it wasn't because I didn't appreciate the story. It's only because I don't like fairytales."

"Tam Lin isn't a fairytale. It's a folk story. One the people in this area take very seriously."

"You cannot expect me to believe in fairies."

"Not at all," he said, taking the biscuit from the plate. He ate it in one bite, taking a swig of tea before he spoke again. "But ridiculous or not, it means something to the people here."

"Does it mean something to you?"

He hesitated before answering.

"Not exactly," he admitted. "To be honest, I've never quite liked them myself. But it's the principle of it."

Faith gave him a sardonic look.

"Bravely defending your heritage against the English?" she asked in jest, but a shadow fell over his face at the mention of English, and Faith wondered if she had touched upon something. She leaned slightly forward. "Tell me, if I were Scottish, French, or some other nationality, would you have been quite as offended?"

"Yes," he said quickly. Then, "Well, maybe. I mean, I suppose not."

"You know, my heritage is not my fault. My parents had me, not the other way around."

That made him smirk.

"I guess that's true," he said. "Tell me, are you more like your mother or father?"

"Neither, I'm afraid," Faith said softly.

"Why? Were they both gentle, well-spoken people who never argued with anyone?"

Faith glared at him, but sensed that he was teasing and threw a biscuit at him. He caught it deftly and took a bite.

"They were, actually. All of those things, and they wanted their daughters to be like that as well. You might not believe it, but once I tried my very best to be the perfect daughter."

Logan's brow dipped slightly and genuine curiosity came over his handsome face.

"Is that so?"

Faith nodded.

"But when they died, I…I guess I became rather angry."

"Angry?"

"Yes. At them for leaving me and my sisters, at the world for taking them, at everyone, really, even though it wasn't anyone's fault," she said, her tone dipping. "I suppose that's not a very good thing to admit, is it? But it's true."

A long silence followed, and Faith was sure she had crossed some unknown line admitting such things to him, but then he spoke.

"Aye. I can understand that."

She glanced at him.

"You can?"

"Children often don't have the capacity to understand trage-dy. Anger is one of the more basic feelings humans and sometimes…" he said, his own eyes shifting down. "Sometimes it's easy to believe that anger is the only thing that can protect us from being hurt again."

Faith's eyes widened. Yes. That was exactly how she'd felt and to hear it said so perfectly, well, she felt suddenly lighter. Leaning forward, she nearly spoke when he leaned back and continued.

"I suppose I can forgive you for being English, as it isn't really your fault."

Faith smiled at his jesting tone and she nodded, tucking away her previous response.

"Well then," she said. "Perhaps we should put our prideful ways behind us and start anew."

Logan's hazel eyes locked onto hers, and she felt a warmth crawl over her.

"Yes. I'd like that."

"Faith Rebecca Sharpe!" Grace's voice echoed into the room.

Faith and Logan turned to see Grace and Arabella standing in the doorway. "What on earth are you doing out of bed?"

"Ah, just taking in the scenery," she said meekly, pushing the plate of biscuits away. Logan pulled them toward himself. "Isn't this the most modern kitchen you've ever seen, Grace?"

Her sister was not amused.

"Come, you must return to bed," she said, coming forward to take Faith's arm as she stood from the bench. "You are not fully recovered yet."

Faith was escorted back down the tiny hallway to the main foyer without so much as a goodbye. As they headed up the grand staircase, Grace finally spoke.

"You likely think I'm being irrational, but I insist that you rest. I know being held up in this room for days is difficult and that you're not terribly fond of Mr. Harris, but you must consider your health."

"But—"

"Now, I am not unreasonable. If you feel well enough in the morning, I promise we can go home. But you must trust me, Faith."

Faith wanted to tell her that she didn't mind Logan's presence as much anymore, but she nodded, thinking the better of it.

"Of course, I trust you, Grace. And you are right. I will stay in the room until you've dictated otherwise."

Bringing her fingers to her forehead, she made a mock salute as they reached the guest room where Faith had been staying, causing Grace to smirk.

"Alright, enough of that. Back into bed."

Faith allowed Grace to help her undress, and soon she was tucked back into her sick bed. Dinner was served some hours later, bone broth and plain tea. Not terribly pleasing, but Faith did not argue.

Once her tray was removed, Arabella was permitted to read to her for an hour, and she, Grace, and Faith spent the evening in pleasant enough company. At the same time, the maids began to pack the sisters' belongings as Grace had decided they could return to Lismore the next day.

"I must say, it's been a grand thing, having you stay here," Arabella said with a yawn as she closed her book. "Even though you've been sick. I hope you've had a pleasant enough stay."

"I have, Arabella, thank you."

"I should like to give you something, to remind you of your time here," she said as her hand dipped into the pocket of her dress.

Bringing her small fist up, she uncurled her fingers and revealed a small, circular piece of amber stone. The light from the lamps shined through it as she held it up between her index finger and thumb, causing it to glow.

"It's lovely," Faith said.

"Isn't it?" Arabella replied, handing it over. "I gave Logan a near identical one before he left for Burma. Amber is lucky, you know."

"Is it?"

"Oh yes. Old Miss Fletcher told me so when I was girl, just before Logan left for war. He had taken me to Glencoe with him for a visit before he left. She gave me one just like this, so that I could give it to Logan."

"Miss Fletcher?" Grace said, coming forward to inspect the gem in Faith's hand. "I've met her. She has a set of rooms behind Dr. Barkley's office." Grace frowned. "Doesn't she have a bit of a reputation for, well, folk medicine?"

"That's a kind way of saying that some people call her a witch," Arabella said, turning back to Faith with a wink. "She's a firm believer in the wee folk."

"Oh dear. Not more fairy tales."

"I don't believe in witches," Grace said. "Nor in talismans, although there is a certain train of thought that a positive attitude can lend itself to good things. There was an English physician, Dr. Haygarth, who did a study about positive influence and imagination. Supposedly, if a patient believes they have been given an effective treatment, regardless of whether they've actually been given something with medicinal value or not, it can make them better. Of course, it's all very subjective."

"The power of positive thinking to cure an ailment?" Faith asked suspiciously. "That seems ambiguous at most."

"It is. But I know Miss Fletcher does have a healthy knowledge about local herbs and remedies for ailments. I've spoken to her a number of times and many locals will still pay her a visit, if they don't agree with or like Dr. Barkley's diagnosis, which is probably why he lets out his rooms to her—to keep his patients close."

"Well, even if it is a superstition, I believe that amber is lucky. It brought my brother home safely, although he did lose his amber," Arabella said off handedly. "Still, I was very pleasantly surprised to find this one, just on the front steps. It was rather magical, really, considering how deep one must dig for it usually." She smiled. "But there it was, just the other day. I thought of giving it to Logan, to replace his, but he's a bit like you, Faith. Only, I'm sure you'll humor me and accept it as a token of my friendship."

Faith's fingers clasped tightly over the small stone.

"Of course, I will. Thank you so much, Arabella."

She smiled, and after bidding them goodnight, she left, soon followed by Grace, leaving Faith alone to finally rest.

The blankets that had kept the chill away from her during the height of her fever were now far too warm. With one leg hooked over the edge of the blankets, she flipped through the book Arabella had given her. It was a recent print about Renaissance painters. Fascinated by it, she was peacefully enjoying herself.

But then, about an hour after her sister left, there was a knock at the door. Glancing up and putting her book down, she wondered what Grace could possibly want.

"Come in," she said, expecting to see her sister when Logan's frame filled the doorway.

She immediately sat up straight.

"Mr. Harris," she said, somewhat shocked. "I, um… What are you doing here?"

"I was told that you were only offered broth for dinner," he said, revealing a bunched-up cloth he held clenched in his fist. "I thought you could stand to eat something slightly heartier."

Faith smiled as he came around the bed, handing her the tied-up napkin. Leaning forward, she untied it to reveal apple slices, a sandwich of bread and cheese, and several shortbread biscuits.

She bit the inside of her cheek to stop herself from smiling too widely. Perhaps she really had been too harsh in her first understanding of this man.

Looking up, she began to thank him, only to see his gaze was focused on her bare ankle. It was the oddest thing. He was completely still and had the strangest expression on his face. For some reason, Faith felt suddenly uncomfortable beneath his scrutinizing stare.

Slowly, she pulled her foot back and snaked it beneath the blankets.

"Thank you," she said, holding up an apple slice. "I do appreciate it."

But Logan didn't answer. Instead, he just looked at her as if some puzzle that had eluded him had suddenly made sense. Faith was about bid him goodnight when he spoke.

"Who was your art teacher, in London?" he asked, his tone uneven.

"Excuse me?" she asked, a minor panic filling her heart.

"Your art teacher. Who was he?"

"Ah, it was Mr. Delaney," she said after a moment's pause to ensure she didn't tell her first teacher's name. "My friend Renee's brother."

"And no one else?"

Her brow scrunched together defensively.

"Who else would there be?"

Logan stared at her as if struggling to decipher her words. But instead of answering her, he asked another question.

"Have you ever had your portrait painted?"

An alarm sounded throughout Faith's body as her eyes widened, and she grew cold. Why would he ask such a thing? She leveled him with a straight stare, unwilling to tell him anything.

"No."

"No?"

"It's what I said, isn't it? No."

Her tone was forceful and unpleasant, but he stepped toward her and leaned over, crowding her. When he spoke, she shivered.

"I don't believe you."

What could he know? Certainly nothing of importance. And yet Faith's entire being seemed to scream out to beware, because he already knew too much.

Suddenly, her breathing felt laborious, and she shook her head.

"Well, I'm sorry you feel that way," she said, pushing his napkin of treats away, ignoring how close his face was to hers. "But if you wouldn't mind, I'd like to get some rest now."

Logan's eyes dropped to her mouth and for the briefest of moments, she thought he might kiss her. She inhaled, worried that there was a part of her that actually wanted him to do so, but that would be insanity. Of course she didn't want him to kiss her. There certainly wasn't an amorous feeling between them, and she wouldn't admit it even if there was. But beneath his analyzing stare, Faith felt her skin grow hot.

"It *is* you."

Faith shook her head. He couldn't know. He couldn't possibly know. It was impossible.

"I don't know what you're referring to—"

"*Odalisque Reclined* by Donovan," he breathed, and Faith felt her heart shatter. "You're the woman in the painting."

Oh, God. This wasn't happening. How could this be happening? She closed her eyes, humiliated and furious, hoping she was still sick and this was some sort of fever dream. But the sinking feeling in her chest was too real to be imagined.

"Why…" she tried at first. "I mean, how do you know that painting?" she asked, refusing to look at him.

"I'm the current owner."

Faith's eyes snapped open, unable to believe what she had just heard. She gaped up at him.

"Excuse me? H-how?" she asked before she could stop herself but held her hand up. "No. Don't tell me. Don't talk to me. I don't want to know."

"Faith—"

"This cannot be happening. This can't happen," she said, suddenly frantic. She pushed the rest of the blankets off her as she swung her feet off the bed to stand, moving around him. "Oh God. You must leave. You have to leave."

"Wait."

"I can't do this. Oh God, how is this even happening?"

"Can you hold on for a moment?" he asked as he reached for her, but Faith wouldn't stay. She pulled away from him, and she could see the look of regret in his eyes, though whether it was about telling her about the painting or not being able to touch her, she did not know. "I only wanted to—"

"Fine. If you won't leave, I will," she snapped, unwilling to discuss it any further.

She stalked toward the door and reached for the door handle to pull it open, but Logan's hand came above her head, holding the door shut. Faith turned as her entire body began to shake with outrage.

"How dare you—"

"Will you calm down for just a moment?"

"Calm down?" she hissed. "How can I calm down when you… You've somehow managed to bully your way into ownership of a piece that should never have left its maker?"

"Do not direct your displeasure at your former paramour at me. I merely stated a price, and he accepted."

"Paramour?" Faith repeated. "How dare you compare what we had to something so, so cheap!"

"Is this the scandal that took you and your sisters away from London last year?" he asked, tilting his head. "I admit, I would never have guessed that you were the cause of your relocation."

"Of course it's not," she bit out. "Not that it's any of your business, but no one in my family knows about that…that piece of canvas."

He let out a frustrated breath.

"Listen, I didn't mean to—"

"To embarrass me? Shame me? Make me out to be some sort of fool? Well, you have," she said hotly. "I thought I had judged you too harshly, but if this isn't evidence that my initial impressions were correct, I don't know what is. You are nothing but a wicked man. A no-good, blackmailing coward."

At the word coward, pain and fury flashed in Logan's eyes, and in an instant, he had his large hands clutching her upper arms in an aching grip. Faith gasped, partly stunned by his audacity but also partially excited, though only the Lord knew what that said about her. Would he hurt her in flash of anger? She doubted it, although she couldn't clearly state why or how she knew that that was a line he wouldn't cross.

After a stalled moment, Logan spoke, his tone grave.

"Say that word again and you'll see how very wicked I can be."

His voice's biting tenor told Faith she had hit a nerve. While she was morosely satisfied to get under his skin, his reaction made her curious. What right did he have to be indignant?

"I knew what you were the moment I saw you," she said, her eyes dropping to his mouth. "Cold and calculating."

"And you're nothing more than a liar," he countered, his breathing uneven.

"A liar? How?"

"Pretending to be all innocent and self-righteous when you're nothing more than a—"

Fury like Faith had never known sprung up within her. How dare this man speak anything to her? Particularly things that she had only privately considered herself. He had no grounds to judge her.

"Say it," she bit out through clenched teeth. "I dare you."

But something seemed to stop him. He only gave her a single shake as if he couldn't bring himself to do any more.

"Arrogant bastard," she hissed after a long moment.

"Conceited harpy."

How wrong she had been when it came to this man. This awful, plotting man. But as her breathing became difficult, his hand approached the side of her face. She pulled back only slightly before mirroring his advance. Her hands came up to his face, and in an instant of madness, she kissed him.

A burst of color, sound, and taste enveloped her senses as Logan stood, stunned into stone. For a moment, she thought he might not kiss her back, but then suddenly, his strong arms wrapped tightly around her—and after that, she was lost. Whatever possessed her at that moment to do such a brazen thing as to kiss him, she did not know, only that it felt as if it were imperative, necessary even. There was an overwhelming need to dominate and demonstrate her autonomy, as though to say her body was her own and no painting or prose created in her image could take any part of her away.

But Logan's mouth possessed her in such a devastating way. Never had she experienced such a torrent of fevered excitement, as if every inch of her had been made to experience every inch of him. It was as if kissing him had unlocked some secret compartment within her, and she was desperate to explore it.

But before her thoughts could even form, Logan's strong arms loosened, and he held her shoulders, pulling away the warmth of his body.

"Wait, wait," he said in a rough whisper, his eyes meeting hers.

They stared at one another, shocked for a moment, before Faith stepped back. Her hands covered her face as if the intensity of his stare burned her.

"Oh God," she said to herself. "What is wrong with me?"

"Faith—"

"No. Do not speak. Please, just go," she begged, moving around him. "Please."

Thankfully, he didn't speak, and when the door opened and closed behind her, she rushed to lock it. Turning, she pressed her back against the carved wood and slid to the ground, shame filling every part of her being.

What on earth was she going to do now?

✦

Chapter Seven

I T HAD BEEN three days since Faith and her sister had left Harris House, and Logan was still reeling from what had happened between him and Faith as he walked the northern path along Loch Fyne with Jaco. Both Sharpe sisters had thanked him the morning after his kiss with Faith. He had tried to make eye contact with Faith as she said her goodbye, but she had refused to even look at him.

Though he couldn't speak to her in front of everyone, he had hoped to reassure her. A comforting nod or an understanding glance would have sufficed. Some hint to let her know that while she may not be pleased that her painting was in his custody, it was at least safe from being seen by anyone else. But she would not meet his eye, so he was unable to make any signal.

He wished he could have discussed what had transpired between them. All good sense had vanished from his mind the moment she had called him a coward. If there was one thing he could not abide, it was being called a coward. He hadn't meant to handle her as he did, and he certainly hadn't meant to insinuate that she was any less in his eyes for having posed for the painting. But he feared that she believed he would say something unkind when all he had wanted to tell her was how infuriatingly perfect she was.

It galled him, even now, to realize how close he had come to admitting that, and while a part of him couldn't help but seethe with jealous fervor toward Donovan, a man who had been permitted to see Faith in all her natural splendor, another part of him was in awe of her reckless bravery.

He only wished she knew that the painting was safe within his possession.

Indeed, Logan had found that he had become rather ogre-like when it came to *Odalisque Reclined*. He had little wish to share it with anyone and even covered it with a sheet when he left his room, hoping to keep the servants' curious eyes off it lest they recognize Faith. Thankfully, no one had said anything, and he meant to keep it that way.

Why he should feel so defensive of her, however, he did not know. She had all but molted back into her banshee-like self when he confessed to owning the painting. But the moment he held her in his arms, he had lost all logic.

There was something shockingly perfect in the way she fit into his arms.

He hadn't even meant to hold her. He'd only wanted to move her aside so he could leave, but when they'd touched, something had seemed to zap between them. Something dangerous and exquisite. Something he had never experienced before. He had caressed her cheek out of sheer need, and she had done the same to him. Then his mind had turned hazy as the desire to touch her consumed him and he had kissed her.

He let out a shaky breath. He needed to get a better handle on himself.

Bending to the ground, Logan picked up a dead pine stick and tossed it ahead. Instantly, Jaco ran away ahead to retrieve it, only to be distracted by some trailing scent as Logan pondered his reaction to Faith. Their kiss had been electric, and though he knew it was ridiculous, he wanted very much to do it again.

Of course, that was something he desperately needed to not think about, for it stirred too many uncomfortable emotions. Bedding women had never been an issue for Logan, but nothing ever ventured past a physical sort of arrangement, and there couldn't be anything like that with Faith. And yet, while the chances of Logan and Faith having an affair were nearly nonexistent, he couldn't help but imagine it. Their brief kiss had consumed his every thought and every moment he wasn't distracted by conversation, he was thinking about it.

But it was a ridiculous notion to consider repeating it. He and Faith were too volatile toward one another, too different. Besides, there was something about Fatih, a quality about her seemed to whisper the word "forever," and he would not be consumed by one woman for the rest of his life and end up like his father.

No. He wouldn't do that.

Logan had tried to be sympathetic toward his father for having lost the love his life, but the old man's loss of joy in life had only managed to leave Logan bitter toward the whole idea of falling in love. He often pitied his father, and he had no wish to become pitiable himself, even with the lure of soft curves, silky curls, and vibrant green eyes.

The sudden deep growl emanating from further along the path caught Logan by surprise. Distracted from his thoughts, he stilled as he looked ahead. Jaco's head was low to the ground, and he was positioned just beyond the crest of a hill. He was in a pre-attack stance. Curious, Logan hurried to see what warranted such a posture.

The wooden path led to an open field that sat beneath the beginning of a mountainous landscape. Just at the foot of the mountain stood an old stone crofter's house. Logan had played there as a boy amongst the overgrown rose bushes that had nearly engulfed the tiny house—but he hadn't been there in years.

"What is it, boy?" he asked, hunching down to Jaco's side to pet the dog's head. "Is it a stag?"

But just as he spoke, Logan thought he saw the flapping of a cloth just around the cottage's corner. Straightening up, he squinted. It was a decent way away, and the wind was blowing, causing the tall grass and heather to wave before him to the point where he couldn't entirely be sure if what he saw was real or merely a shadow.

Jaco's growl intensified, and while Logan was curious, he did have a standing appointment to meet with Graham. If he went to inspect the building, he would likely find nothing… but still, he stared. This land butted up against his own. If there was any danger here, he needed to be aware of it. But the longer he observed the cottage, the more he was convinced it was some sort of shadow playing against the bramble bush that covered the corner.

He rustled Jaco's head.

"Come on, boy. Let's go."

Logan hadn't ridden his horse in the hopes of exhausting himself, but by the time he reached Graham at the northern half of the shore, he had barely even started to build up a sweat. He was used to the rocky terrain, and he was in the process of wondering if he should try running when Graham's tall form entered his vision.

Dressed in his usual dark jacket and matching pants, Graham stood with his back to Logan, gazing out over the loch from his favorite fishing spot. Why Logan continued to pursue this foolish sport, he did not know, but he was eager to speak with Graham if only to learn how Faith was doing since her departure from Harris House.

He only hoped that Graham had left his wife at home this time.

"Oy!" he called out, never the sort to sneak up on anyone. Graham turned around, flashing him a smile. Logan made a point to look around. "Is your bride not with you?"

Graham had recently made it a habit of bringing his wife, Hope, with him on fishing excursions. Logan hadn't minded at first, except when she began landing the damn fish almost before her line had been cast. Her natural ability surpassed even her husband's, and while most men might be aggravated by it, Graham only ever puffed his chest out, proud as the day was long about his wife's talent.

"Not today, I'm afraid," he said as Logan and Jaco reached the water's edge. Graham bent down to pat the dog on the head. "She isn't feeling well."

"Oh? I'm sorry to hear it," Logan said.

"She's saying she's all right, but she was pale yesterday, as well as today. I was going to send you a note to cancel, but she insisted I go," Graham said, eyeing him. "I hope she didn't catch anything from Faith."

Logan looked straight ahead as he dropped the wicker basket slung across his chest to the ground.

"Miss Sharpe appeared to be in perfect health when she left Harris House. Besides, I doubt her sister would have let her leave if she had felt otherwise."

"Aye, that Grace is a stern one," Graham said, a sense of brotherly pride in his tone. "She was the one to convince me to come today, actually. Said there was nothing to worry about concerning Hope and that it would do her good to get some rest without my bothering her."

Logan smirked, privately amused by Graham. He had always been so self-possessed, so sure of himself and his purpose—which had always been to regain Lismore Hall, the ancestral home that his father had gambled away to Lady Belle thirty-some years ago. When he had learned that her nieces were going to inherit, he had been so determined to not like the Sharpes, particularly Hope, but then had fallen madly in love with her. Now, he was the bane of every bachelor's existence: a happy husband.

It was tiring to be around him sometimes, Logan acknowledged. A man should never be so overtly pleased with himself or his family. It led to complacency since it left one with little to no reason to strive to better one's situation. Logan would certainly never be so content.

"How does Miss Sharpe fair?" Logan heard himself ask as he baited his line. "She seemed well enough when she left my house."

"Very well. And my wife wanted me to thank you for taking

such good care of her. Especially considering well…You know."

Logan paused and glanced at his friend.

"Do I?"

"Well, considering you two don't get on. Hope was very grateful that you kept her in such good spirits."

It shouldn't have been surprising to hear. Logan and Faith had rarely kept their contentious feelings for one another hidden. Yet he found himself irritated. Mildly so, like when a twig is caught in one's sock. And even though no one knew what had transpired between them, he wanted to make some sort of amends.

"It was no trouble. I believe Miss Sharpe and I have cleared up some misunderstandings between us."

"Oh?"

"Yes. It seems we were both rather unfair to one another based of unfounded preconceptions," he stated slowly. When Graham didn't answer, he looked at him, only to find his friend staring at him with an odd sort of expression. Instantly, Logan's guard rose. "But perhaps I was too quick to assume that our hostility for one another was in the past."

Graham's brows knit together, and he looked down. After a moment, he spoke.

"Well, that would explain why she was so quick to defend you yesterday."

Logan paused in his activity.

"Defend me? How so?"

"Hmm?" Graham said, looking up. Then he shook his head. "Oh, it was nothing really."

He would have to ask plainly, he thought. Taking a deep breath, he returned his gaze to the south shore.

"What happened?"

His question, practically an admission of interest, hung in the air between them for some moments before Graham answered.

"It was a small instance. Lady Belle's former secretary, Rose, came to visit yesterday."

"Did she?" Logan asked. "She and your cousin Jared have barely shown themselves ever since they got married."

"Aye, no doubt Rose has kept him to herself all these months. She'd been in love with him for an age," Graham said with a grin. "Well, she stopped by and learned about Faith's stay at Harris House. She made a comment about how difficult it must have been to be in your company for so long. Grace spoke, going on about your hospitability, when Faith suddenly interrupted."

"What did she say?"

"Only that yours was as good a house to get sick in as any."

Logan's shoulders dropped, annoyed that he would be so interested in such an irreverent comment. That was hardly a compliment, yet Graham was smirking.

"A testament, to be sure," Logan said sarcastically after a moment.

"She also said that Harris House was the finest home she'd ever been to."

Logan instantly regretted the burst of ego that bloomed within his chest. She liked his house, did she? It was a small, throwaway piece of information, but something about it made him swell with pride.

"Is that so? A blaring tribute from one like Miss Sharpe."

"I certainly thought so."

Despite the conversation changing then to talks of business and weather, Logan found himself wholly engrossed in the idea that Faith had enjoyed her time at Harris House despite being sick. And despite having learned that her nearly nude portrait now occupied space there. He wished she could visit again but quickly pushed the thought from his mind, knowing it was unlikely.

Faith would likely never return to Harris House knowing that *Odalisque Reclined* was there and he couldn't blame her. It must have been shocking for her to learn that such a revealing painting was in the hands of her former sparring partner. If he were honest, he would admit that it had been difficult reconciling that the woman in that painting was his Faith.

No. Not his Faith. Good God, what was wrong with him? He didn't want any claim to her, yet the words had popped into his head so suddenly and effortlessly. Surely he had lost his mind. Faith was not his, nor did he even want her to be.

Still, by the time he left Graham and Logan and Jaco started their journey home, all he could think about was her, in his house once more, staring at his vast collection of art as they argued about the meaning of each one. And what they might do after such arguments played out in his mind, followed by a slew of erotic images.

He bit his tongue, trying to shake such intrusive thoughts. Yes, it was best to steer clear of Faith. From now until at least the end of time.

Chapter Eight

"I'M THINKING ABOUT returning to London," Faith announced one evening, nearly a week after returning home from Harris House.

The entire family was sat in the parlor, each in the middle of something as they all turned to gape at her. Graham had been helping Grace find a book on medieval medicines while Hope was embroidering some sort of quilt. Aunt Belle sat at her desk, tending to her correspondence, her manservant Andrews faithfully standing behind her as he always did.

It seemed everyone was surprised by Faith's sudden proclamation, but she had been toying with the idea of leaving for days. Since learning that Logan was now the owner of *Odalisque Reclined*, she had been plotting an escape from Scotland. The shame that festered within her heart, particularly after kissing him, was enough to make her want to run away and never return. If only she could be sure Logan would never reveal the painting to anyone. Of course, Faith doubted he'd be so generous and wouldn't believe him even if he gave her his word. Not after Donovan had so easily broken his promise.

At first, she'd had ideas to steal the painting or, at the very least, ruin it somehow. She had some paints in her room that she could throw on it, but the thought of going to Harris House made her leery. There was no way on God's green earth that she would ever be able to look Logan in the eye again. Which is why she decided her best choice was to flee.

Forever.

"London?" Aunt Belle said with disdain. "Goodness, my dear, why would you wish to return there?"

Faith held her chin up.

"I've always had an idea to return to London and I think now is as good a time as any."

"But why?" Hope asked, dropping her embroidery to her lap. "It seems rather sudden."

"Yes, you've not mentioned it before now," Grace added. "Has something happened?"

"No, nothing has happened. And just because I haven't mentioned it doesn't mean I haven't thought about it. Which I have. In great detail, actually."

"But you can't go alone," Hope said. "Where would you stay?"

"I could stay with Renee. I'm sure if I write her, I could persuade her to ask her parents to allow me to visit for an extended period of time. And who knows? If I were to meet someone, I might stay forever."

Faith knew she was being slightly outrageous, wildly tossing out the idea that she might meet a suitor, but then she couldn't bear staying in Lismore. Not with that painting only an hour's walk from where she slept. What if Logan hung it in his house where guests might see it? What if his father or sister saw it? Faith could feel herself grow warm with embarrassment. She couldn't bear it.

She looked around the room, noting the apprehensive glances she was receiving. She must be genuinely shocking them.

"I see no harm in going to London," Aunt Belle said at last, addressing the rest of the family, though her silver stare held Faith's. "If our Faith wishes to leave Scotland, we should be supportive of her."

Faith smiled unevenly, not entirely pleased, while Hope seemed at a loss for words. She turned to her husband, who appeared equally as dumbstruck.

"Er, well, I don't see why not," he said, unsure, as Hope stood up, facing Faith.

"You cannot go," her sister said. "It's just not feasible."

"Why not?"

"Because. It's too far from the rest of us and you can't beg to stay with friends."

"Surely she wouldn't beg," Aunt Belle interjected. "Would you, dear?"

Faith shook her head, glad to have at least one person's support.

"No. Absolutely not."

"It's still out of the question," Hope said defiantly, and Faith stood up.

"Who made you matriarch?" she snipped, glad to be starting an argument. If Hope became upset with her, leaving would be easier, and her sister would most likely be happy that she was gone. "You have no right to tell me how to live my life."

Hope frowned, appearing hurt. Faith bit the inside of her cheek, hating to see her sister distressed, but she needed to be away from this place.

"I don't want to dictate your life," Hope said, her tone softening. "I just don't know why you suddenly wish to return to London. It's been over a year and I've not heard you speak of the city in nearly as much time. We have a home here and we've all been very happy—"

"I don't deny that," Faith cut in. "But I don't wish to stay here."

"Whyever not?"

"Ladies, ladies," Aunt Belle said, waving a bejeweled hand above her head as if to settle them down. "There is no need to argue. If Faith wishes to go to London, then she may go, of course. We will not hamper her desires. And I will accompany her." Faith gave Hope a self-satisfactory grin. "In three months' time."

Faith's smile faltered as she glanced at Aunt Belle.

"Three months?"

"At least, my dear, at least. While London may be the crown jewel of high society, Glasgow has quite a vibrant atmosphere itself. Not to mention, that I am patron to at least a dozen charities and societies that require my attendance, particularly because I was unable to do so last year with my illness."

Faith began to chew the inside of her cheek.

"But the London season will be over by then."

"A fine time to go, in my opinion," Aunt Belle said, standing up. Andrews took a step forward, but she waved him off. "That way the crowds have all gone and one might enjoy the city quietly. Unless there was some specific person you wished to see, my dear?"

Faith shook her head.

"No, not particularly—"

"Good. Then we will leave the first of August," Aunt Belle said. "As for now, I will retire. I'm afraid I've stayed up far too late. Good night, all."

A murmur of good nights followed Aunt Belle as she left, leaving Faith and the others in tense silence. Once Aunt Belle was well and gone, Hope took several steps toward Faith.

"I do not know what brought this desire to move to London, but it's not the greatest of timing."

"Why not?"

Though Hope didn't speak, she gave Grace a peculiar glance, which made Faith somewhat uneasy. She was about to ask what was going on when Grace spoke.

"Because we are throwing Aunt Belle a surprise birthday party."

"We are?" Graham asked.

"You are?" Faith asked.

Hope appeared frozen, as if the information was new to her as well before she began nodding her head enthusiastically.

"Yes, of course," she said, though it didn't sound convincing. "Aunt Belle will be seventy-six this year, and that is a milestone."

"Is it?" Graham asked, frowning.

"Of course," Hope said quickly, giving her husband an unusual look. "And it's just a little shocking that you would want to leave in the middle of that."

"Well, I didn't know there was going to be a party. Had you told me about it, I might have waited until afterwards. Besides, Aunt Belle said we shan't leave until August."

"Yes, that's true," Grace said to Hope. She moved away from the bookshelf and reached for Faith's hand as they sat on the sofa. "I guess we just assumed you would be here to help."

"Well, I will be, won't I?" Faith said.

"What I mean to say is, we're just surprised, that's all. You've not mentioned London in such a long time, and I guess Hope and I assumed that you no longer wanted to return."

That was true. Though Faith had once been desperate to return to London, her desire had waned since coming to live in Scotland, and in more recent days, she hadn't much thought about returning.

She began fretting about what it would be like to run into Logan again.

Faith tried not to display her turmoil, but she was sure her anxiety was painted all over her face. She tried to push it away. She simply needed to avoid him for the next several weeks, and she would be able to, hopefully, leave this country and never see him again.

"It matters little," Faith said, trying to focus on something, anything that would distract her from Logan. She turned her head to see Hope and sighed. "So, tell me. What is to be involved in this birthday celebration?"

Hope looked slightly panicked and gave Grace another pleading look. Grace cleared her throat, drawing Faith's attention once more.

"Well, we were just about to send out invitations. Tomorrow," she added hastily, her eyes flickering to Hope again. "Which is why we all must go to Glencoe tomorrow. You will come, of course. We've several things to settle. Flowers, food stores, decorations, and fireworks."

"Fireworks?" Graham repeated.

"Of course. Seventy-six is a very important birthday."

"But is it?" Graham asked again, confused.

"Yes," Hope said firmly to her husband, who smirked at her tone.

"Very well then," Faith said, looking at Hope again. "But isn't her birthday only a few weeks away?"

"Yes, which is precisely why we must stary organizing immediately," Grace said, going to her knees before the small table that sat before the sofa. "Hope? Bring me a sheet from Aunt Belle's desk. We will start with making a list."

"Perhaps I should leave you three alone then. I wouldn't want to get in your way," Graham said, walking behind Hope. He leaned close to her ear. "Tomorrow, noon?"

The blush that came to Hope's cheeks made Faith discreetly glance away. Though Graham and Hope had been left alone during the early months of their marriage to do whatever it was newlyweds did, it seemed the return of Faith, Grace, and Aunt Belle had caused a bit of claustrophobia for the couple, who had taken to visiting the old hunting lodge at the northern edge of the property once a week to allow them some privacy.

But Hope apparently would not let him leave so quickly.

"Stop that," she whispered, apparently embarrassed that he would be so brazen as to mention something everyone knew about. "And you can't leave. You know everyone of importance within a hundred miles. You can help us make the invitation list."

"I suggest you write my uncle. Laird McTavish knows everyone."

"It'll be too late before he responds. We must have these done and sent out tomorrow." Hope gave him a pleading glance, and of course, Graham sighed and came forward.

"Very well. Are you ready, Grace?"

"Yes," she said, studiously crouched over her paper as Graham began to list off a dozen names, all families and friends that Aunt Belle had grown close to during her thirty-year residence at Lismore Hall.

Faith was suspicious of the whole matter, but she couldn't deny her love for her aunt and was privately glad to have such an event to celebrate the woman whom Faith had come to view as a surrogate grandmother. And in her heart of hearts, she had to admit that she felt rather more fondness for Aunt Belle than she had for their actual grandmother, Belle's sister. Where Grandmother Alice had always tried to dissuade Faith from being too impractical, or too consumed by her own interests, Aunt Belle had nurtured Faith's choices.

She understood that she and Aunt Belle had shared an independent streak, and while she was happy to celebrate someone who had lived life on her own terms, Faith wondered if she was as brave as her elderly great-aunt had always been.

"—Logan Harris, of course, as well as his father and sister," Graham said.

"What?" Faith said suddenly, causing Grace to stop.

"What is it?" she asked, looking down at her list. "Did we already add them?"

"No," Faith said, leaning forward. "But Lo—ah, Mr. Harris doesn't like us. Why would we invite him?"

Hope's brow lifted incredulously.

"Faith Sharpe, what manners you have. Of course, we will invite the Harris family."

"I'm not say to exclude his father or Arabella, but Lo—I mean, Mr. Harris," she said slowly, as if to chastise herself, "has never liked us. And he's very loud about his dislike for the English." When no one spoke, she sighed. "I just don't see why we should bring him here if he's going to do nothing but drink our wine and complain about us and the guest of honor."

Grace's mouth tightened and shifted slightly as it did when she was conflicted. Graham appeared confused while Hope came forward.

"Mr. Harris might not have always gone out of his way to be pleasant, but he has always been perfectly courteous at least to Grace and me," she said. "Not to mention his friendship with Graham. And Aunt Belle has always spoken very fondly of him." She paused before adding. "And I should think, after he was so accommodating during your bout of sickness, that you two might have come to an understanding."

Instantly, Faith stood up.

"What understanding? I assure you; Mr. Harris and I have no understanding." Everyone stared at her, confused at her overreaction. Faith exhaled, suddenly aware of how foolish she was being. "Very well. Invite whomever, but I think I will follow Aunt Belle and retire. I'm not feeling myself."

"I hope you are not having a relapse," Grace said, concerned.

"I'm sure she is fine. Simply tired. Aren't you, Faith?" Hope asked.

Though she could explain it, Faith knew Hope was giving her an exit. She tried to smile but failed and left the room. She heard Graham say something along the lines of that he was not particularly interested in hearing the family dissect her behavior, causing a surge of gratefulness toward her brother-in-law to shoot through her.

At that moment, all she wanted to do was to fall into her bed and sleep away her misery.

Chapter Nine

A THICK, GRAY fog engulfed a sweat-slick Logan while hazy flashes of British canon fire and echoes of Burmese rifles echoed around him. He had been trapped in this dream a thousand times, but it felt as visceral and as terrifying as the actual day every time.

The vessel that had taken him and the other troops up the Rangoon River, a vessel called the *Medusa*, had run aground. While half the men had been dispatched to try and figure out how to get their ship free, the others had been dictated to watch for the enemy, as their presence was heavy in this part of the jungle.

The heat and humidity had taken its toll on a handful of troops, including Duncan Carlyle. He had been below deck, suffering from the strange fever that swept over nearly half of the soldiers. He had just come topside and called out to Logan, who turned to face him.

"Duncan, what the devil are you doing out of bed?" Logan asked in a mocking sort of way.

While he had been concerned for his friend's well-being, the jungles during a war were hardly a place for pampering someone back to health. If Duncan was up and walking, he was likely well enough to fight. After having been down for nearly a month, it was obvious that he was finally ready to escape the sickroom.

"I can't stand it in there anymore," Duncan answered, coming up the railing. He placed his elbows on the wood. "I swear, every time I started to feel better, I'd just contract something new from one of the other men. It's a rolling stone, down there, isn't it? Recovery and reinfection, over and over again." He shook his head looking into the dense jungle. "I've a better chance topside."

"Well, if you're feeling better, I won't stop you. Although, Jeanne will have me quartered if you end up catching some sort of pox that might scar that ugly face of yours," Logan said with a smirk.

That made Duncan smile.

"Jealous that I've such a pretty wife and you're stuck cuddling sheep back home?" he teased.

"It's not sheep I keep company with."

"Oh no, that's right," Duncan said, with a jovial nod. "It's cattle."

Logan had nearly quipped back when the first blast happened. Everyone dunked their heads as chaos erupted all around them. He looked up to his side after a second, wondering why Duncan hadn't dropped when he saw blood spurting from his shoulder as his body tipped. Standing up, Logan tried to grab him, but Duncan was already swinging back. He grabbed at Logan's collar, snapping the leather strap that held the small, circular amber charm that his sister had given him before he left Scotland. An instant later, Duncan fell over the ship's railing before Logan could stop him.

Jolted awake and drenched in sweat, Logan's eyes opened wide in the darkness. The gentle growl of Jaco reverberated through the room as his heart raced. He tried to swallow, but he found it difficult. Pushing back the covers, he launched himself off the side of the bed. Bare feet touched the ornate carpet that covered the wood floors as he crossed the room to a table, where a pewter pitcher of water sat. He poured himself a glass and gulped it down while Jaco's head nudged at his hip. His hand dropped absently to the dog's ears.

"It's all right," he said into the dark, more to himself than the dog. "It's all right."

Jaco whined, seemingly worried about his master. Walking toward the bedside table, Logan reached for a small, brown glass bottle and shook it. Empty. Dr. Hall had given him laudanum to help with his sleep, and while Logan didn't like using it, he couldn't deny that it helped him sleep. Unfortunately, he was all out.

Groaning, he turned, noting the faint gray light that shone through his window. Whether it was the moon or the early morning sun, he did not know, but he decided to get dressed. He would go to Glencoe that day to see if Dr. Barkley had any laudanum to give him as he tried to shake the nightmare from his body.

Once dressed, he went to the kitchens to find something to eat. Mrs. MacGregor always left him a plate of cheese, bread, and biscuits at the ready. After eating, he tossed a piece of cheese to Jaco and returned to his room. Usually, he would walk the halls, admiring the art pieces that took him away from his dreams, but lately, there was only one painting that could stave off the horrible memories of Burma.

Lighting several oil lamps in his room, he removed the sheet that hid *Odalisque Reclined*, sat on his bed with his back against the foot post, and observed the piece. Jaco turned in two wide circles and lay down at his feet. Faith's spirited, come-hither facial expression seemed less playful tonight, and Logan was sure she was practically frowning at him. Obviously, he was seeing things, but the longer he looked at it, the more defensive he became.

"I don't see why you're so upset," he murmured, causing the dog's head to perk up. "It's not as though I've hung it on display for the whole house."

Jaco tilted his head, apparently confused.

"And now the dog thinks I'm losing my mind for talking to a painting," he murmured, his eyes following the yellow velvet fabric painted over the curve of her hip. His jaw tightened. "If you're going to be mad at anyone, it should be Donovan. I'm not the one who sold it. I would never, ever, sell a portrait of you.

Not to anyone."

No, he certainly wouldn't. Besides the fact that it was close to a masterpiece, Logan had found that he had become rather possessive over this piece, even though the stillness of the painting unnerved him. In real life, Faith possessed endless facial expressions, sharp words, piercing glares, and a rather adorable smirk that would cross her face whenever she thought she outwitted someone. It had annoyed him a great deal at first, but now he found it appealing, if not downright erotic.

He wondered, not for the first time, if Faith had had a physical relationship with Donovan. *Of course she had*, he thought, ignoring the bitterness that rose in his throat. Though he hadn't ever met the man except through their correspondence, Logan disliked him. No, he detested him. What sort of man had someone like Faith in his confidence and then betrayed her as he had? It was apparent when Logan told her about buying the painting that she had been stunned by the artist's treachery. The expression on her face was one of heartbreak. The sort of look a tossed-aside lover might have.

It burned his insides to think that someone had hurt her. He wished he could demonstrate what a proper lover should be, *could* be to a woman like Faith. Although that was highly unlikely. Faith wasn't in any rush to see him again, and he couldn't blame her. She was mortified and likely would avoid him forever now. It was just as well. It was becoming too easy to be in her presence, and the added desire he had begun to feel toward her was undoubtedly as unrequited as it was unwelcome. It would be best to simply follow her lead. If she ignored him, he would do the same and save her from further embarrassment.

Still, he sat and looked at the painting for a long time. When the first streaks of true morning light finally entered his room, he got up, stretched, and covered it back up.

He left his room and found his way to the dining room, where he discovered his father dozing off in his seat and Arabella, her brow pinched with worry.

"Early day, today?" Logan inquired upon entering the room.

"Yes," Arabella said, her voice scratchy, as though she hadn't slept much. "Papa did not sleep well last night. I'm afraid he hasn't slept well for the past several nights."

"He's not the only one," Logan mumbled as he sat, nodding to the servant who poured him coffee while Arabella gave him a tense look. "What?"

"You needn't be so cavalier about it."

"About what?"

"Papa's health."

"What am I to do for him?" Logan asked, annoyed that he was arguing this early in the morning. "He mopes about this place every day, tucked away beneath his plaids like an invalid waiting to die."

"Logan!"

"Tell me I'm wrong," he countered as his father snorted. They both looked at him, waiting for him to wake, but he didn't. Logan peered back at his sister. Didn't she understand that they couldn't help him when he did not wish to be helped? A man without the desire to live would have his way sooner or later. Logan had accepted it a long time ago. Why couldn't she? "He's been this way for years, Arabella. He has no desire for life."

"He wasn't always like this," she argued. "He was different when you were away."

"Oh, that's right," Logan said sarcastically. "When I was in Burma he was the image of good health. No doubt because I was out of the country."

"It wasn't because you were gone."

"No, it was because if I died over there, he'd have to sit up and pay attention to life so that you might find a husband. Which I'm sure is the only reason he's holding on now, as limp as that hold may be."

Arabella stared daggers at her brother, but she held her tongue. Perhaps he should have let the matter rest there, but he was in a frightful, argumentative mood, so Logan leaned over the table.

"What? Say I'm wrong. Make any valid point and I will concede on the matter."

"You're so *damn* unfeeling when it comes to Papa," she said in a blistering whisper. Logan was surprised that she cursed. "Why are you so harsh in your judgment of him?"

But Logan didn't want to speak it out loud, didn't want to admit to his sister that he had argued with his father when he had first joined the service, telling the man that he had enlisted in an endeavor to get away from Scotland in general and him, in particular, since he had run out of sympathy for the old man who had let his grief consume him.

Logan leaned back against his high-backed chair, reaching for his coffee. The bitter, hot liquid burned his throat, but he barely registered it. He glared at his sister.

"If you're so concerned about his sleep, you should come to Glencoe with me today."

Arabella's brow quirked, confused.

"What? Why?"

"I'm going to see Dr. Barkley for something."

Arabella gave their father a concerned glance.

"But I can't leave him like this."

"Like what? Sleeping? He won't even know you've gone."

"But what if something happens?"

Logan nearly let a biting retort slip but inhaled slowly instead as a plate of food was placed before him.

"Do whatever you wish then."

They ate the rest of the meal in silence, and then went their separate ways. Logan hadn't expected to see her again until after his return, but when he was ready to go, Arabella had come hurrying down the stairs, dressed in a pale-violet day gown. His brow went up at the sight of her, but she barely acknowledged him as she hurried out the door.

The ride to the village was quiet, though not for lack of trying on Arabella's part. She always tried to find some common ground between herself and Logan, searching for a bond that had been severed when he left for war. In truth, they hadn't been terribly close as children since Arabella was seven years Logan's junior. Still, she tried to connect with him time and time again, only to be rebuffed.

It wasn't that Logan didn't like his sister. On the contrary, he was very fond of her. Arabella was an intelligent, caring young woman, not prone to pouting or bouts of stubbornness. She was delightful, which was why Logan kept his distance. He didn't wish for his cantankerous disposition to rub off on her. Not to mention that the empathy she felt for their father irked him. It was best to stay out of each other's way.

Upon reaching the bustling village, Logan was regretfully reminded that it was market day for the local livestock. Dozens of farmers had brought their fattest pigs and cows to be sold to the butcher or possibly individual families. This, of course, made town exceptionally crowded, and as Logan got out of the carriage, he helped his sister out just as a gaggle of geese scurried across the dirt road, barely avoiding being trampled by a group of pigs.

"Blast," Logan muttered under his breath. He did not like crowded places. "A fine day to come to town."

"Oh, it's just a little busy," Arabella said, standing on her tippy toes to see over the crowd. "Shall we see if the doctor is in?"

Logan gave his arm to his sister, and they walked down the street. Three distinct ridges, known as the Three Sisters of Bidean Nam Bian Mountain, towered over the village, partially hidden by low-lying clouds. It seemed the weather was determined to stay miserable and wet this early summer.

Dr. Barkley serviced most in the council area, though he did share his offices with Dr. Hall whenever he was in town, which was once a month at the least. The small, whitewashed cottage that served as their office sat in the center of town, flanked on one side by a draper and, on the other, a chemist who aided in filling the doctor's prescriptions.

Logan and Arabella purposely approached the building, knocking on the black-painted wooden door. The excellent doctor opened the door within moments, and his white brows lifted.

"Harris, Miss Harris," he said with a slight nod. "To what do I owe the pleasure?"

"You aren't busy with a patient, are you?" Logan asked as the old man stood back to let them in.

The small house was divided by a wall that ran the length of the building. The front room acted as an office and reception space while private examinations were handled in the back. Logan was aware that old Miss Fletcher, the so-called local witch, lived upstairs. He hadn't been fond of the old woman since she had convinced his sister that talismans and tokens of amber were good luck, and he gave the ceiling a sour look as he moved toward a wooden table that stood against the far wall opposite a small pot stove.

"No, no," Dr. Barkley said, waving his hand. "I was just on my way out actually. I've not another appointment until..." He patted his vest pocket, looking for something. His fingers dipped into the shallow breast pocket, and he pulled out a silver pocket watch. "At least an hour." He looked up. "What can I do you for?"

Arabella stepped forward.

"Papa has not been sleeping restfully these past few nights," she said. "No amount of chamomile tea helps, and he refuses spirits."

"Does he?"

"Yes. He says alcohol only makes his dreams more vivid and he doesn't wish them to be."

The hesitation in Arabella's voice caused Logan to stare. There was something she wasn't saying, and he wondered what his father had told her to make her appear so sad.

"Ah, well, that it does for some. That it does. Very well," the old man said, turning his back on them as he headed toward the desk beneath the front window that overlooked the street. He hunched over and, after picking up his pen, scribbled something on paper. "Take this," he said, handing it to Arabella. "To the chemist next door. He'll give you some laudanum."

"Thank you, Dr. Barkley," Arabella said. "And is Miss Fletcher home?"

"I believe so," the doctor said, giving her a speculative look. "Why? You're not looking for a love potion or anything, are you?"

"Oh no," Arabella said, her cheeks turning pink. "I only wanted to say hello."

"She's a fool, Arabella, don't waste your time," Logan said.

"She's an old woman, who has been very kind to me. And you, if I do say so."

Logan rolled his eyes, not willing to argue over magical nonsense with her again. Instead, he sighed.

"Very well."

Arabella smiled.

"Lovely. After I say hello, I shall go next door then?"

He nodded at her as she made her way out of the little cottage. Once she was gone, the doctor gave Logan a knowing glance.

"I suppose you wish for some as well?"

"If you would," Logan said as the doctor opened one of his drawers at his desk.

Pulling out a small, brown vial, he handed it to Logan. Dr. Hall had arranged to keep Logan's supply at the office, for which Logan was grateful.

"That last one lasted a little longer this time, didn't it?" Dr. Barkley asked. "Nearly two weeks longer."

"Is that so? I've not paid attention to it."

"I have," the doctor said. "In fact, if I were to guess it, I think you might not need it in a year or so."

Logan pocketed the small bottle.

"You're an optimist, then."

Dr. Barkley shrugged.

"I've been accused of worse," he said before letting out a humorous huff. "In fact, I've been called a traitor to my profession at least twice today."

Logan's brow furred. Dr. Barkley had been the town's physician for nearly thirty years. Whoever would accuse him of poor practice was a fool.

"By whom?"

"Well, just this morning, Mark Finley said he'd take his ailments elsewhere, if there were any other place he could go."

"But why?"

"Because I'm letting the Sharpe girl apprentice with me," he said, taking his coat off the coat rack and putting it on. "I must admit, I was apprehensive about it. But with Hall off in Glasgow, I've no other eager students to teach. Besides, she's smart as a whip, that one. Did a fine job tending and diagnosing her sister while she was under your care."

Logan's shoulders tensed at the mere mention of Faith, but he tried to shrug it off as he followed the doctor out of the cottage.

"Indeed," he said as they both set off in the same direction along the crowded street.

"I should like to speak with Lady Belle about finding her a surgeon's apprenticeship, actually. She's a fine mind for it, I think, and she doesn't have the malady of fainting at the sight of blood."

"Is that so?"

"It is. I suppose I'll be able to talk to her at Lady Belle's surprise party next week."

Logan glanced to his side.

"Is there such a party?"

"There is. I only received my invitation this morning, from the middle sister, actually, not ten minutes before you arrived."

"Faith is in Glencoe?"

"Yes. All three of them are," he said, his eyes squinting as he looked over the bustling street. He pointed a finger diagonally across the road. "There they are now."

Logan's head turned, and there, sat on that ridiculous petite Connemara horse, was Faith. It had been days since he saw her, and he was amused and aggravated at how his heart seemed to hammer beneath his chest at the mere sight of her. It was ridiculous to be so blatantly excited and miserable at seeing her sitting proudly on the too-small pony. Her honey-brown hair was pinned beneath a black, curved-brimmed top hat, and she was dressed in a brass-colored habit, with black piping stitched up the front of her chest in a military fashion.

Hope stood beside her horse, speaking with Graham, while Grace was just getting up on hers. Faith sat sidesaddle, as was expected of gently bred women, but her rigid back seemed too stiff as the horse moved from side to side in agitation as a large drove of pigs made their way down the street.

She was nervous. How he knew, he couldn't begin to understand, but she was. Impulsively, he stepped in her direction, wanting—no, needing—to get to her, but in an instant, a sickening dread flooded his veins as everything moved in slow motion.

The honking of several geese, frightened by a dog working to keep a flock of sheep in line, scared the pigs, which rushed toward the edge of the road. Faith's horse, Sweetness, reared up suddenly, turning midair before letting out a frantic neigh. Grace's horse shifted to avoid the commotion while Faith's hands gripped the reins as the horse twisted and took off, her hat dropping to the ground amongst the shouts and screams of busy passersby.

"Faith!" one of her sisters screamed, but Logan was already on the move.

Without hesitating, he ran forward, shoving his way through people and farm animals alike until he reached Hope's horse. He barely registered her panicked expression as he tore the reins out of her hand, hopped onto the horse's back, and took off after Faith.

All the noise from his surroundings seemed to die away as he galloped after her, down the country lane and across the stone bridge that led out of the village. The road led into the forest that sat between the town and the mountains. As best he could see from trailing behind her, Faith's body was hunched over, and it appeared as if she were desperate to hold on.

Logan rode faster, urging his horse to a breakneck speed. He could grab her horse's reins if he could only get to the side of it, but the surprisingly fast pony would not yield. When a fork in the road appeared before them, the animal hesitated, and Logan seized the opportunity to gain the upper hand, driving his horse faster up along the side and snatching the reins with deft precision.

All at once, the trampling of the horses' hooves died away, and within moments, Logan was off his horse, pulling Faith off hers as he held her tightly against his chest. Her entire body shook, flooding him with waves of fierce protectiveness that surprised him.

He held her for long moments, squeezing her as if he could absorb her fear. He barely even realized that he was laying kisses on the top of her head. He even kissed the spot between her brows that creased whenever she was deep in thought, unable to stop himself. The softness of her body against his was as provocative as it was necessary. Nothing had ever felt more natural to Logan than holding her protectively in his arms. Gently caressing the back of her neck with one hand, he murmured foolish, sweet nothings to calm her.

"It's all right. You're safe now," he whispered, his tone raw as a tremor moved through her. "My darling, it's all right."

The bare skin of Faith's neck was cold and clammy, but it was her silence that unnerved him most of all. She was most likely in shock, and he didn't know how to rouse her from it.

"Can you not speak?" he said, pulling back a fraction to look down at her as she clung to him. "If I knew a mere horse ride could rob you of your speech, I'd keep a stable full of wild ponies to silence you."

The soft teasing seemed to break the spell over her. Blinking, she pulled back, though she didn't release her grip on his coat. Her green eyes flashed with uncertainty.

"How can you—"

But the relief he felt at the return of her ability to speak was almost too much for Logan, who had feared that she might not shake the near-death experience, and he leaned forward to kiss her. Taken off guard, Faith pulled back at first, only to lean forward forcefully, her grip tightening to keep him from moving away from her.

Her lips were relaxed but parted as the velvet swipe of her tongue touched his, and he was overcome by a barrage of heat and yearning. Every muscle in his body reacted to her; every inch of skin begged to be touched by her slim hands. He was aflame as his mouth searched hers. *Only a moment longer*, he told himself, though every exquisite exhale from her seemed to pull him closer. His hand dropped to her breast, and he had begun unbuttoning the front of her dress when a set of hooves sounded in the distance.

Groaning, Logan stopped and tore away from her, leaving her to stumble slightly as he regained control of himself. They had waited too long to return, and he wasn't surprised that someone had followed them, though, at that moment, he was brutally unprepared for the desperation that engulfed him.

Breathing heavily, he turned back to see her standing there, staring back at him slack-jawed as the distant noise came closer.

"Are you all right?" he asked roughly. Faith nodded, though she seemed unsure. "Say it."

"I—I'm all right," she said, her tone shaky.

Of course she wasn't, but as Graham's black horse appeared around the bend, there was little else he could do for her, so Logan tried to steady his breathing as his friend stopped.

Graham was off his horse in an instant, coming up to Faith.

"Thank the Lord," he said. "You gave your sisters a right

fright back in town."

"I—"

"It wasn't her fault," Logan snapped, surprised at his anger aimed at his friend. "What the devil is she doing riding a horse meant for someone half her size?"

Graham's brow lifted quizzically as he looked at his friend.

"I beg your pardon?"

"She's too tall for that damn pony, and if she were riding a proper animal, not something so skittish, she'd not have taken off in the first place."

Logan knew it was unfair to attack Graham, but he wasn't sure how to express himself. He was angry, terrified, aroused, exhausted, and utterly frustrated, mostly by the fact that none of his feelings could be dealt with in the way he would wish.

"Now, see here," Graham started, but Faith came forward, holding her hands up between the two.

"Please," she said, her tone slightly steadier than before. "I am well. I just wish to see my sisters."

Begrudgingly, Logan glared at Graham before reaching for his horse's rein. In a swift, singular motion, he was back on the animal and moved it toward her, holding out his hand to her. She only stared at it.

"Come," he commanded quietly. "You'll ride with me. Graham can walk your horse back."

With a tentative glance at her brother-in-law, Faith took Logan's hand, and he pulled her up as easily as if she were a blanket floating in the wind. He wrapped one arm around her waist, holding her against him as they began to move down the wooden path at a snail's pace, back the way they came.

After a while, they crossed the stone bridge and returned to the kilt shop where Faith's sisters had remained. Both women were frantic as they caught sight of Faith, hurrying toward her with Arabella in tow. Though he didn't wish to, he let Faith go, helping her into her sisters' waiting arms.

"Oh, Faith, are you all right?" Hope asked. "My God, we

were so scared."

"I didn't think Sweetness could move that fast," Grace said, patting Faith's hair. "Were you hurt?"

"I'm fine," Faith said as the two crowded her.

Hope's eyes peered around Faith's shoulder.

"Thank you so much, Mr. Harris. I hate to think what would have happened if you hadn't been here to go after her."

"Of course," he said, brushing off the comment as Faith turned in her sister's arms. His gaze locked with Faith's. "I'm just glad she's not hurt."

"It was all very heroic to watch," Arabella said, bouncing on her toes as she faced Faith. "Are you sure you're all right?"

"Yes," she answered, giving Arabella a half smile. "Thank you."

"Well, I will come to check on you in the next day or so. At the very least, we'll be at Lismore Hall in a week's time."

"We will?" Logan asked, confused.

"Yes," Arabella said, holding up an invitation. "Mrs. MacKinnon has invited us to Lady Belle's birthday celebration. But it's a surprise, so you mustn't tell her about it."

"Ah. Well, we will see you all then. Come, Arabella," Logan said, taking his sister by the elbow and escorting her away from the Sharpe sisters as quickly as possible.

Arabella glanced back over her shoulder as they hurried down the street.

"Why did we leave so abruptly?" she asked, but Logan didn't reply.

To answer her truthfully would be a mistake, particularly since he didn't quite understand it himself, but the longer he was in Faith's presence, the harder it was to leave, and if he didn't do so quickly, he feared he might never do so at all.

Chapter Ten

THE MORNING OF Belle's surprise party was difficult, particularly because it had fallen on Faith to keep her aged aunt distracted. At the same time, the rest of the house made preparations for the evening celebrations. Why they had decided on a surprise party, Faith did not know, but she was hard-pressed to keep Belle occupied in her office.

Ever flanked by her faithful manservant, Andrews, Aunt Belle was in a fiery mood. Somehow, all her correspondence from the day before had gone missing before it could be sent out, and she was forced to rewrite those letters on top of the ones she had intended to write and send out today, causing her to be ornery.

"What lummox misplaced my letters?" she muttered as she scribbled frantically along a sheet of paper. "Disgraceful."

"I'm sure they'll show up, Aunt Belle," Faith said from the settee. Her legs were curled beneath her body as she tried again to read a paragraph of the art book in her hands. "I wouldn't fret about it."

"Do I appear as though I'm fretting, my dear?" her aunt asked, perturbed. "What I am, is angry. What sort of person misplaces letters? And what's worse, my own staff can't point the finger at the correct culprit, which means they conspire against me."

Faith rolled her eyes.

"That's a stretch, even for you, Aunt Belle."

"Do not try to argue. I've never been so outraged in my entire life."

Faith closed the book, giving up her reading attempts, and stood up.

"Perhaps Andrews misplaced them?" Faith said teasingly, trying to get the man to smile, but he didn't.

Andrews rarely smiled, and he seldom spoke.

"Nonsense," Aunt Belle said, waving her hand. "If there is one person in this household I trust more than Andrews, I do not know them."

The slightest twitches pulled at the corner of Andrews's drawn mouth, and Faith smirked. If Andrews was dedicated to Belle, then the feelings were mutual.

But just then, Belle stood.

"I'll find them. I've no time to rewrite all my letters. I'll be here until dusk."

Faith turned, looking at the porcelain clock that sat on the mantel. It was already four o'clock. She only needed to keep Aunt Belle busy for another hour before the halls would be cleared, and she could escort her to her bedroom to dress for dinner. Only when Faith did that would she suggest a far fancier evening dress than usual and would goad her into wearing her finest gown, which was being pressed at that very moment.

"Ah, Aunt Belle," she said quickly, hoping to distract her. "Can I ask you something?"

"Walk and speak, my dear. I've already wasted half the day," the old woman said as she crossed the room.

Her recovery from her ailments the previous year had been astonishing, and she was able to move much quicker now than before. Determined to keep her in this room, Faith opened her mouth and let the first thing that came to mind fall out.

"What was it like being King George's mistress?"

Belle's forward progress halted immediately as a discouraging cough came from Andrews. Glancing between the two, Faith waited for Belle to turn around. Slowly, the matriarch spun toward her, and though Faith had been anticipating a startled expression, she only saw something akin to glee in the old woman's silvery stare.

"What a question," she said gently, her eyes on Faith. "What's promoted this sudden interest in my relationship with Georgie?"

"Um," Faith started, unsure why she had even asked.

Perhaps because it was one of Aunt Belle's favorite topics. She wasn't shy about her relationship with the king and spoke at length whenever prompted, but something else had pushed Faith to ask about this, specifically, even though it was a subject she usually avoided.

But today, she found that she wanted to know about the cardinal relations between a man and a woman.

Ever since Logan had kissed her in the doorway of her room at Harris House, Faith had been tormented with the wildest and the most vivid daydreams, explicit thoughts that made her blush from head to toe. And after he had rescued her from her spooked horse, he had held her so protectively against him, and kissed her so passionately, that she had thought of little else since.

Faith shook her head, desperate to remove such thoughts but her curiosity remained.

"Well, I suppose…" she tried, but still, she could not think of something to say.

"Is it because you find yourself in a similar quandary?"

Faith's eyes snapped to her aunt's.

"Heavens no."

"Oh, I don't mean that you're seeking to be someone's mistress, my dear," Aunt Belle said as she made her way to the settee. She patted the cushion next to her, prompting Faith to come and sit down at her side. "I only mean to say that, has someone caught your attentions the way dear Georgie was ensnared by my charms?"

Faith's mouth pulled up into a smirk. Even at seventy-six, Aunt Belle was confident of her appeal and wasn't wrong. The old woman was quite charming. And part of that charm, so far as

Faith could tell, came from her utter frankness and total lack of shame. Even though speaking to an innocent young woman about romantic affairs would be taboo in most households—Lord knew Hope would disapprove—Faith knew she only had to ask, and Belle would reveal everything she knew.

Which was tempting, to say the least. She had many questions she wished to have answered, but she wasn't sure how to ask. Her eyes flickered to Andrews, who was staring straight ahead.

"Don't mind him, dear. Andrews is a locked box."

Faith shook her head.

"Still, I don't think I could…"

"Very well. Andrews? Leave us, please."

"My lady," he said with a nod.

He exited the room, closing the door behind him, and Faith was sure he would stand guard on the other side.

"Now, tell me. Why the sudden interest in my affair with the king?"

"Well, I suppose it's not so much about what occurred between you and um, His Majesty, particularly, but rather what prompted it."

"What prompted our affair?"

"Yes."

"That's easy. He was madly in love with me."

Faith smiled.

"Yes, but why did you go through with it? Haven't you said that he had to ask you three times before you even considered him?"

Aunt Belle eyed her.

"Are you asking if I loved him?"

"Yes."

"Well, if I'm being honest, no. Not at first. But then, Georgie was very persistent."

"But if you didn't love him, why go through with all of it?"

Aunt Belle stared across the room; her stare glazed over as if she was remembering some long-ago memory.

"Well, it was a number of things, really. Georgie wasn't the only person infatuated with me. I had made quite a success of myself on the stage, which had brought me to the notice of the highest members of society. I had several offers from several very prominent peers. I even entertained a few of them, but Georgie was different from the rest."

"Because he was royalty?"

"Oh, no. Because he was a dreamer," she said languorously. "He always had these supercilious ideas about life and love. To hear him explain it was really annoying, but somewhat exciting. I could get swept away in his daydreams and, I often did."

"But didn't you find it, difficult, to… well. To… you know…" Faith tried as her cheeks warmed. "Go through with *it*, when you didn't love him?"

"You mean lay with him? Not at all," Aunt Belle said, only to quickly amended her words. "I mean to say, while being with someone in that way is certainly better when you're in love, there is a certain *je ne sais quoi* to being with someone with whom you share a level of animosity."

"Animosity?"

Belle's eyebrows wiggled.

"Oh yes."

Faith frowned.

"Did you have animosity toward the king?"

Belle sighed and leaned back slightly.

"Yes and no, I suppose. He was certainly sure of himself when we first met and I found his arrogance trying. He thought he was terribly clever and when I cut him once or twice, he became prickly."

"How so?"

"Oh, would that I could remember exactly, but even if I could, I wouldn't tell you," she said with a wink. "However, Georgie would not be deterred. He was determined and in a bout of madness, I may have challenged him."

"In what way?"

Even at seventy-six, Belle's wrinkled cheeks turned crimson.

"It's really not for innocent ladies to hear, my dear."

Her gaze drifted to the opposite wall where a painting Faith had completed for Belle last Christmas hung. It was a portrait of Belle's sister, Alice, painted from one of the sketches Faith had done of her the winter prior to her passing. Belle had adored it and, much to Faith's surprise, had hung it up on the wall in the office.

Faith was sure Belle was worried that Alice would have found their entire conversation inappropriate. But she had to distract her.

"Please," Faith asked, leaning forward, pulling her aunt's attention back to her. "I won't tell anyone."

"I doubt very much you would even be able to bring yourself to repeat it," Belle said, giving her a thoughtful look. She seemed to debate whether or not to continue, but then she smirked. "But what harm could it do? As long as you don't think to do something as reckless."

"I wouldn't," Faith said quickly. Too quickly, apparently, for Belle hesitated. "I promise. Besides, who would I even consider challenging?"

Though Belle didn't say it, and Faith tried to keep her face neutral, they both knew exactly who she would confront. But then one of Belle's brows lifted, and a flash of satisfaction shone in her eyes. Only for a moment, but Faith found herself wondering what Belle had to be so pleased about.

"Very well," she said, sitting up straight. "I told Georgie after the ninth or tenth time of him coming to my dressing room that there wasn't any place in my heart for him and that he should move on. He countered, saying that we might share a single kiss, so as to prove him wrong. In defiance, I offered him an entire evening to prove that there was nothing between us."

Faith's intake of breath was soft, and though she knew her aunt had done many wicked things in her life, she hadn't ever heard word for word about the deeds she had done. Belle continued.

"Being nothing more than a man wanting, he accepted, of course, and we decided on the night. I will not tell you any details, for even I'm not so brazen, but I will tell you that after our evening together, both of us were changed."

"For the better?"

"For better or worse, I cannot say, but we were different. My prejudice against him softened significantly, as my gamble had not worked, and his arrogance softened as well. He was far more regular after that." Faith nearly spoke, not understanding, but Belle continued. "What I mean to say is, Georgie became much more human after that. He was no longer the haughty prince who was next in line to the throne. He was merely a man who, due to the circumstance of his birth, could not act like his true self or even be permitted to marry whomever he wanted." Belle looked at Faith. "Can you imagine telling a king who he is allowed to marry?"

"No," Faith said. "I cannot."

"Regardless, I doubt I would have married him even if he had been allowed to do so," Belle admitted.

"Why?"

But Belle only shook her head. She may have had to tell herself that for so long to lessen the sting of not being able to, and perhaps she had come to believe it, but Faith had her doubts.

"It's of no matter. Still, with me, Georgie was able to be at peace with himself and the world." Belle's gaze turned distant again before adding, "And so was I."

A bittersweet expression came over her aunt's face, and Faith felt suddenly unsure. It must have been terribly unfair to not be able to be legally, officially together as a married couple, and yet, Belle and the king had found a small piece of happiness together, as immoral as it was. Perhaps because Faith was feeling particularly sympathetic or because it happened so long ago, she couldn't quite find fault with their relationship, even though she knew it wasn't proper.

Faith wondered how Belle had felt toward the king and wondered if it wasn't similar to how she felt about Logan. Of course, Faith didn't have any sort of feelings toward Logan except contempt.

Well, perhaps that wasn't exactly true. She was grateful that he had saved her from that disastrous horseback riding incident. And while their early meetings had sparked some friction, she had to admit that she might have eventually befriended him, if he hadn't obtained her painting. She had even begun to enjoy his company before learning about that. A part of her had even argued that it was rather forthcoming of him to admit to having it, but it didn't matter. She and Logan were nothing like Aunt Belle and King George.

"Oh goodness," Belle said suddenly, shivering. "You've made me nostalgic, my dear, but I'm not one to languish in the past. Now, I really must get back to trying to find those letters."

Faith's gaze snapped to the clock. A quarter of an hour left. She still needed to keep Aunt Belle from going.

"Wait," she said quickly, just as Belle began to stand.

She turned to face Faith.

"Yes, dear? What is it?"

"Um, Mr. Harris," she blurted out. "The elder Mr. Harris, that is."

Belle gave her a curious look.

"Yes?"

"Do you know much about him?" she asked, uncertain. "I met him when I was at Harris House and he was very kind, but there was a sadness to him I couldn't quite understand." Belle's brow quirked, and Faith pressed. "It's only that, you know everyone within a hundred miles, and I thought you might be able to tell me a bit about him. I'm quite fond of Arabella, as you know, and wouldn't want to broach any topics that she might find, well, uncomfortable."

Belle's brow lifted as she sat back down, seeming caught off guard by the question.

"Well, let's see. I met Mr. Harris some twenty years ago, I believe. Yes. Yes, I remember because Mrs. Harris was quite excited to meet with me, although she was heavily pregnant at the time. She had been away from England for nearly a decade and longed to speak with a fellow countrywoman. I made a point to visit her upon learning about her, as she was in confinement and could not pay any calls herself, hoping to strike up a friendship. Not many of the locals particularly liked me when I first came here, but that was only because they didn't know me." Belle was so sure of herself that it made Faith smile. "She was one of the first friends I had in this area, you know. Although, the friendship didn't last very long."

"Why is that?"

"She left, only months after I came to retire. Perhaps four months? Five? I'm not quite sure. All I know is that Mr. Harris was desperately in love with his wife, and she was desperately in love with not being in the Highlands."

"Oh?" Faith said, a hint of guilt emerging from the depths of her memories.

Hadn't she once told Logan how much she wished she could be away from the Highlands and back in London? A pinch of regret nipped at her senses as her hand reached around to the back of her neck.

"Yes. Unfortunately, I believe she fell out of love with Mr. Harris once she realized she couldn't keep her Highlander in London. It wasn't a surprise, of course, that they would have to move here, but I believe she had a different idea of what life would be like so far north."

"Did she ever discuss it with you?"

"Her dislike for Scotland? Oh yes, almost constantly. She didn't like the weather, the isolation, the mountains, the lochs or even the people. She was desperate for news from London and I told her all I knew, but I had quite finished with town life at that time and wished to mourn my previous life privately."

Faith quickly did the math in her head and figured that Aunt Belle had come to Scotland not long after George had died and William had been crowned king.

"She left so soon after her daughter was born," Faith said, pressing on. "Arabella told me as much when I was at Harris House."

"Yes," Aunt Belle said gravely. "And you know, my dear, that I do not cast judgment on anyone. But that particular incident did test my patience."

"I think it's awful."

"And it was, but it is not my place to judge anyone. Not after the way I've lived my life. Whatever reasons Mrs. Harris had, I'm sure I do not understand, but I will not criticize her."

"Then you are a better woman than I," Faith said.

"I'm a better woman than most, my dear, but that is beside the point," Belle said haughtily, and while Faith was sure she was jesting, she couldn't help but take note.

"Is that why Mr. Logan Harris is the way he is?"

Belle's head tilted.

"What way is he?"

"Well, he's… He's always been so…"

But the words would not come. All that annoyed Faith about Logan had dissipated, only to reemerge into something different now, and she wasn't sure who he was anymore. He had been kind to her since her stay at his house; he had even saved her since then. Not to mention his deep appreciation for art.

But she could not forgive his ownership of that painting. Mainly because of what it had meant to her when it had been painted.

Belle waited patiently for Faith to continue, but Faith stood instead and began pacing the floor, trying to solve the problem.

"Can one find someone attractive, even if they're rude and brooding and overall ill-tempered?" she asked out loud and to no one in particular. "It just seems the opposite of what one would look for, doesn't it? I mean, it simply makes no sense."

"No sense at all," Belle agreed, allowing Faith to continue.

"And if it doesn't make sense, then how can it possibly be something sustainable?"

"How is *what* sustainable, my dear?"

Faith opened her mouth to answer but closed it. She couldn't answer because she wasn't sure what she was talking about. Instead, she rubbed the back of her neck with her hand and stared across the room.

"Nothing, I suppose."

"Well, if you mean to ask how Georgie and I got on being so unsuited for one another, I'll simply leave you with this. Love finds a way."

Faith watched Belle as she stood up.

"And was it love between you two?"

"Oh yes, my dear. It was."

Nodding quietly to herself, Faith felt even more confused than she had at the beginning of this revealing discussion. She might try to speak with Logan about what she did not know, but the very idea was unsettling. Her embarrassment over the painting was still at the forefront of her mind, and she couldn't bear to even consider what he might think of her.

But perhaps she was judging him too harshly, assuming he would think the worst of her? He had kissed her ardently after the runaway horse incident and seemed genuinely concerned for her wellbeing. Whatever the case, Faith knew that she would eventually have to speak with him, and it would undoubtedly be tonight during the ball.

Faith finally permitted Belle to leave as the clock struck five o'clock, exiting the room first to ensure the hallway was clear. Andrews stood just outside the door and winked at Faith briefly to indicate that the coast was truly clear.

"Shall we go to dress for dinner then?" Belle asked, coming up behind Faith.

"Yes, but what do you think of tonight, wearing your finest dress?" Faith suggested.

"Tonight? But why?"

"Oh, no reason."

Chapter Eleven

THE BALLROOM AT Lismore Hall was not a large room. Indeed, it didn't compare in size to the vast ballrooms of the Mayfair homes of London where Faith had spent time. But it had been decorated beyond compare for that evening's festivities, and Faith was certain that she had never seen a more stunning room. The wood panel walls had been washed and waxed, causing them to shine, and with the chandeliers ablaze with dozens of candles above their heads against the barrel-vaulted ceiling, the room was filled with a golden glow.

Everyone for nearly fifty miles had been invited, some traveling from as far as Cumbria to attend. Nearly every member of the McTavish clan had come, which accounted for nearly half the attendees. The Earl of Clyde and his wife had also arrived, with their four daughters, as well as a dozen of professional men from Glasgow. Even old Miss Fletcher had been escorted by Dr. Barkley. Surprisingly enough, she looked nothing like a witch, and was dressed in a very simple, very stylish gray gown, with her salt-and-pepper hair was pulled back in a tight, demure bun.

At least seventy people were mingling and carrying on as Aunt Belle entered the room, and a robust cheer echoed throughout the home upon her entrance. A single, twinkling tear rolled down the old woman's cheek as she realized what was happening, understanding that they were all there for her. They had come from far and wide and on short notice, all in honor of Belle's seventy-sixth birthday.

"What's all this now?" she asked as she came into the ball-room.

She was dressed in an amethyst-colored gown adorned with diamonds and her beloved emeralds. Faith had insisted that she wear her emerald tiara, a gift she had received from the king himself over forty years ago. At that moment, she appeared ageless in the company of so many who loved her. She was flanked by Hope and Graham, both of whom were watching her, smiling.

"Happy birthday, Aunt Belle," Hope said, kissing her cheek.

"Oh, my dear, did you plan this?" she asked.

"We all did. Graham, Faith, Grace, and I."

Belle turned to see Faith, who had hurried away after helping her aunt pick out her jewels for the evening. Faith wore a simple, pale-lemon-colored tiered gown with white piping that came off the shoulders, as was the latest fashion. Grace was beside her, wearing a blue dress with intricate lace trim.

"Is that why you kept me locked away in my offices all afternoon?" she asked, bewildered.

"I'm afraid so," Faith said, coming forward. "I hope you'll forgive me."

"Of course, my darling girl."

"And your letters weren't lost," Grace added. "They were sent out with the morning post."

Belle's mouth dropped slightly.

"What a rascally set of girls you all are," she said with warmth before adding, as she turned to the crowd, "Let it be known that my grandnieces get their wits and their wiles from my side of the family. A warning to all of you." Everyone laughed. "Well, don't let me stop you. Let the dancing begin!"

The musicians took up their instruments with a raucous cheer, and a galop dance began. Graham escorted Hope to the center of the room as dozens of couples followed suit. Belle made her way slowly through the crowd, greeting all her guests with the utmost sincerity.

Their surprise had been a success, and while Faith was glad for it, the impending meeting with Logan would not leave her mind. Surely she should busy herself with something—anything, really—but she found that she could not. Instead, Grace came to stand next to her.

"I think this party is a rousing success, don't you?" Grace asked, peering around the room. "Nearly everyone we invited came."

"Which is a surprise in and of itself considering how late the invitations went out."

Grace made a face.

"Do not be sour, Faith. The idea came to Hope and myself rather late, and while it may not have been a fully formulated plot when we explained it to you, the results speak for themselves," she said, gesturing her hand about the room. "Don't you agree?"

Although London etiquette required much more preparation for a party of this size, Faith had to admit that it had come off rather nicely. Rolling her eyes, she smiled as Grace gently elbowed her.

"Yes," she admitted, joining Grace in her survey of the room. "It did turn out very well. Oh, and look." Faith said as her eyes landed on the tall man with short-clipped hair standing near the glass doors that led out onto a small balcony. "Is that not Dr. Hall standing with Laird McTavish?"

Grace's head whipped around, and after a moment, she spoke.

"It is! You know, I've been told by Dr. Barkley that Dr. Hall is quite the reformer when it comes to medicine. Dr. Barkley believes that if I can persuade Dr. Hall to write me a letter of recommendation, I might be able to gain entrance into the University of Glasgow."

"Really?" Faith asked, stunned. "Dr. Barkley said that?"

Grace bobbed her head up and down quickly.

"Oh yes. In fact, I think I should attempt my pursuit right now."

"Oh, but Grace," Faith said, reaching for her sister's hand to stop her.

Grace gave her a funny frown.

"Yes?"

It wasn't any of Faith's business, indeed, and her sister's desire to study medicine at a university had been known and talked about for months, but a part of Faith worried for her. What if Dr. Hall refused her in a particularly harsh or cutting manner? What if he, like so many others, thought to make a joke or unkind comment about Grace, whose mind often neglected the tedious social decorum everyone else followed? With Grace's hopes so high, that sort of blow would be devastating.

That was not to say Grace was fragile. In most cases, she took everyone's prejudices gracefully and forgave them, believing that if they knew better, they might not be so judgmental of her. But when she truly set her heart on something, she could be deeply wounded when she was met with a lack of understanding.

Still, it was too much to convey now, and instead, she simply squeezed Grace's hand.

"Good luck."

Grace smiled and turned away, leaving Faith just as the pale-pink vision that was Arabella came toward her.

"Faith!" Arabella said. A quick glance told Faith that Mr. Harris senior was not nearby. "How are you?"

"I'm well," she answered with a smile. "How are you?"

Arabella took Faith's hand and tucked it into the crook of her arm as she pulled her into a close walk.

"Very fine indeed, but I'm glad to hear that you are, as well. We were so worried about you after that incident with the horse in the village. I told Papa all about it when I returned home. How frightening it was and how heroic Logan was in his response."

"Quite heroic," Faith said softly. "Er, is your father in attendance?"

Arabella frowned, her blonde hair shimmying at the shake of her head.

"No, unfortunately. Papa wasn't feeling very well, but he insisted that I come with Logan."

"Oh. Well, I hope he is not under the weather?"

Arabella waved her free hand.

"Papa goes through spells where he cannot sleep. He's terrible company during them, but I do worry. Perhaps you can come visit one day? He so enjoyed it when you came last."

Faith swallowed, unsure what Logan would think about seeing her in Harris House again. But she had enjoyed Arabella's father's company when she had been there.

"Perhaps," was all she said when a dark form crossed her path, causing her to look up.

Logan was dressed in gray-and-black tartan, with a vest and evening jacket against a starched white shirt. Faith was instantly frozen beneath his intent, hazel stare as all the air vanished from her lungs. While she hated to admit that she had missed him, especially since their last meeting was only a few days prior, it was worse to realize that the true torture was to be in his presence.

"Miss Sharpe," he said, his deep voice wrapping around her like a warm length of plaid.

"Mr. Harris," she said, her eyes trailing down to the glass he held.

"Arabella, if you insist on using me to play fetch, it's unsporting of you to move," he said, handing his sister the glass.

"Forgive me," she said, playfully abashed as she took the glass from Logan. "I was just inquiring whether or not Faith has recovered from her horse ride in Glencoe."

"I see. And have you?" he asked, his tone somewhat worried.

"I have, thank you," she said as the music ended.

The crowd around them moved as a waltz began to play.

"Oh, a waltz! Your favorite, Faith," Arabella said, turning to her brother. "Logan, you must dance with Faith. She loves waltzes."

"Oh, no," Faith said quickly. "That's quite alright—"

But Logan didn't ask. Instead, he took her hand and led her onto the dance floor. Though no one seemed particularly interested in the two, Faith was sure the entire world was staring at them.

"What do you think you're doing?" she whispered harshly.

"If we don't dance together, my sister will prattle on about it indefinitely."

"Why?"

"Because she's annoying."

Faith squared her shoulders.

"She is not. And that's not a very nice thing to say about your own sister."

"Forgive me," he said sarcastically. "But she's been nattering on about you for days. It seems you are her favorite topic."

"Whatever for?"

"Worried about your poor nerves, as she says, due to your pony ride."

Faith scowled.

"It wasn't a pony ride. And I'm perfectly fine. I was from the moment the horse stopped," she said, lifting her chin. The knowing glance from Logan reminded her that the horse wouldn't have stopped without him. She cleared her throat. "Thank you, for that."

"Don't mention it," he said gruffly as they spun about the room.

For some reason, there was hostility between them again, and while Faith wasn't sure why, she was grateful for it. This was the Logan she knew, the Logan she could handle, and even though their bodies swirled and danced together in perfect synchronicity, she couldn't help but feel as if a barrier lay between them.

"What?" he asked abruptly as they came back together.

"I didn't say anything."

"No, but your brow is creased, and whenever your brow is creased you tend to be deep in thought."

The familiarity of his comment made Faith warm with glee and annoyance.

"It isn't polite to comment on one's appearance."

"So you've mentioned."

"And yet you still insist on insulting me?"

"I didn't insult you."

"You do every time you comment on my looks."

"What about when it's a compliment?"

"A creased brow is hardly a compliment."

But then Logan's eyes darkened, and he leaned forward. She was sure he would say something biting, but then he spoke, and her heart began to beat wildly.

"And what if I were to tell you that your creased brow causes me a great deal of consideration, hmm? That I can focus on little else whenever it appears because I'm besieged with the need to know what you're thinking? To learn what has caught your attention and what I might do to procure whatever it is that you suddenly desire?" he paused as his voice lowered to a whisper. "What would you say to that?"

Faith's throat became tight, her mouth dry. She could not fathom why such a statement should make her eager for things she did not understand. But the tone of his voice, both annoyed and seductive, made her heart constrict.

"I would not know what to say," she answered breathlessly. "Except that it seems you have too much time on your hands."

To her surprise, Logan let out a bark of a laugh. Though she didn't believe what she'd said had been particularly amusing, the light in his hazel eyes gave her a significant amount of pleasure that pooled in her belly, even as she tried to appear indifferent.

"You're a conundrum, you know," he said as they danced. "I'm never sure where to place you."

"You're the first to say such a thing," she said truthfully. "Everyone always just assumes I'm difficult, simply because I know my own mind."

"That you do, but you seem to be a cacophony of conflicting

traits. Cold and hot, rigid, and flexible."

"How so?"

His brow lifted as he began to list off a number of observations.

"Well, for instance, you've made it clear that you don't care for fairytales, but my sister tells me you accepted one of her good luck talismans. Why is that?"

"Because it was a gift. It would be rude not to accept."

He shook his head.

"I don't believe that. I did at first, but since becoming better acquainted with you, I think there's a part of you that is very taken with the idea of magical realms and the like."

She laughed, though not loudly.

"That's preposterous."

"Is it?"

"Yes," she said firmly. "I simply didn't wish to be impolite."

"That I don't believe either. Since when have you been concerned with propriety? You've always made it a point to turn up your nose to everyone since arriving in Scotland."

"That is false," she argued. "On the contrary, I've acquired a healthy number of friends and acquaintances since coming here, including Arabella. I like her very much." She paused, before adding, "Jeanne has also become a particularly trusted confidant."

A strained look flashed in Logan's eyes.

"Has she?"

"Yes."

"I suppose I should not find that surprising. She is a fearsome sort."

Faith laughed. "You say that as if it's a bad quality to have. For my part, I'm quite taken with women who do not bat their eyelashes demurely, waiting for a man to tell them what they're worth."

He shook his head.

"No one would ever accuse you of that, to be sure, but then I cannot help but believe there is some other side of you." Logan spun her away as the music reached a crescendo, only for her to come back into his arms. He leaned forward to speak softly into her ear. "The side that not even your closest friends or family knows about. How I wish to know more about *that* Faith. Who is she really and what does she desire most?"

She swallowed hard before remembering that this man was in possession of the one thing that could ruin her entire life. She tried to pull away, but he held her close.

"Let me go," she whispered quietly so no one around them could hear.

"I wish to talk to you first."

"There's nothing to discuss."

"I beg to differ, but we shan't discuss it here."

"Will you destroy it?" she asked, her eyes not meeting his.

She had come to the conclusion that the painting needed to be destroyed. To have such an unmistakable likeness out in the world was dangerous, and the only way she would be free from it was if it were no longer about. When he didn't answer right away, she eventually lifted her gaze to find his unreadable face.

"Destroy it? You mean the painting?"

"Yes. Will you?"

His head tilted a fraction, his brow creased.

"The thought never crossed my mind."

"So, you won't destroy it?"

"No."

What good feeling she had felt for him dissipated.

"Then we shan't discuss anything, Mr. Harris," she said as the song finished. "Good bye."

With that, she turned on her heel and hurried off the dance floor, worried he might try to follow her. Thankfully, she was alone by the time she reached her sisters, and for the next hour or so, she kept her distance from Logan.

Surely he could see why she was so desperate to have the piece of art destroyed. Not only was it evidence of a time in her life when she hadn't any foresight, but it also reminded her of

Donovan and the promise he broke to her. Of course Logan had no way of knowing about that. Faith had never explained it. But even without explaining it, he had to realize that for a lady of her status, having a nude painting of oneself out in the world would be dangerous. Even more so now because it wasn't far away in Paris where she had no desire to go, but directly in the center of her current community.

Whenever she thought of it, she felt filled with shame. Not only because she had been so foolish as to trust Donovan with the painting's creation in the first place, but also because his willingness to sell the painting served as proof that she hadn't meant nearly as much to him as he had to her. It was a revelation that had stayed at the outer edges of her mind since she'd received his letter, but now that she focused on it, it was so blatantly obvious. Donovan had never truly loved her; worse, he had used her feelings for him against her by coaxing her into a sense of comfort to disrobe and pose for that damn portrait.

As the night's celebration wore on, Faith's mood sank further and further. Eventually, her sisters' concerned stares and questions caused her to retreat from the ballroom, but she found the entire hall was packed with merrymakers.

Bitter, sad, and increasingly uncomfortable from the heat generated throughout the house due to the number of people, Faith thought to retreat to her room early, only to catch a glimpse of their cook and several footmen carrying a towering cake into the dining room. Knowing she would not be able to slip up the stairs without being noticed, she altered her route to Aunt Belle's office instead hoping to find a reprieve there. But as she approached her aunt's office, she suddenly saw Grace taking long, purposeful strides toward the room, entering it quickly and all but slamming the door behind her.

Then, from the opposite side of the hallway came Dr. Hall. He peered over the other guests, seemingly searching for someone with an apologetic look on his face, and Faith had the awful feeling that the doctor had crushed Grace's hopes. Faith was sure Grace had locked the door to deter any followers. But then, Dr. Hall spotted Faith and started to walk toward her.

Oh no. Whatever had taken place between the doctor and Grace, Faith did not want to be a part of it. She turned, trying to leave, but was trapped by a pair of giggling ladies when she heard the doctor speak behind her.

"Miss Sharpe," Dr. Hall said upon reaching her.

Faith winced before turning around.

"Dr. Hall," Faith replied, making her voice icy.

The man's brow dipped slightly at hearing her tone, but he seemed ready to ignore it.

"I was wondering if you had seen your sister come through this way?"

"Yes, I have," Faith said, deciding to be purposefully obtuse. "Nearly every day."

The doctor's brow furrowed, and he opened his mouth to speak, but no words came out. Apparently, she had confused him.

"Right," he finally said after a moment. "And did you happen to see her this evening with Miss Fletcher?"

Faith frowned.

"I did not."

"Well, if I could ask you a favor—"

"I'm terribly sorry, Dr. Hall, but I'm all out of favors tonight," she said, noting the surprise in his eyes. "Good evening."

Turning on her heel, Faith hurried away without looking back. She wasn't sure what had transpired between him and her sister, but Faith wasn't interested in hearing any apologies. She had long since tired of men apologizing to her sisters for this and that.

Deciding that she would find no peace inside, she concluded that some fresh air might be best for her. Borrowing one of the cloaks that hung from the rack in the corner of the foyer, she went outside and headed toward the walled garden that sat at the western side of Lismore Hall.

Making her way out the front doors and down the stone

steps, Faith inhaled deeply as she walked around the front of the house, along the stone wall to an iron gate that separated the front landscape from the back. Unlatching the metal hook, she pushed the door open and passed through it.

There was a large pond covered in lily pads and beautiful white-and-pink blooms. Patches of lavender and mint had been planted together, giving the air a fresh, sweet scent. Along the wall that climbed the western border of Lismore grew a massive rose bush that produced hundreds of apple-sized white blooms.

It was an enchanting place, yet Faith could hardly appreciate it. She found an intricately carved stone bench that sat near the stream that fed the pond. Seating herself upon it, she brought her elbows to her knees and leaned forward with her chin in her hand.

As the muffled music from the ballroom mixed with the crickets and natterjack toads that croaked along the edge of the water, Faith sighed. If only she could figure out a way to get that painting. It was evident that she needed to take it back into her possession, but how? Perhaps she could sneak into his house and steal the blasted thing. But how could she leave with it? It was far too large for one person to carry.

As she was pondering the idea, a low, dark figure on all fours appeared to her right, scaring the life out of her.

"Oh!" she said, startled as she stood up. She was just about to flee when a familiar cold nose pressed into her hand. "Jaco? Oh, damned if you didn't frighten me."

Faith dropped to the ground without thinking about her gown and hugged the shaggy black animal around the neck.

"The charm of this garden always seems to catch me off guard," Logan's deep voice echoed behind her. "But hug a man's dog and he's liable to fall in love with you."

Faith twirled around awkwardly from her crouched down position to find Logan leaning against the apple tree.

"What are you doing out here?" she asked, standing. "And what's Jaco doing here?"

"He's rarely too far from me whenever I leave Harris House, even if I explicitly instruct that he be kept indoors while I'm away." Logan bent down as he came forward, scratching the dog between the ears. "When he was still a pup, I would fish early in the morning, leaving him in the kitchens because I believed he was too young to follow me. But he always got loose and found me."

"He followed you?"

"Yes. He has a hell of a nose, this one," Logan said, tussling the dog's head back and forth playfully before standing up.

"And what about you?" she asked. "What are you doing out here?"

"Trying to find a moment's peace from the party," he said, kicking an unseen stone down the water's edge. "What are you doing out here?"

As he approached, the moonlight highlighted his silhouette, and Faith's breath caught. He really was dashing in his kilt and evening clothes, and she vaguely remembered how she once loathed how beautifully proportioned his mouth was. He wasn't frowning at her as he once did, though the knit in his brow made her curious.

"The same," she said softly as he came around the bench. To her dissatisfaction, he sat next to her. "But I was not searching for any company. Particularly not yours."

He shook his head and looked forward.

"I do not know how to redeem myself in your eyes. I did not seek out *Odalisque Reclined* knowing your connection to it. If I had, well…"

"If you had, you'd have paid doubly for it, I've no doubt."

"Oh yes, because your half naked body is exactly what I want hanging about my home."

The rumble of his voice as he mentioned her body made her dizzy, but she ignored the thunderous beating of her pulse.

"If it is so grievous to you, I think you should have no want for it."

"And what should I do with it?"

"Burn it," she said emphatically.

The offended expression that crossed his handsome face caused Faith's stomach to clench.

"Out of the question."

With her temper rising, Faith stood, eager to be out of his reach.

"I don't see why not. You don't even like me—"

"I like you." She made a disbelieving sound, and he stood. "I do," he insisted, "albeit not in the usual way."

"What is that supposed to mean?"

His hand lifted to the back of his neck, and he rubbed it, trying to find the right words.

"I don't know. You're combative, always have been since the moment we first met."

"Me? You're the one who has been rude from the start."

"Regardless of all that, it doesn't detract from my feelings toward you."

"So what? You like sparring with me?"

"No. Well, yes, but…" He shook his head. "I don't know what it is about you. At times I'm sure there is not another living creature on this earth who aggravates me so."

"How very kind of you to say," she said sarcastically as she turned to leave.

"But then other times…"

The drop in his voice made her stall. Waiting, she only heard his gentle breathing. Peering over her shoulder, she watched him.

"Other times what?"

"Other times, I feel like I'll go mad if I don't touch you."

The raw honesty in his tone made Faith's heart hurt. Yes, she knew that feeling. The feeling of wanting to drag him down to the ground and roll around, if only to feel his hands on her.

Faith swallowed, desperate to keep such emotions off her face.

"Well, I hope you will keep such thoughts to yourself, because I—" She tried to say that she didn't feel the same, but the words stuck in her throat.

Before she could adequately answer, Logan's hand touched her cheek and rocked her slightly back before pulling her into a searing kiss.

A dozen glass bowls breaking at once was the closest Faith could come to describing what it was like, being caught in Logan's kiss. The pure exhilaration of doing something so reckless and downright dangerous, coupled with the simmering desperation that had simmered within her for weeks, caused a combustible reaction.

She stood on her tippy toes and pushed back against him viscerally, craving to be consumed by this man. There was no reason for her to be so infatuated with someone who aggravated her as he did, particularly when he owned something that could destroy her. Still, this limitless desire to be overwhelmed by him in every way made her shake with need.

He pulled away too soon, leaving her dazed and falling forward.

"Tell me," he spoke, his breathless, ragged voice filled with yearning. "Tell me that there is not something between us."

"There is n-nothing—"

But he kissed her again, almost as if he could banish her foolish words, and for a moment, she wished he could.

Despite everything that had happened between them—their arguments, and their circumstance regarding the painting—Faith was utterly enthralled with Logan's kiss. She was a willing victim of his dominance, if only for the few moments they shared here and there.

But the painting did separate them, and as much as she longed to continue, she knew she could not give in. She pushed at his shoulders, tearing her mouth away from his as they both gasped for uneven breaths.

Focus, she scolded herself silently. She couldn't let Logan's kisses distract her from the fact that he refused to destroy the one thing that kept her in constant worry.

Logan's full mouth pressed against her temple as they both breathed unevenly.

"What will it take?" he asked quietly after only a few moments. "Anything."

Faith's mind barely understood what he meant. What was he asking?

"Wha—"

"There is desire here, Faith. I can barely contain it. Every time you are in the room, I'm beyond myself. Tell me, what it will take to have you?"

As his meaning dawned on her, a cold, cutting drip touched the back of Faith's neck while a distant rumble sounded. Grateful that her face was pressed against his shoulder, concealing her shock, Faith held onto him, unsure how to answer. Then he spoke again.

"I know Donovan hurt you. I know he betrayed your trust, but I promise, I would never treat you in such a cowardly manner," he said. "Not if you chose me as you did him."

Faith's brow scrunched together as her mind reeled. Did he…did he think she had slept with Donovan? A shiver went through her as she began to understand.

"I—I don't know," she stuttered, still hiding her face as her mind reeled.

"I know Donovan's disloyalty has burned you and I know it would be outrageous to ask you to trust anyone again, but the passion of painters, by your own admission, is exclusively to the canvas. Whatever transpired between you and he, I doubt very much your needs were met and I find the idea of seeing to said needs to be the most pressing matter in my life currently."

Faith couldn't believe what Logan was saying. He thought that she and Donovan had been lovers and, more, that she had been dissatisfied with him. It was overwhelming to hear. Did he really think she was so carefree with her virtue?

But perhaps that was hypocritical of her. She had *wished* to be

Donovan's lover. The fact that their relationship hadn't reached that level was due to his circumspection, not hers. He had repeatedly rebuffed her, calling any physical relations between an artist and his muse tainted.

But this man—this solid, living, breathing man who was kissing up and down her neck at that very moment—wanted her. She knew she should pull away, that she should be wholly offended by his offer, but she kept her mouth shut. For nothing in the world had ever felt so wonderful as being held by this man.

"I would never betray you, Faith," he whispered softly into her ear after another few moments, causing her to shiver. His mouth moved up to her temple. "I only wish to explore what lies between us." He kissed her brow and her eyes closed. "Let me show what it can be like."

Lord forgive her, she wanted to say yes, but to do so would be ludicrous. She couldn't agree to have an affair with this man, or any man. It would ruin her.

But ruin her for what exactly? Marriage? Faith never had any desire to marry anyone. She surely didn't have any prospects. Yet did he really believe her to be such a wanton?

She rolled her head back as Logan's hands moved around her waist, pausing for a moment.

"Faith?"

"Hmm?"

"Are you… Are you without a corset?"

Faith's eyes snapped open.

"Ah, yes," she said, avoiding his gaze. "I'm under medical orders not to wear one while my lungs recover from the bout of pneumonia."

He watched her for a moment before answering.

"Oh."

Faith's eyes closed tightly as her cheeks began to heat up. Could she behave any more promiscuously? If he found her naked in his bedroom, she doubted he'd be much surprised.

But an idea popped into her head at the thought of his bedroom. The painting. It was in his home—possibly even in his bedroom. And if she was his lover, she'd have access to it. She'd be able to destroy it. *Yes*. That was a good enough reason to accept his ludicrous proposal. That and the fact that she would be leaving for London in only a few months' time anyway, which would give her some distance once she finally ruined *Odalisque Reclined* once and for all.

"Yes," she whispered into his shoulder, fighting the pleasure she felt as his arms tightened around her.

"God, Faith," he said roughly after a moment's more of kissing her temple and then her cheek. "Are you certain?"

"Yes," she said, although she'd never felt more uncertain of anything in her life.

It was outrageous, dangerous, and exceedingly satisfying to agree to his offer, and while she would be sure to regret it one day, tonight was not that day.

His mouth found hers once more, and the aching burn of shame that bubbled within her at the thought of becoming a man's mistress melted away somewhat. As long as she was in his arms, there could be no wrong in the world.

But eventually, he pulled back, and she grieved for the loss of something she didn't fully understand.

"When shall we met?"

Faith gazed up at him. Passion and something akin to joy shone in his eyes, and her stomach tumbled. What was she doing?

"I don't know," she said. They were interrupted by the distant sound of cheers from the hall. They both turned to face the building. "I think we should be getting back. The cake will be served soon."

"Yes, I suppose we should part for now," he said, holding her hand as he escorted her to the gate. When they reached it, he squeezed her fingers gently, then let her go. "I wish I could take you away this very minute."

"To Harris House?" she asked, wondering if it would be as easy as that, but Logan shook his head.

"No. Not with my family there. It would be too hazardous."

"I can be discreet."

Faith could see the corner of his cheek pull up, even with the moon at his back.

"I'm eager too," he said softly. "But I won't risk your reputation."

"It's my reputation to risk," she pressed, trying to convince him. "Harris House is the only place possible."

"Easy, love. We'll figure it out. I'll send word in a few days."

She tilted her head.

"Are you leaving?"

"I'm afraid so," he said, the hint of a smile on his lips. "I don't think it would be wise for me to be in your presence anymore tonight, lest I make a fool of myself somehow."

Faith smiled.

"No more a fool than I," she said softly, turning to leave, but he gripped her hand again.

Faith gazed into his eyes and her stomach flipped. Logan was staring at her with such intensity that she almost felt guilty for her secret motive for agreeing to this ridiculous affair. He brought her hand up to his lips and pressed his mouth to her knuckles.

"You are no one's fool, Faith. No one's."

She knew that he meant to buoy her spirits regarding Donovan, but Faith realized in that moment that he would never forgive her for what she was planning to do.

Logan left swiftly, with Jaco close behind him. Faith stood there for a few minutes once she was alone, contemplating everything that had just happened. Logan would undoubtedly hate her once she ruined that damn painting, but she couldn't just let it continue to exist. Such tangible evidence of her relationship with Donovan, and his disregard for her, was too much for her to bear. It needed to be destroyed.

Didn't it?

Faith's head dropped into her hands. She was about to head back into the house when a far away voice suddenly called out.

"Faodail..."

Faith froze. Was someone beyond the garden wall? Was it Logan? Frowning, she turned around, searching the garden. There was no movement, no hint of another living person, and nothing moved to save the plants as a blustering wind swept through the grounds.

Still, she had the uncanny feeling that she wasn't alone.

"Hello?" she called out, but no one answered. Confused, she called out again. "Hello? Is someone there?"

But there was no sound except the music coming from the house behind her. Perhaps it had been the wind? After another moment, she turned to head inside, repeating the bizarre word she thought she had heard.

Chapter Twelve

Whatever had possessed Logan to approach Faith with the irrational, ridiculous, and all together asinine idea of starting an affair, he did not know, but the words had dropped from his lips almost on their own accord. That she had accepted surprised him greatly, but now in the light of day, he was reconsidering his impetuous approach.

He never would have even considered such a thing if he hadn't been certain that Faith and Donovan had been lovers. To be sure, he had no concrete evidence that such had been the case, but it was hard to imagine that anyone could be in Faith's presence and not be taken in by her. Particularly if she had been disrobed. Between her fiery back talk, her vast knowledge of art, and her overall charismatic persona, Logan was positive no man could resist her charms.

And if she had been willing to take one man for a lover, she might be willing to agree to another.

As, indeed, she had.

Though he was astounded that she had accepted his offer, part of him was put out by the idea that Faith had been with someone else. Even though it cleared the path for them to have an affair now, it still fired his jealousy. But perhaps he was being too idealistic about it. If she were innocent, there would be no way to have her without marriage, and marriage wasn't an option for Logan. Not since his return from the war.

The war. Logan hadn't been comfortable laying with a woman since before his time in Burma. It had been a nagging issue when he'd returned, one that he had tried to deal with in Glasgow whenever he visited. But it wasn't that he couldn't perform. On the contrary, he could more than satisfy any partner's needs, but the whole ordeal was done rather coldly on his part. It was a business transaction to be done as efficiently as possible, and the ladies at Madame McHenry's brothel were always capable, but the pleasure of the act was lost to him.

Still, it was Logan's preference to dally with professional women versus the country lasses of Glencoe, such as the barmaid at the Stone and Stag Pub or a number of farmers' daughters who always tried to catch his attention whenever he was around. At least with a professional, he need not fear finding himself caught in some sort of dire situation.

Which, of course, made his dealing with Faith all the more hypocritical. She wasn't a prostitute nor a carefree country girl. She was a lady, the granddaughter of an earl, and while a wicked part of him was aroused by the idea of laying with a woman so high born, he felt at odds with himself over his reasonings.

He was very much enticed by the idea that Faith wasn't as perfect or virtuous as she had always appeared to be. To take part in a secret affair with a woman who had been so dismissive of him at first was tantalizing, to say the least. Which is why he could not stop thinking about the letter he received from her the afternoon following Lady Belle's party.

Lismore Hunt Lodge. Tomorrow at noon.

F

It would be embarrassing to admit how his body had reacted to such a brief letter. Six words to set his blood ablaze, tapping into an unseen pool of desire such as he had not felt in years. Already the hours in between seemed filled with months rather than minutes. And what a clever minx. The hunting lodge was a perfect place for a rendezvous.

The Lismore Hunting Lodge was a stone building set in the

northern part of the Lismore estate. Graham had lived in it before he married Hope and moved into the hall, but it had been vacant for some twelve months, save when it was used for after their deer stalking retreats.

It was the perfect place to commence their affair, and when Logan finally reached the copse of tall Scotch pine that hid the gray stone hunting lodge the next day, he could barely contain evidence of his eagerness.

The lodge was modest in size, especially compared to Harris House, but it was large enough to sleep twenty men comfortably. A staff of four had lived there when Graham was in residence, but as they were no longer needed full time, they had been let go to seek other employment. Temporary help was hired as needed during the hunting seasons.

Its seclusion from the rest of the world made it an ideal place to meet. As it came into view, Logan saw Faith standing at the top of the stone steps in front of the green-painted front door. His heart began to beat hard against his chest, a reaction that he tried to convince himself had nothing to do with Faith herself, merely his excitement at the start of an affair.

Faith was dressed in a blue-and-green striped gown covered mostly by a dark, intricately styled cloak. It was gray wool but trimmed with a gold-and-yellow tartan, a plaid that gave Logan pause.

That was Duncan's family plaid.

Faith must have noted his hesitation, for her friendly smile shrank away.

"Is everything all right?" she asked as he came off his horse.

"That cloak," he said, taking the rein of his horse in his hand. "Where did you get it?"

"Oh," Faith said, smiling again. "It's Jeanne's. She left it during Aunt Belle's party and I thought to, well, borrow it, so that no one would recognize me. Though no one knows I'm here."

Relief coursed through him as he let out a breath. He hadn't been aware of how affected he was by seeing something that reminded him of Duncan wrapped around Faith. It had been surprising, to say the least.

"Are you all right?" she asked, breaking into his intrusive thoughts.

"Yes," he said unevenly. Her one brow arched higher than the other, and he knew she didn't believe him. "Truly," he said, trying to fill his voice with as much certainty as possible. He didn't wish to speak about Duncan now.

"No, you're not," she challenged. "What's wrong?"

"Nothing's wrong."

"Liar," she pressed, and he felt the familiar teasing he always did in her company. "Tell me."

Her command was infuriating and arousing all at once. He could see that she wasn't likely to let it go, even though it was a trifle.

"That," he said, nodding to the hem of her cloak, "is Carlyle plaid."

Faith looked down before raising her face, frowning.

"Yes, and?" she asked before it dawned on her. Jeanne had once explained that Logan had served with her husband and that he grieved the man's death in the war. Her face fell. "Oh. Oh yes, of course." A stilted silence hung between them as Logan's horse hooved the ground. Faith shook her head. "I'm sorry to have worn it."

"There's no need to apologize, he said. "It's neither here nor there."

"But it makes you uncomfortable."

"It does not."

She quirked her head.

"It does. Your face became drawn when you saw it."

Logan scowled.

"It did not."

"It did though," she insisted before taking a breath. "There's no reason to deny it. I certainly haven't the faintest idea of your experiences, but there is no shame to them, I'm sure."

"How would you know?" he asked, his tone harsher than he'd intended, instantly quieting her. Logan silently scolded himself before continuing. "I don't wish to talk about it."

Faith nodded. "Very well."

Blast. This wasn't how he had envisioned their first coupling to start. Inhaling deeply, he cast his eyes around, searching for her pony, deciding to change the subject. "Where is your horse?"

"I walked," she said, another smile pulling at the corner of her mouth. "I'm quite unlikely to ride again until I manage to forget my last jaunt."

"I see," he said, turning his horse about. "Well, then…shall we go in?"

Faith's eyes widened slightly, and she stepped away from him.

"Uh, let's first put your horse in the stables."

"The stables?"

"Yes. We wouldn't want to be discovered, would we?"

Pragmatic of her, he thought with a nod.

"Lead the way."

Faith walked across the pine needle–covered drive to a C-shaped stable. She walked past the first five stalls, stopping before the first stall hidden from view upon the first entrance. It was obvious that she'd put some serious thought into how to ensure they wouldn't be caught and for a moment Logan wondered if what they were doing wasn't in her best interest. Evidently, his apprehension shone on his face because she reached for his hand, almost reassuringly.

"Just in case," she said.

He led the horse into the stall and closed the grate before turning to face her. Whatever suspicious inkling he had felt a moment ago melted away. Faith's green eyes all but shined at him, and his breath caught in his throat. She was beautiful, but he had seen many beautiful women before and none of them had affected him as she did. He couldn't explain it. It was more than her heart-shaped face and perfectly arched brows. The way the corner of her mouth quivered between smile and sneer, or the way her eyes would widen when he said the right or wrong thing. It was so many nuances that her painting could never reproduce, and he was grateful to have her in the flesh.

Her curled, honey-brown hair was pulled back, and he longed to run his hands through it, to hold her head to his and kiss her into oblivion. Giving in to his desires, his hand touched her cheek, which she leaned into.

Not for the first time, he considered how fortunate he was to have found himself in this predicament. While he and Faith had started out at one another's throats, the unfolding of their situation had seemed almost serendipitous.

"You know, had you told me a year ago that we would be involved in a secret rendezvous with one another, I'd have believed it."

Her brow lifted.

"You would not have."

"I would," he said, his thumb gently rubbing the edge of her jaw. "From the first moment I saw you, I thought you were an arrogant, conceited thing," his voice dipped as fire lit her eyes. "And the most beautiful creature I had ever seen."

The last bit caught her off guard, and she looked down.

"I thought you were an egotistical prat," she said, glancing up. "And I was right."

"Were you?" he asked, a hint of danger in his tone. She nodded. "Well then, what an unfortunate situation for you to be in. Perhaps you should have taken better care."

He leaned forward, his mouth nearly on hers when she spoke.

"It's you who should be cautious, Logan."

At the drop of his name, Logan felt a flame engulf him as he bent down to kiss her. Instantly, her hands came up over his shoulders, the faint pressure of her fingertips digging into his skin, emboldening him.

Though he was no stranger to physical acts of love, the feel of

Faith in his arms was at once familiar and foreign. He knew the motions that were expected of him and had been praised for his ability to coax a lady into a euphoric state, but this was different. He knew Faith, knew her anger and annoyance, her wit, her likes and dislikes. A bizarre yearning to please her in all ways bubbled within him as their kiss deepened.

His hand moved to the back of her skull, his fingers snaking through her hair. Her head tipped backward, and he kissed down the column of her neck as a soft moan escaped her mouth. The sound aroused him, and he pulled her closer as his other hand drifted up from her side to the mild slope of her breast. Caressing her through the cloth of her gown was terrific but not enough. He needed to undress her.

His hands came up the row of buttons that ran down the center of her torso, searching for the top one, but as soon as his finger began to toy with her gown, a distant sound of hooves sounded, pulling him from his task.

"What the…" he said, turning away from Faith.

She cleared her throat, reaching for his chin as he focused back on her.

"Logan, please," she said softly.

His mouth caught hers again, but the sound grew, and he soon pulled away again.

"Faith, wait," he breathed.

Seemingly distracted, Faith nodded dazedly before her eyes focused as she heard the noise. Shaking her head, she glanced over his shoulder.

"What is that?"

"Shh," he said, staying her with his hands. "I'll be right back."

Logan walked cautiously down the stables, pressing his back along the wall. Two black horses appeared through the thicket, yielding just before the front steps of the lodge. Logan pulled back in an effort not to be seen, but as he recognized the happy, almost giddy couple, his own arousal was extinguished.

Graham was the first off his horse, and he quickly picked

Hope up by the waist, swinging her down off the animal as her riding habit twirled out. Her gentle giggle as he did so made Logan aware that he was witnessing a very private moment.

"I'm sorry," Hope chirped. "That business with Aunt Belle took far longer than it was supposed to."

"Aye, I almost left without you."

"You could have." Graham made a face as if to say he would never leave her, which seemed to please Hope. She tugged at the lapels of her husband's coat. "Well, all's well that ends well. We have all afternoon now."

"That we do," Graham said, his tone low, his hand caressing her cheek. "Shall we?"

Hope nodded enthusiastically as he led her into the stone lodge, closing the door behind them. It seemed someone would have a rendezvous today, but it wouldn't be Logan. He returned to Faith.

"Who was it?" she asked.

"Your sister and brother-in-law," Logan said, perturbed.

"Really?" Faith said, though something in her tone told him that she wasn't exactly surprised. "How strange."

He exhaled slowly. "We can't possibly continue this now." Pausing, he glanced at her. "Any ideas?"

"I suppose we could always try Harris House?" But before she even finished, he was shaking his head.

"It would be impossible. My father hasn't left the house in months and my sister is far too aware of the goings on around her."

"Perhaps they might take a trip? To Glasgow, for instance."

"What would my father do in Glasgow?"

"I don't know," Faith said. "Visit friends? Take in the sights?"

"No. It wouldn't work. Besides, there are plenty of other places we might meet. For you to come to Harris House would be far too perilous for your reputation."

Faith gave him a small smirk.

"How chivalrous," she said sardonically. He opened his

mouth, but she lifted her fingers and pressed them against his mouth. "Perhaps tomorrow then? A quarter to eight in the morning, by the flat rock near Loch Fyne."

Anticipation stirred deep within Logan.

"Very well. Tomorrow."

With a teasing glance, Faith nodded, and pressed her lips to his once more, kissing him with a heat that he had not noticed before. How strange. But the next moment, she was off, hurrying from the stables with her hood pulled over her head as she headed back toward Lismore on foot.

It felt like a thousand hours until their planned rendezvous. Logan hadn't anticipated sleeping so soundly the one day he desired to be up, but when his eyes opened the next morning, he found the morning light was already shining through his window.

Without a second thought, he rushed to dress and tore out of the house with Jaco close behind, quickly saddling his horse so that he could make it to the rock on time. Faith was already there when he reached it, leaning her hip against the stone as she looked over the loch. Her expression was pensive, and Logan was curious as to why, but when she saw him, it melted away, leaving only her seductive smirk in its place.

God, how he wanted to shake the self-satisfaction from her being. Not in an attempt to smother her confidence but to challenge her core senses.

He came off his horse quickly and reached for her, bringing her body against his as he kissed her. She was caught by surprise but soon enveloped him in her arms as he leaned her back over the flat rock, kissing down her neck.

"Wait—"

"I've been tormented all night," he confessed, more to himself than to her, as he made easy work of the front of her gown. It was a corseted front scheme, and he pulled at the strings to free her from her restraints.

"As have I," she breathed, her arms wrapping around his head as he loosened the front of her dress. "But you must stop."

Stop? Not for all the rice in Burma. He had slept so soundly because his dreams had been far too vivid—yet they paled in comparison to the real thing. He needed to taste her, to touch her skin with his own. He was just about to pull her chemise down when a voice sounded somewhere, not too far off.

"Faith!" Grace's voice called out, causing Logan to freeze.

"Blasted hell," he whispered harshly into her bosom.

Was there no privacy in this world? He lifted his head and saw an apologetic Faith staring up at him.

"I tried to tell you."

"What is your sister doing here?"

"She forges for medicinal herbs and thought to come with me when she caught me leaving through the garden."

"Faith?" Grace's questioning tone sounded closer.

Pushing himself up, he righted his jacket and helped Faith as she tended to her dress. Once she was done, he leaned forward.

"I can't take much more of this," Logan whispered into her ear, causing her to shake. "I nearly bit through my fork at dinner last night."

Faith, the chit, had the audacity to smile.

"Patience," she said as if that solved everything.

"I'm glad you find this amusing."

"It *is* amusing. It's also inevitable. If we must conduct this liaison, outside in the wild, we cannot be surprised when we are interrupted. And unfortunately, there are too many people between Lismore and Harris House for us to find any privacy, so yes, you must show patience."

"Patience until when?"

"Well, without four walls and roof that someone isn't constantly barging into, I don't see when we could begin this…" she said, her voice trailing off. "Unless you have an idea where we can go, I'm afraid this affair is over before it has even begun."

Logan stared at Faith. Her face was blank, but he was confident she was leading him to an answer she wanted. She had mentioned Harris House twice, and while he had tried to avoid it, it was the only place where he could be in command of his environment. But he wouldn't take her there while his father or sister were in residence.

"I suppose we might try the hunting lodge again. What about tomorrow?" he asked, but she shook her head.

"I've a horse-riding lesson with Jeanne tomorrow and then I'm to accompany Hope to the vicar's house."

"Faith, where are you?" Grace's voice sounded much closer now.

Faith gave him a pleading, sorrowful look before moving away from him, heading toward her sister's voice.

"Here I am!" she called, turning to give Logan a last glance.

Logan reached for his horse's reins and quickly walked him back to the trail. His presence could have been explained away as a coincidence if Grace had spotted him, but the less they were caught in each other's company, the better. Everyone assumed they didn't care for each other, which was a fine cover, but it needed to remain intact.

Figuring out how to have an uninterrupted meeting with Faith plagued him for the rest of the day. If he could only be with her for a few hours, this nagging need would dissipate—or at least be hoped it would, because it was beginning to have adverse effects on other parts of his life. Apparently, he was far shorter with his staff and his family.

Surprisingly, a letter arrived around dinner time that evening from Lady Belle. She requested that the art pamphlets he had borrowed be returned the next day. He could have sent them over with a servant, but the prospect of seeing Faith again was too tempting to resist. Though he doubted they would find much privacy, he still felt the need to be near her, so the following afternoon, he made his way to Lismore Hall through the rain.

Upon entering the library, which Belle used as her private office, he saw the old woman sitting behind her desk with a tea set just being set down by a maid. Her faithful companion, Andrews, stood behind her, barely acknowledging Logan's appearance.

"Harris!" Belle said excitedly, looking up from her work. "Excellent timing, I was just about to have some tea. Would you care for some?"

"No, thank you," he said, handing over the dozen pamphlets he held.

He set them on the corner of her table.

"Thank you for letting me borrow these. They were most helpful."

"Oh, I'm glad," she said as she stood.

"I'm surprised you kept them for so long. Some date back several years."

"I do enjoy keeping things. It's the historian in me," she said, coming around the desk. "You know, I have gossip pages somewhere around here from the year my sister made her debut. I've kept them for nearly sixty years."

Logan chuckled, perplexed.

"Why?"

"Oh, why do people do anything? Because I enjoy them," she said, staring at him as silence settled around them. "So. How are things going with you?"

Though he knew she couldn't possibly understand what had been happening in his life, Logan pinned her a steady glance.

"As well as they can, I suppose."

Belle made a strange little "humph" noise as if displeased by his answer. He was about to inquire as to what troubled her when she peered over his shoulder suddenly.

"Ah! Faith my dear, could you come in here, please?"

Logan turned around to see a startled Faith stop abruptly in the doorway. Evidently, the sight of Logan was shocking, for her eyes were wide, and her cheeks seemed somewhat pale. He took a step toward her instinctively before remembering that they were to not demonstrate any actual friendly feelings in front of an audience.

His hands balled into fists.

"Aunt Belle," Faith said, coming into the room. Her chin dipped a fraction. "Mr. Harris. To what do we owe the pleasure of your company?"

"I was just returning some pamphlets to Lady Belle," he said, motioning with his hand behind him at the desk where he had placed the booklets. "I thought you were—"

He stopped himself before he could finish his sentence.

"Thought what?" Aunt Belle asked, almost intrusively.

"Ah, I was just, um, returning from my lesson with Jeanne," she said, turning her hands out against her skirts as if to display her riding habit. "The rain stopped us again."

"I see," Logan said, his tone somewhat rough.

An electric heat seemed to pass between them. Logan was unsure if the unannounced meeting was affecting him, but all he wanted to do was take her by the hand and escape Lady Belle's company so he could have Faith to himself.

As if she could read his mind, Aunt Belle cleared her throat and stepped around him.

"Andrews, would you help me with something? I've quite forgot my need for, erm, my walking stick."

Faith looked at Belle, her gaze worried.

"Are you not feeling well again, Aunt Belle?"

"Oh, it's nothing. The rain wreaks havoc on my poor old bones. Andrews?" she said, making her way to the door briskly before suddenly stopping. She began to limp as if suddenly remembering to do so. "Shall we? I'll only be a moment, my dear. I'm sure you can entertain Mr. Harris while I'm gone."

Andrews briskly followed his lady and closed the door as if on purpose. Alone with Faith, Logan could barely resist the urge to come toward her. He needn't, though, because as soon as the door handle clicked, Faith came to him.

She was on him instantly, kissing him as her tongue searched his mouth. He was aroused immediately, though the urgency of her kisses made him wary. Placing his hands on her upper arms, he pushed her back slightly.

"Faith?"

She shook her head.

"I can't bear this," she said, husky. "It's too much to be constantly tormented."

She sought his mouth again, but he resisted, much to his own displeasure.

"Well, it can't happen here."

"It can't happen anywhere. It can't happen at all," she pouted as she kissed him.

Logan knew. He felt the same way, but this was madness. They couldn't possibly be caught in one another's arms in her family's library. There would be consequences that neither of them were prepared for, so he pulled back.

"Faith, wait," he tried, and to his dismay, she obeyed.

In fact, she moved entirely out of his reach. Wrapping herself in her arms, she stopped several feet away. Belle returned then, and judging by the expression on her face, it seemed she wasn't very pleased either.

"Well, Harris, I've told the cook you were staying for dinner," she said, approaching her desk.

"Ah, I actually cannot—"

"It will be no trouble," Belle said, ignoring him. "I just saw Graham in the hallway and told him you were here. He mentioned something about a confectionary nightmare he wanted to discuss with you?"

Logan nearly began to argue with the old woman, but the confectionary nightmare was not an issue he could just brush aside. Evidently, he had business to tend to. With a passing glance at Faith's back, he nodded.

"Very well. If you'll excuse me."

Unchanneled angst and unresolved passion made Logan nearly unfit to be in polite company for the rest of the afternoon. Thankfully, Graham was in an equally poor mood as they discussed their investment in a confectionary factory in Glasgow. One of the new ovens built for the space had become too hot, and a fire had broken out. No one was harmed, but a prominent building corner had been burnt, and the factory was compromised. It would take weeks to fix and much money, but Logan could barely focus on that.

When dinner was served, he sat across the table from Faith, who, by chance or circumstance, had worn a gown with a particularly low neckline. For an hour and a half, he had to converse politely with everyone, doing his best to ignore the growing need to have her.

By the time the final course was served, Logan could no longer stand it. Faith served herself a honey mousse that had been invented by the Lismore cook. He felt his throat dry as she brought up the silver utensil, parting her lips to consume it.

Though he had been in an actual war, this was torture.

After dinner, he made his goodbyes to the family. Faith was nowhere to be seen. Perhaps she had decided to end this ridiculous attempt at an affair before it had even begun. He left the house, heading toward the stables. A young stable hand sat on a stool in the corner, his arms folded across his chest and his cap pulled down over his eyes, sleeping soundly. Logan didn't bother to wake him. Upon reaching his horse's stall, however, Faith appeared.

"Hello," she said softly, and it took every ounce of strength in Logan not to reach for her.

Instead, he simply stared. That seemed to make her uncomfortable, for she began to shift from side to side.

"More like goodbye, isn't it?" he said after a moment, fixing his horse's saddle.

It pained him to see the disappointment in her green eyes.

"Is that the way of it then? It's too difficult?" she asked as he pulled his horse out. Thankfully, there didn't seem to be any stable hands around. "We're to give up before we even start?"

"What would you have us do?" he asked, letting his aggravation sound. "I can't bloody well take you up against a stable wall, can I?"

The sting of his too-honest words caused Faith's mouth to drop open, and he felt like an ass. She certainly didn't deserve to be spoken to so harshly. She swallowed and shook his head.

"I'm sorry," he said, disgusted with his reaction. "I just don't know what to do."

"Nor do I."

Her tone seemed unsure. He wanted to fix it, but how? He sought a guarantee to be uninterrupted the first time they lay together, and if that meant shipping his family to Glasgow, then so be it.

Yes. That was the only place he could think to manage true solitude for them.

"Very well. It will have to be at Harris House. Give me a week's time to settle my father and Arabella. I'll send word the day of."

Faith nodded once and abruptly turned away from him.

"Until then," she said over her shoulder, though she didn't stop.

Yes, until then. He wasn't sure how he would make his father leave Harris House, but he'd find a way, no matter what it took. He wasn't a gentleman, had never claimed to be one, and his attempted affair with Faith was immoral, but his craving for her was too much, and it needed to be sated so that he could put his torment to rest.

— ❧ —

Chapter Thirteen

A FTER NEARLY A week of sabotaging their rendezvous, Faith was finally on her way to Harris House.

Arranging for interruptions to keep them apart hadn't been easy or pleasant, but it had had to be done. The first had been easy enough to arrange. Hope, and her husband visited the hunting lodge weekly, as a way to spend some uninterrupted quality time together. Everyone in Lismore Hall knew about it, and Faith had used that knowledge to her advantage. She knew Hope and Graham would be there to interrupt Logan and herself and it had worked.

The second meeting had been even easier to sabotage than the first. Grace went out every other morning to harvest her medicinal plants. Faith and simply suggested the right time and escorted her sister out, causing Logan more frustration. It was the only way she could think of to get him to bring her to Harris House.

But when Logan had shown up unexpectedly at Lismore Hall, that had jarred her. To see him without warning had affected her most embarrassingly, and she had all but thrown herself at him the moment they were left alone.

That had not been part of her plan. What was wrong with her? Blessedly, he had shown more sense than she had in that moment and had pushed her way before anyone walked in on them.

But her plan had finally worked. Faith had made Logan desperate enough to finally bring her to Harris House. And once she was inside, she would ruin *Odalisque Reclined*. Then she would flee to London with Aunt Belle and hopefully never think about Logan Harris again.

But that was more easily said than done. Faith couldn't explain it, but the idea of never seeing Logan again hurt her heart. There was an honesty to their dialogue that she had never experienced with anyone else. While she knew she was lying to him about her reasons for seeking an affair, it still felt as though she could tell him anything and he would simply accept it.

Except her wish for the painting to be burned. For some reason, he wouldn't give her that. And for that reason alone, she had to go through with her plan.

Looking up at the dimly lit Harris House, she felt a whirlwind of emotions. Fear, excitement, resentment, lust, and, to her surprise, regret. There was something undeniable between her and Logan. Something real and tender. Had they not met the way they had, perhaps if he hadn't come to own *Odalisque Reclined*, they might have been able to explore a more honest connection. But fate had dealt them this hand, and Faith could not change it.

Taking a deep breath, she walked at a fast pace, eager to be out of the woods. Though she had never been the sort to be afraid of the dark, she could swear that during her walk from around the loch, she heard someone call out that word again.

"Faodail!"

It had stopped her in her tracks at first, but then she had picked up her skirts and hurried as fast as she could. Why she was being haunted by that word, she didn't know, but she felt as though a ghost of sorts was after her. *Faodail.* It was certainly not English. Thankfully, Harris House was in her sight.

She dug her hand into the pocket of her cloak and wrapped her fingers tightly around the small, circular amber Arabella had given her. Even though Faith didn't believe in silly things like luck, she wasn't so arrogant as to not hedge her bets.

Also in her pocket was a letter opener that she had borrowed from her aunt's desk. It wasn't very sharp, but it was pointy and Faith only needed something that could pierce the canvas.

Yet with each step toward Harris House, Faith's confidence in her plan faltered. Logan would likely be in a rage when he realized her deception, but what did it matter? As long as she eliminated the damn painting, she would be free.

So why did she feel so unsure?

She headed toward the northwest corner of the house, where she had told him in her letter she would meet him. He had countered, stating that he wouldn't let her sneak around the forests at night, but Faith was never one to do as she was told. She had feigned a headache, asking not to be disturbed, and then left two hours before she told him she would. Admittedly, she felt like a burglar, sneaking around in the dark.

"Psst…"

Faith halted in her tracks. She searched the night for a silhouette, a shadow, anything that might show her who was there, but the darkness was too great.

"Hello?" she whispered, only to be suddenly seized upon.

She nearly shrieked when a hand came over her mouth. A solid, hard body pressed against her, and a familiar, deep voice sounded in her ear.

"How did you get here?"

"I walked, of course."

"Walked?"

"Yes, all by myself."

"Impudent little fool," he said, humor and annoyance mingled in his tone. "I was just leaving to get you."

"Well, there's no need to now," she said, looking around. "Where's Jaco?"

"Locked away in the kitchens with a slab of beef. I won't have him distracting us."

"Oh, the poor dear."

"'Poor dear' nothing. He was gnawing on a bone when I left him, happy as can be."

"Still, I hate to think of him locked away."

Logan gave her a sardonic look.

"For someone who doesn't like big dogs, you've become awfully attached to that mutt."

Faith smirked, amused by Logan's jealousy. It wasn't her fault that the pup was so attached to her.

"Shall we, then?" She moved toward the back entrance into the house, but he redirected her with his strong hand. Surely they weren't going to walk through the front door? "What are you doing?"

"Taking you inside."

"But what about the servants?"

"They've all been given the evening off. And after a grueling argument with my father, he and my sister have gone to Glasgow for several days. We are quite alone."

"Are we?" Faith asked, surprised at how delighted she felt at that sentiment.

"Aye."

She was sure that her cheeks were turning several shades of pink. Faith ducked her chin as Logan escorted her across the lawn to the front of the house.

It was sheer madness to consider doing something like this. She would be discarding her chastity for the sake of saving her reputation by ruining the painting. But Faith had concluded that ruining herself with Logan would be the lesser of the two evils. If that painting could see the light of day, she wouldn't be able to deny her involvement, and no amount of talk could get her out of it.

Besides, Faith had also decided that once she and Belle left for London, she would make a point to explain to her aunt that she had no desire to marry, instead choosing to live her life like Belle. An independent, if sometimes eccentric, spinster. It only made sense. The idea of marriage had never held much promise to Faith, especially since leaving London. After her failed romance with Donovan and her half-hearted attempt at a relationship with

Renee's brother, which had really only been an attempt to overcome her heartbreak after Donovan, Faith didn't think she would ever be inclined to marry. Not when it was so obvious that she lacked the confidence a woman needed to manage a relationship.

Once they finally crossed the threshold, Faith shifted from one foot to the other lost in her thoughts. She jumped when Logan reached out and touched her shoulder. Whipping around, Faith let out a frantic little huff of breath, and Logan's charming smirk faltered slightly. He went to remove her cloak, but she clutched it tightly to her throat, causing him to pause.

"I didn't mean to scare you."

"I'm not scared," she said almost instantly.

"No," he replied, his hand coming to her cheek. "I doubt there's anything in this world that could scare you."

"I'm sure there is something, I've only not found out what yet."

The gentle rumble of laughter that came from Logan sent a shiver down Faith's spine. His hand touched her back, and she swallowed as he led her up the stairs.

This was it. They would retire to his room, undress, and lay together, and afterward, while he slept, Faith would find the painting, destroy it, and flee. All she had to do was keep her wits about her.

The walk down the hallways was perhaps the fastest and slowest she had ever experienced. Though this entire plot had been her idea, she wasn't sure how she should feel. Frightened, of course, because she had never done anything like this and wouldn't be able to take it back once executed. But she had also anticipated what it might be like, particularly with someone like Logan.

Donovan had always been so kind and soft-spoken. He'd always ensured that she was comfortable in his studio and had never once allowed her to pursue her desires for physical intimacy with him because her reputation was too important.

On the other hand, Logan believed that her reputation was already decimated. Would he think that she was experienced? All Faith had ever witnessed of coupling were a handful of farm animals during her time in Cornwall. It had seemed natural enough, and it was why Faith continued to rationalize that virginity wasn't so important. Animals and people did this sort of thing every day, had been doing it every day for thousands of years. Which was what she kept repeating to herself. It wasn't important.

But it is necessary, Faith noted as they reached his room. As much as she didn't want it to be, she knew it would likely be the only time in her life that she would be with someone, and that alone emboldened her. If she would be a spinster for the rest of her life, at least she would know what she was missing out on.

Of course, there was also a chance that she wouldn't like it. What a blessing that would be.

"Faith?"

Looking up at him, Faith realized that he had asked her something. Shaking her head, she spoke.

"Forgive me. My mind was somewhere else."

Logan's gaze became thoughtful, and he tilted his head.

"Where was it?"

"Oh, who knows?" she lied, looking at the bedroom door. Fear was creeping up her spine, and for an instant, she thought of delaying their encounter. She opened her mouth and blurted out the first thing she could think of. "Faodail?"

Logan stared at her, seemingly half surprised and half charmed.

"What?"

"Faodail," she tried again, changing the pronunciation slightly. "Or fao-dail?"

"You said it correctly the first time," he said, the corner of his mouth hitching up. "Where did you learn that?"

"I haven't, actually. I've only heard it."

"I see."

"What does it mean?"

"It means, 'lucky find.' Though it's sometimes used as an endearment, as well."

"Oh." Faith's mouth quirked, confused. Upon glancing up at Logan, however, she hurriedly shook her head. "Oh no, I'm not disappointed."

"Are you sure?"

"Yes," she said with a smile. "It's just, I've heard it twice now and I don't know why I keep hearing it."

"Perhaps the fae are calling out to you."

Faith gave him a biting glare.

"Do not torment me with fairytales, Logan. I've no room for such frivolities in my life."

"Nor do I," he said before peering at the door. He looked back at her. "I wanted to caution you. The painting is here."

"Is it?" she asked breathlessly as he opened the door, and they walked in.

Parisian green walls adorned with gold leaf trim surrounded them. A crown canopy hung over a large bed. The furniture was dark wood and heavily carved. Zodiac symbols had been painted around the room, with the ceiling done to mimic a night sky.

It was oddly fanciful and artistic. The corner of Faith's mouth quirked. What strange decor for a bedroom.

Looking around, she noticed a large, rectangular shape covered by a white sheet sat leaning in the corner of the room. A wooden chair stood close to it as if someone had sat there, inspecting whatever was hidden beneath the cloth.

Faith's heart began to thud agonizingly in her chest. It had been at least two years since she had seen it. The last time she had laid eyes on it, she had been in love and so sure of things. She had been very proud of Donovan upon its completion, even though she thought he had painted her far too flatteringly. Still, she turned to face Logan, whose face was carefully blank.

"Is that it?" she asked, and he nodded. "Why is it covered?"

"I've not permitted anyone to see it," he said, moving around her. "That's why it's not hung up. And also, why it's in my bed chambers."

Faith removed her cloak and placed it gingerly on one of two high-backed chairs before facing the painting once more.

"Why haven't you allowed anyone to see it?" she asked, unsure.

But Logan didn't answer. Faith realized that he wasn't entirely sure why he'd kept it to himself.

"Logan," she said, causing him to look at her. "Why have you kept it away from everyone?"

A moment passed between them, and when he opened his mouth to speak, Faith felt her heart pinch.

"When I first saw it, I knew it was you almost instantly," he said, moving slowly across the room toward it. "I was shocked, to say the least, and tried to rationalize that it must just be a coincidence, with a model who merely happened to look like you. I mean, what are the chances that I would come to own such a piece of work?"

"I can't figure that out either," Faith said, standing behind the wooden chair. "It seems impossible."

"It shouldn't have even happened, honestly," he said. "I was interested in a pair of paintings by Marchelies. You know him, don't you? The French artist?"

Faith nodded. "Yes, I'm aware of his work. Weren't *Faustus in the Garden* and *Faust in his Study* recently on display in the Salon?"

Logan smirked at her knowledge.

"Yes. I had every intention of acquiring those exact works, but when I mentioned my intentions for those pieces, your aunt actually instructed me to buy something from Donovan."

Faith's head snapped around, her wide eyes on him.

"She did?"

"Yes. Was she aware of Donovan and who he was to you?"

That was a loaded question, but Faith answered it anyway.

"No. No one ever knew what Donovan meant to me."

A heavy silence settled between them. Faith felt like a fool for admitting such a thing to Logan. But then, he had no way of knowing that Faith's feelings for Donovan, as strong as they had been, had all been one-sided.

"May I ask you something?" he asked, and Faith nodded.

"Yes, of course."

"Were you in love with him? Donovan, I mean."

An outrageously personal question, and yet, what they were about to do was perhaps the most intimate thing two people could do. In light of that, maybe it was silly of her to think that anything would be out of bounds. To her surprise, she shook her head.

"I thought I was."

"What did it feel like?" he asked, and she turned to face him. He shrugged. "I'm curious."

"What being in love feels like?" she asked, and he nodded. "I don't think I ever had a good understanding of it," she admitted.

She looked back at the sheet-covered painting. Would it look like she remembered?

"Can I see it?" she asked suddenly, annoyed with herself for becoming maudlin.

Logan nodded, pulling away the white fabric, revealing a sight that had haunted Faith for two years. Laid out on a bed of pillows, her waist wrapped in yellow velvet, was Faith. Turned at the waist, she stared seductively over her shoulder at the viewer. Faith bit her lip at the sight of her uncovered breast and felt her cheeks warm.

Of course Logan thought she had slept with Donovan. This was a painting of a siren, a woman who had known a man's touch, and she was, well…She was not this woman.

"The velvet was actually blue," she said softly. "But he changed it to yellow, at my request."

"Yellow is a better contrast for the background. It was a good choice," Logan said. "You are fond of yellow, aren't you?"

"I am," she said, pointing to the peacock feather. "And that was actually a goose feather. He had to paint the peacock from memory."

"Is that so?" Logan asked, turning his focus away from the painting. She looked at him as well. "You know, I've studied this piece for longer than I'd like to admit."

"Have you?"

He nodded. "I have and while initially, I believed it to be a true masterpiece, I've experienced a growing dissatisfaction with it."

Faith's brow scrunched.

"Why is that?"

"Well, if I'm honest," he said, stepping toward her, "I think I find it lacking because the subject isn't quite right."

Faith frowned, looking back at the painting and then at him.

"What is lacking?"

The corner of Logan's mouth pulled up slightly.

"It cannot speak."

Faith blinked.

"What?"

"It cannot speak, or argue. It has never once even attempted to insult me." He faced it once more. "It has done your physical likeness justice, that is true, but I'm afraid that it does not capture your soul. It does not—cannot—speak to your virtues, or your vices."

Faith squinted at him.

"What vices?"

Logan smirked.

"Your inability to be proven wrong, for instance."

"If I were ever wrong, I might see your point."

"But you were wrong."

"About what?"

"About me," he said. "About why I won't destroy this painting."

She turned back to stare at him.

"You mean you *don't* like having something which to black-mail me with?"

The air between them turned thick, and Logan watched her with a seriousness that hadn't been there before.

"I would never use this painting against you," he said. For a moment, Faith wanted very much to believe him. "I don't like the idea of it having such power over you."

"Power over me?" she repeated with a humorless chuckle. "You believe this has power over me?"

"I do," he said intently as he took another step toward her, practically touching now. "I think this Donovan fellow must have used your feelings for him against you. I think, perhaps, you were far softer before he betrayed you. I hate to think that the hurt he caused you somehow molded you into what you are now."

Faith's words caught in her throat. Donovan *had* hurt her, but not quite in the way Logan believed. She knew he thought the artist had used her and thrown her to the side once he had had his way with her, but the truth was more innocent and somehow more pathetic.

"And what am I now?"

"Frightened."

"Ha," she said, the word shaky as she spoke.

For a devastating moment, she wanted to explain everything to Logan—that she'd never given Donovan her body but that she'd thought she'd given him her heart...only to discover later that she hadn't even known what love was. That she had been too young and too proud to listen to reason. But she was too cowardly to confess all that to him, and her head dropped.

Seeming to mistake her quietness for shame, Logan's hand came up, curving beneath her jaw as he tilted her face back.

"Let me help you forget him," he said softly as he leaned forward.

In all honesty, Donovan's vague memory could barely compare to Logan.

Donovan had been dark haired and pretty, with soft hands and a youthfulness that had played to her young heart. He had been gentle but in a delicate way that had made Faith feel uncomfortably like a porcelain doll. On the other hand, Logan was entirely and unmistakably a man in his prime, and he treated her like a woman—one who had strength and vitality and passions of her own. The hard lines of his face, the strength of his hands, and the rawness of his being both unnerved and delighted Faith in the worst way.

Logan may have challenged her, but his challenges were never condescending as Donovan's reprimands had been. And best of all, he seemed just as eager to touch her as she did him, as opposed to Donovan, who had eagerly and earnestly run from her advances.

"Can you?" she asked softly, playing into this game that she didn't understand.

"Will you let me try?"

She nodded absentmindedly as she pressed her cheek into his hand. He exhaled with a satisfied growl before his mouth landed on hers.

The magnetism between them was instant. Faith's hands instantly went up to his neck, fingers snaking through his hair as she held him to her. His hands were bruising and powerful and everything that Faith had ever imagined.

There was no reason for hesitation. Faith had expected to feel scared at this moment, but she only found herself thinking one thing.

Finally.

Yes, it was outrageous to think, and it certainly didn't speak to her being a lady, but Faith wasn't in a drawing room surrounded by society. She was in Logan's arms, and all she wanted to do, all she was going to do, was exactly what she wanted.

Even if she didn't know quite what that was.

Clawing at his coat, she continued to kiss him as his hands fell to the front of her dress, working to free the six large, black buttons. He was efficient, untying her overskirt and continuing to kiss her. Soon, she was standing in only her chemise, petticoats, and corset.

Shocked at the speed with which he'd undressed her, Faith ignored the growing panic she felt in her heart.

"Turn around," he said, lifting his mouth to her ear as he gently twisted her about.

His hands moved up the tight lacings of the back of her corset. If she had any idea what to expect, it certainly wasn't the gentleness with which Logan seemed to handle her. He didn't treat her as if she was fragile but rather as if she was precious, and it warmed her heart to be handled so.

With the same speed as before, he loosened the strings of her corset, removing it in a matter of moments. Turning her in his arms, Faith couldn't help but feel they were moving too fast. She lay her hands on his chest, and he thankfully paused in his actions. To her surprise, a faint color broke over the bridge of his nose.

"Ah, I'm rushing, aren't I?" he asked, his tone unsure. "I'm sorry. I've not done this in a while."

Faith watched him, amazed that he would confess that. The tenseness displayed in his hazel eyes made her empathetic. It seemed he was nervous too.

Slowly, Faith raised her hand to his cheek.

"Truly?" she asked.

"Aye."

"Why not?"

His muscular shoulders shrugged, and a cloud came over his face.

"It's not been particularly important to me recently, I guess."

"But isn't it always important to men?"

His gaze caught hers.

"Lumping us all together, are you?" He gave her a teasing smile. "Tsk, tsk. That's bad form, isn't it?"

Faith felt embarrassment swelling within her.

"How was I to know that, well…"

"Different men felt different things?" he chided, and she playfully slapped his chest. "My, for such a forward, independent sort of woman, you really are a conformist."

"I am not," she argued.

"Then perhaps you'll let me show you how different men can be?" he asked, dropping a kiss on her nose.

Heat crawled up the back of her neck.

"Yes. But slowly, if you don't mind?"

"Slowly is just how I like it."

"Is it?"

He gave her a slight nod, and she pulled him toward her until their lips touched once more. Kissing Logan was the most stunning activity Faith had ever experienced. It was as if all her desires melted together to create a combustible yearning.

Logan's mouth slowly moved across hers, and Faith melted into him. Her eyes closed as he dragged his mouth across her skin, licking and nipping along her cheek until reaching her ear, where he teased her, eliciting a gasp.

He turned her again, his arm coming across the top of her chest as his other hand moved over her stomach and further down. Faith's eyes flickered open, and she saw the painting staring back at her with an almost curious gaze.

"Do you know how often I've thought about this?" he murmured into her ear, moving his hand to hers.

Gripping her fingers gently with his, he tugged them toward the top of her legs.

She felt both of their hands on her most intimate parts, causing her to flinch.

"Easy," he whispered, stroking her with his fingertips. "I had a dream just like this—of me using your own hands against you."

She bucked beneath his caresses as he continued to lay a string of kisses along her neck. His other arm pulled back across her chest, his fingers softly kneading at her breasts. Faith felt like her bones had disappeared, and she fell against him wholly as his grip tightened.

"Sweet Faith," he said as his hands reached down the side of her thigh, gathering her chemise in his fist, pulling it up over the swell of her backside.

He pressed his hips forward, and though he still was dressed, Faith could feel the substantial weight of his manhood pressed against her. Instinctively, she arched backward, but an uneven chuckle escaped him as he again turned her in his arms.

"Not yet, love," he said, though his voice was husky.

She nodded, pretending to know his meaning, and allowed him to move her back against the bed. As her head fell back against the pillow, Logan knelt in front of her. Confused, Faith tried to sit up, but his long arm held her beneath the sternum, not letting her up.

"But what…" she asked when his mouth kissed the top of one knee and the other in lieu of answering.

It was strange, but she fell back to support herself on her elbows as his mouth moved slowly along each leg.

"Logan," she said, growing more worried the higher he went.

"Let me, love," he asked.

Faith wasn't sure what he was asking, but then he kissed the inside of her hip bone, his tongue dragging across the hot skin before reaching the center of her.

Faith bucked, trying to sit up as a wave of euphoria and humiliation washed over her.

"Logan, y-you can't."

He picked up his head, lust hazy in his gaze.

"I've wanted to taste you since the day you pushed me into the loch."

Faith's mouth dropped open.

"Have you?"

"Yes."

"Why?"

"I have a theory," he said, returning to his work. "Now let me test it."

Faith's brow arched with a question, but the next moment his tongue was… good God, it was inside her, and she was shaking. It was unfair at how easily she obeyed him, but then her body seemed to be grappling with some building feeling that overpowered everything else. It was as though her soul was expanding, and the longer he tasted her, the closer she came to exploding.

"Logan," she breathed, her hands going to his hair to try and push him away. "I can't…I can't…"

But he only continued, holding her hands down to her sides as a torrent of rapture fell over her. Her hips bucked, but he wouldn't be removed, and Faith was sure she might die.

"Logan!"

He stood before her momentarily, looking down at her with fascinated longing. He tore off his shirt, revealing a surprisingly muscular torso scattered with the white scars of former injuries. His muscles, tightly knotted bulges from his arms down, gave her the idea that he must lead a far more active life than she had previously assumed.

However, Faith's courage drained when he went to undo his pants. She turned her head hastily to look up at the star-studded ceiling. When he came over to her, he seemed aware of her hesitation.

"Do not fear, love."

Fear? Was that what she felt? Perhaps, but more than that, she thought she might expire from need, particularly when he brushed against her swollen flesh. Her eyes shut tightly as he pressed into her.

"Here. Give me your hand, Faith."

She lifted her left hand, and he took it, pressing it against his torso and dragging it down his stomach until she felt the warm pillar of his erection. Startled, she nearly pulled away when she heard him gasp at her touch, but he kept hold of her hand, and for that, she was grateful. She needed to lean into his instruction if he was to believe that she was experienced.

But her tightly shut eyes were probably giving her away.

"There is nothing to be ashamed of, love," he whispered, though his breath was ragged, matching her own. "Please don't close your eyes. Look at me."

"I can't."

"Faith," he said, his voice strained. "Look at me."

Her eyes flickered open, and she gazed up into his intense stare. She would never forget the look in his eyes when he pressed into her. A pained gasp escaped her, and he paused, confusion written over his face.

"Faith?"

She nodded swiftly, needing desperately to be filled by him, regardless of the pain.

"Yes," she said. "Please, Logan."

He sank all the way into her, and with a blistering gasp, she absorbed his invasion. He withdrew after a moment, only to push in once more. While the invasion was undoubtedly aching, it was also fiercely satisfying in a way that was unfamiliar and new.

"Faith," he moaned, making her name sound almost like blasphemy. "How can you be so…"

But thankfully, he didn't finish his words, instead focusing on his movement.

Faith noted with gratitude that the pain had subsided. His mouth fell to her breast, and the gentle grazing of his teeth caused her to arch. He licked at the tip of her breast, drawing one into his mouth, awakening a new euphoric feeling emerging from beneath the pain, Faith focused on it as Logan continued to move within her, and soon she was lifting her buttocks up, trying to take as much of his as possible.

"Logan," she whispered, her eyes on his. "I think… It's happening again."

"Yes, love," he whispered, his mouth dropping to her ear. "Come around me."

She couldn't say whether or not his soft command triggered it, but Faith's entire body seized. All too soon, Logan withdrew from her, leaving her yearning and empty. Warm liquid fell like droplets against her stomach before Logan fell bodily on the bed beside her.

Faith watched him as both her and his erratic breathing subsided. He lay on his stomach, his face turned to see her, and for the briefest of moments, Faith wondered how lovely it might be to be in the man's bed for years to come.

She swallowed then, blinking away the thought as she looked back up to the starry night–painted ceiling. It was a foolish and dangerous thought, because she had no intention of staying in Scotland, let alone this house. Nor would she be welcome here once she did what she'd come to do.

Logan's hand reached for hers, fingers intertwining in such a supportive, intimate way that Faith nearly pulled away. A sweet, seductive smile crossed his mouth.

"My God, Faith. How are you so perfect?"

Lost for words, Faith shook her head.

"Don't be ridiculous."

"I'm being honest," he said, reaching for her. She curled her legs up as his arm wrapped around her.

It was early yet, but weighted drowsiness fell over Faith as the warmth from Logan's body sunk into her bones. She closed her eyes, letting herself fall into a peaceful rest for a moment—just a moment.

But soon darkness engulfed her, and she was fast asleep.

Chapter Fourteen

THE WARM, SLIGHTLY ticklish brush of a man's leg against hers caused Faith's eyes to open instantly, and though she did not move, her heart began to beat erratically. She knew exactly where she was and what had happened, but she didn't know what time it was. She had fallen asleep, blast it.

Her eyes shifted up, to see the windows. Darkness. Thankfully, there was still time to go through with her plan.

As slowly as she could, Faith began to shift and slide her body away from Logan, freeing herself from his arm, which was still held her around the waist. All she could do was pray that he slept deeply.

Please let that be the case.

Faith slipped lower, and then rolled gently and painstaking slowly out of his reach. His sudden deep inhale caused her to freeze, but then his breathing evened out and he was once again sound asleep.

Finally at the edge of the bed, Faith stood up, naked. A shiver coursed down her spine as she walked toward the cloak that had been draped across the back of the high-backed chair that sat before the fireplace. The flames had died down and only the glowing embers lent any light to the room. Slipping her hand into the cloak's pocket, the tip of the letter opener stabbed the palm of her hand, causing her to stifle a yelp.

She glanced back at Logan's prone form, which lay undisturbed. Turning back, she carefully picked up the cloak and fished out the letter opener. Once grasped firmly in her hand, she faced the painting and took a step toward it.

This was it. All she had to do was stab it—once, twice, a dozen times, it did not matter. As long as the canvas was punctured, it would be ruined and she would be free. But the longer she stared at it, the more uncertain she became.

It really was a beautifully executed piece. If only Donovan had changed her hair color, or drawn her eyes closer or father apart, or even made her nose smaller, it would have been enough to disguise her identity and she wouldn't have to destroy it.

But destroy it she must, she reminded herself as she took a deep breath.

Faith turned her head a fraction, gazing at Logan as he slept soundly with his face half buried in a pillow. A small part of her heart pinched. He seemed, for once, completely at rest. The constant shadow that haunted his waking eyes wasn't visible in this dim light, and the peace he found in sleep smoothed out the lines of his brow. She wanted to touch his forehead. She wanted to place her lips in between his eyebrows, so that she might remember, many years from now, what it was like to kiss a man she lov—

Oh. *No.*

Faith squeezed her eyes shut and shook her head. That was not what she'd meant to think.

Refocusing on the painting, Faith lifted the silver letter opener in front of her. She had to do this. If she didn't, there would always be something out in the world that could control her.

But a voice in the back of her mind argued with her logic. Logan would never try to use it against her. And it seemed he only appreciated it as a splendid work of art, which it was.

A slight tremor stole over her clutched fingers. She covered them with her other hand as she took another step toward the painting. The tip of the blade scratched against the raised paint of a brushstroke, just at the subject's mouth. She could do it. She *had* to do it.

But a moment passed. And then another. And soon a whole minute had gone by and Faith's arm dropped to her side.

As much as she wanted to destroy it, she couldn't bring herself to do so. Whether it was because she couldn't go through with betraying Logan, or whether it was because of her genuine love and adoration for art, Faith couldn't bring herself to stab it. Which meant that she would absolutely have to go to London now, because she wouldn't be able to bear living so close to this painting. It was too dangerous. Heaven forbid someone within her circle should come to Logan's house and see it, even by accident—they would recognize her, and it would cause a scandal.

At least when it had been in Paris under Donovan's protection there had been a small comfort believing that no one would ever be able to buy it. But Donovan had sold it, along with the last bit of her belief that he cared enough about her to keep it close to him.

Quietly, she replaced the letter opener in her cloak pocket and returned to bed. She would have to leave Scotland for good, and the thought felt suddenly painful. She didn't want to leave her family, or friends, or even Jaco, but it was too much of a liability to stay.

Shaking slightly, Faith tucked herself beneath the covers. Unconsciously aware of her presence next to him, Logan rolled, scooping her into his arms as he pulled her against his chest, leaving her to lie awake in his arms and wonder when and how and why she had ever fallen for Sir Logan Harris.

Chapter Fifteen

A DEEP, ALMOST paralyzing slumber had fallen over Logan after laying with Faith. It had been years since he had slept so soundly, and when he finally woke, he was resistant to open his eyes. He must have reached over to cover them in a blanket at some time during the night, for Faith's naked body was pressed against his beneath a length of warm wool.

Faith's golden-brown curls were spread out along the red counterpane. Logan could smell the heather in her hair as he inhaled. She turned, rolling onto her back as she slept. A small crease between her dark brows told him she was having some sort of difficult dream. He leaned forward to kiss her cheek, then her jaw, and pulled back to see the crease disappear.

God, she was perfection. Their coupling had felt so easy and natural, as if they had been made strictly for one another and no one else. He wanted to kiss her awake and retake her, but remembering that he had fallen asleep before cleaning them up last time, he guiltily pushed the blanket off himself and got up.

Dipping a towel length into a ceramic bowl holding water near his shaving table, he wrung it out and returned it to the bed. Lifting the covers, he felt a moment's remorse at the idea of having to disturb her sleep. She had rolled onto her back and stretched her legs straight, enticing him, when Logan noticed something.

Like strokes from a paintbrush, dark rust stains covered parts of her legs. Frowning, he bent closer. Had she been bleeding? It certainly seemed so, though she wasn't any longer. *Perhaps her monthlies had started*, he thought as he brought the cloth to her thighs. She shivered slightly at the coldness of the fabric, but as he cleaned away the marks, another more unsettling idea came to mind.

Had Faith lied about being Donovan's lover?

No. She hadn't. She couldn't have. It would be preposterous to lie about something so important. Why would she even agree to start an affair with him if she was still innocent? It wouldn't be because she was in love with him, that was for sure. The animosity between them had been palpable from the start.

But why wouldn't this nagging feeling let him go?

He cleaned the washcloth and then returned to the bed, where he resumed washing Faith's legs. The coolness from the cloth caused her to stir, and she rolled from side to side, seemingly trying to fend off waking up. Pulling her legs up to curl beneath her body, her eyes blinked. The tiny crease between her brows appeared once again as her eyes adjusted, and then, in a swift moment of panic, she sat up, her face strained with worry.

"Oh God, what time is it?" she asked, staring at Logan as he sat in the wooden chair. Her eyes dipped to the cloth in his hand. "What are you doing?"

"Cleaning. I passed out before I could do so earlier."

A deep blush covered Faith's cheeks as she avoided eye contact.

"You don't have to. I'm perfectly capable—"

"It's no worry. I'm just trying to take care of you."

"I don't need anyone to take care of me."

Logan let out a frustrated puff of air as he stood up. She was a conundrum, but he had started to believe that they could be at least civil to one another. Watching her wrap her arms around her bent knees, he saw a range of emotions displayed on her face, and he wondered what he had done to upset her. Had he been too rough? He didn't think so. Bumbling maybe, but he hadn't done this in a while. She either, he supposed, for the pain that crossed her face had been…

The pain. It had been painful, yet he hadn't stopped, too consumed with his desire, he supposed.

The realization of it all dawned on him as he stared at her. She avoided his gaze as she huddled herself into a ball.

"Faith," he said as gently as possible, even as a ball of exasperation mounted within him. She refused to look at him. "Darling, look at me."

A pause, and then.

"I don't think can," she said so softly that his heart nearly broke.

He was apprehensive about reaching for her, worried that any physicality might frighten her, but he did long to comfort her, even if a part of him was furious. But he couldn't react with fury. She was obviously worried, and he rarely saw his Faith shaken. Why had she lied to him?

Tentatively, Logan's hand reached out, stroking her exposed ankle. She flinched slightly but did not pull away.

"Love," he began, thumbing the base of her ankle. "Tell me. Tell me that wasn't your first time."

Her eyes lifted at that moment, locking with his, and he felt his heart swell and break all at once.

"Would it be so terrible if it was?" she asked meekly.

Logan's eyes closed as he groaned. He let go of her ankle and rubbed his face with his hands, desperate to try and understand her actions. He couldn't quite accept the idea that she had been so taken with him that she thought to ruin herself this way, so why would she have done it?

"Why, Faith? How could you have done this?"

"Me?" she said instantly, pulling her legs beneath her to kneel on his bed. "You're the one who approached me, lest you forget."

"Yes, and you said—"

"I didn't say anything. You assumed I slept with Donovan."

"And you didn't correct me," he said, his tone agitated. When she didn't reply, he continued. "What the devil were you thinking?"

"What does it matter?" she snapped, holding the blankets to her neck, covering her naked body. "It happened. There's no changing it."

"Yes, but it didn't happen the proper way," he said, leaning over the bed. "You should have told me."

"Why? Then you would have backed out of our affair," she said, her tone peevish. "And I wanted it."

Pride shot through his chest at her words, but he tried to push it away. He was glad she had wanted him so, but it didn't change that he had now taken her innocence. And he intended to do right by her. But she spoke first.

"It doesn't matter, does it? We both got what we wanted," she said, her tone brittle as her green eyes fell to the canvas behind him. "And now I can go to London with an education that other spinsters lack. At least I'll know what I'm giving up."

Faith began to move off the bed as her words sank in. London? Spinster? What the devil was she going on about?

Turning on her as she gathered her clothing, he moved behind her.

"What are you talking about? Why would you go to London?"

Faith straightened up after grabbing her petticoat, standing at her full height before him.

"I'm going to London with Aunt Belle in a few weeks. We will be staying in her townhouse, the one where I lived with my sisters before coming to Scotland."

"For how long?"

"Indefinitely," Faith said as she picked up her overskirt hanging on a wingback chair before the fireplace.

Logan's temper began to rise.

"What the blasted hell do you mean 'indefinitely'?"

"Just that," she quipped as she began to dress.

"Then what was all this about?"

"It was… It was what it was," she said unevenly. "I don't see a reason to name it. There's no need to, as I've no intention of staying in Scotland."

Her eyes shifted to the bed, and Logan's anger began to bubble dangerously high.

"Like hell you aren't staying here," he said viciously through gritted teeth. "You can't leave. Not after what we just did."

"Why?" she asked coolly, though her voice seemed frail. "It was a simple affair and they never last, do they?"

"It wasn't an affair. I took your innocence," he said, reaching for her as she buttoned up her dress.

"Oh Lord, do not call it that," she said shakily, but her eyes would not meet his. "I only wanted… I don't know what I wanted anymore. Except to go home and think, I suppose."

"You're not going anywhere," he said, coming up behind her. "Not until we settle this."

She turned, her body mere inches away from his.

"It's already settled. I will go home, and you will never mention this to anyone. Nor will I and perhaps we will see one another in twenty years and have a good laugh—"

That was it. His hands gripped her upper arms and shook her slightly.

"I don't know what's come over you, but that is not the way any of this is going to go." Faith opened her mouth to speak but apparently thought better of it and shut her mouth tightly. "Now, I want you to sit there," he said, nodding to the wingback chair. "And just relax. I'm going to draw you a bath—"

"Oh, you really shouldn't—"

"And you're going to take as long as you like, do you understand? In the meantime, I'll figure out how to break this to everyone."

Faith's eyes snapped to him.

"Are you mad? We're not telling anyone that you bedded me."

"Well, of course not," he said as she visibly relaxed. "But still, we need to come up with an explanation of some sort—

otherwise, there will be too much confusion when we announce our intent to marry."

The expression on Faith's face was almost comical if it weren't for the fact that she was already shaking her head.

"No. No. Absolutely not, no," she said, trying to break free of his arms even as he held her still. "Let go."

"What are you talking about?" he asked, yielding to her wish. "You couldn't possibly think that I wouldn't offer for you after all this."

"All what?" she asked frantically. "You assumed I had slept with Donovan. Would you be offering if that had been true?"

"Well, no—"

"So, there is no reason for you to do so now."

"I disagree."

"Then we are at an impasse," she said, finally managing to pull away. She got back to work finishing with her dressing. "I will leave, right now, and if you'd like, we will never say another word to one another ever again. I think that seems a fair trade."

Logan's brow scrunched incredulously as she sat in the wing-back chair and reached for one of her shoes.

"Are you suggesting that our coupling can be payment for silence?"

She stood up from tying one of her boots.

"When you say it like that, it does sound rather… Anyway… Um, yes?"

"Absolutely not."

"You're being unfair."

"And you're being ridiculous."

"Look, Logan," she said after finishing her task. "Obviously this isn't what either of us expected and while I appreciate the…chivalrous offer, I must decline."

"I'm not being chivalrous, Faith," he growled, reaching for her again. He held her against him and inhaled. "I want you."

The words fell from his lips almost in a whisper, and Faith's shaky disposition seemed to settle. She looked into his eyes, and

Logan's breath hitched. She really was breathtaking.

"You do?" she asked.

"Yes."

"But… why?"

The tone of her question nearly broke Logan's heart. Didn't she realize who she was? Yes, she was feisty, prickly, and argumentative, but that was just a fraction of her. She was brilliant and beautiful, caring and kind, fiery and formidable. Why, there wasn't anyone in the world that he should like better to marry. And while he'd never intended to marry anyone, the circumstance being what it was, it was the only thing to do.

"What a thing to ask," he said as he bent to press his mouth to hers. "I want you, Faith. Because you are witty and wicked. Because you are argumentative and strong. Because when I think of any part of you, whether it be your eyes or hands or heart, I can't seem to function." He paused, fearing that he had exposed too much. He swallowed. "I just… I want all of you."

He kissed her, and her eyes closed as she turned pliable in his arms. He was already planning what to do with her after her bath when she pulled back slightly and spoke.

"But marriage…"

"I'm not some villain, Faith, despite what you've thought of me."

"I never…" she started but bit her lip, unwilling to finish her thought.

"Now granted, I hadn't considered marriage as situation I would ever find myself in."

"You needn't still—"

"But as I'm not some bastard who uses people, I must propose it." He found her hands and squeezed them. "I'm not a blackguard, Faith, and I can't have taken this from you without doing my duty."

"Your duty?" she repeated, almost as if she were offended. "As what? A solider?"

"As a man."

"You needn't feel obligated."

"I *don't* feel obligated," he pressed, getting annoyed. "I mean, yes, I suppose I do in some ways, but did you not just hear all that I said? I want you, Faith. I want you and I want to continue having you."

Her throat worked up and down, and Logan's mind wandered back to the bed. God, how he wanted her. But she was probably too tender to try again tonight. His hands moved up her wrists, gently rubbing her arms. There were so many other ways he might bring her to ecstasy if only she'd let him demonstrate.

"And if I told you that you could have me as much as you liked without marriage, what would you say?"

Logan paused in his actions, drawing back to stare at her. He wasn't sure why she was being so difficult. All he'd offered was marriage, and she was acting like he was trying to take her right arm. He might be offended if he weren't so damn wild about her, but then a small, forgotten part of his past seemed to call out to him.

Don't beg her to stay.

He had unwittingly fallen into the same situation his father had been in. Pursuing a woman who wanted nothing to do with him or Scotland. But this felt different. Faith wanted him; he knew it. He could feel it in how she reacted to him. But then why was she being so difficult?

Slowly and painstakingly, Logan let her go and took a step back. He would not beg her to stay.

"I would say that is generous. But no."

A flash of shame and fury flickered in Faith's eyes.

"Very well," she said as she gathered her things. "Then I suppose this is goodbye."

"I should escort you—"

"No," she said, seemingly unable to meet his eyes. "No."

Without another word, without even a nod, Faith gave one last, piteous look at the painting that sat behind him and left. Logan let her go, bitter about long-ago injuries from his past. He wouldn't beg her to stay, not like his father had begged his mother.

He wasn't sure how long he stood there, staring at the doorway through which she disappeared, but he was sure it was a long time.

At some point, he got dressed and began his usual haunting of the painting gallery. The longer he walked, the more annoyed he became with the situation. Why had she kept the truth from him? And why was she so determined to leave for London? He couldn't imagine that her sisters were pleased with her plans. As different as the three of them were, Logan knew they shared a deep love for one another, and he doubted they were happy with Faith's desire to go to London.

And why London? He supposed she probably had some friends there, but hadn't she fled that city when she and her sisters had become the subject of some scandal? She might be ostracized upon her return, and what friends she thought she had might refuse to see her. And then what would she do? Go about a solitary life, shunned by polite society? She would grow old all alone, miles away from everyone who loved her.

It was contemptible, and what's more, it made no blasted sense.

The idea of Faith leaving forever made him unreasonably livid, and by the time the servants returned to their duties around noon, he had all but decided to go to Lismore Hall and force her to marry him.

But, of course, that would be impossible. He had always sworn never to want a woman who didn't want him, and now he found himself in that exact predicament. But this situation was different from his father's—or at least that's what he told himself as he readied his horse to venture over to Lismore.

Faith wanted him, he knew it. She felt what he felt. He dared not say what it was, but it was, at the very least worth investigating.

Taking the main road instead of the path around Loch Fyne,

Logan began reciting what he would say to her in his head. She would argue, he was sure, but it didn't matter. He would simply present the situation to her in a way that would—

BANG!

Logan dropped his head instinctively as a shot rang out around him, a flock of blackbirds scattering from the trees. His horse neighed at the loud sound, breaking into a gallop when Logan reined up, turning back.

A hunter, no doubt, who had drifted too far south. But as he searched the dark woods that lined the northern edge of the road, Logan felt the hairs on the back of his neck raise.

BANG!

A bullet whizzed past his ear, and his horse started once more. This was no accidental misfire. Someone was shooting at him on purpose.

Turning quickly, Logan kicked his horse. They took off just as another loud bang sounded behind them. The horse's hooves must have kicked up some rocks, for Logan felt a spatter of weight against his leg as another shot let loose.

Heart racing as he rode at a breakneck speed, Logan's mind went completely blank, his entire focus trained on a single resolution: Get away. He might have gone after the culprit if he had been able to spot him, but the thicket had been impenetrable, and he had no doubt that whoever was trying to kill him had been nestled in the thick bramble.

Who would want to kill him? His mind reeled with possibilities, but he was sure he had never wronged anyone so much that it would inspire someone to commit murder.

He raced away as fast as he could, soon realizing that the shooter must not be on horseback, because no one followed in pursuit. But that didn't stop him. He rode fast and hard to Lismore Hall, arriving just as Graham exited the house.

His friend gave him a questioning expression as he came down the steps. A footman appeared, taking Logan's reins.

"Logan," Graham said, concerned. "What are you doing

here?"

"Someone's shot at me."

Graham's gait stalled.

"Excuse me?"

Logan came off his horse swiftly, fixing his jacket as he did.

"I was shot at. Three times on my way here. On purpose."

"Are you sure?" Graham asked. "It could have been a lost hunter, or a—"

"No. It was intentional. I swear it."

"Come in and tell me more," Graham said, twisting around. "I was just on my way to Glencoe, but it can wait."

"I don't wish to disrupt your day," Logan said. "Besides, the magistrate needs to be informed there's a mad man loose. I would appreciate it if you saw to it that the proper authorities be informed."

Graham nodded.

"Of course."

"Thank you. Now to attend to what I had planned to do today."

"What is that?"

"I've come for an audience with Faith."

Graham, who had been walking side by side with Logan, paused as he entered the house. Graham didn't follow him in, Logan was sure he heard a "Good God, why?" come from him.

The foyer of Lismore Hall was open and ancient. The dark paneled walls and flagstone floors harkened to an older time, unlike Harris House. Faith was undoubtedly in her room, but Logan wasn't so forward as to knock down her bedroom door, so he went directly to Lady Belle's study. The old woman was there, of course, sat at her desk with her faithful Andrews standing guard behind her.

She looked up and blinked, evidently flabbergasted to see him.

"Goodness, Mr. Harris, you're here so much I wonder if you've moved in," she said, sitting back. "To what do I owe the pleasure of your company today?"

"I demand a word with your niece."

"Ah, very good. Which one?" He gave her a tight-lipped stare as she bloody well knew which one. Lady Belle nodded, seeming to intuit that he wasn't in the mood for games. "Oh yes. *That* one. I'm sorry to inform you that Faith is not feeling well. From what I'm told, she had breakfast in her room this morning and barely ate."

"I want to see her. Now."

The tips of Belle's silver brows notched up at his command.

"My, you seem rather hostile this morning. I hope you are not unwell?"

"One tends to be hostile when one is shot it."

"Shot at?" she repeated, genuine concern on her face. "By whom?"

"If I knew, I wouldn't be here. Now will you summon her or do I have to march up those stairs and bang on every door until I find her?"

"Goodness, Mr. Harris, it was not I who shot at you, so I would please ask that you remember your manners." She turned to her manservant. "Andrews, go fetch my niece. Tell her Mr. Harris is here and he's in a frightful mood."

Andrews nodded and left, leaving Belle and Logan alone. A question that had been nagging at him since the previous night burned within him, and he needed to ask her before Faith arrived.

"Lady Belle, something has been bothering me for some time and I wish you would truthfully answer a question for me."

The old woman's expression shuttered.

"Of course," she said evenly, in a tone that made him think she would say anything but the truth. "Ask away, my boy."

"The painting that you suggested I buy from Donovan. *Odalisque Reclined.* You were aware that that artist was a friend of your niece's, were you not?"

Belle did her very best to appear surprised.

"Was he?" she asked, her tone too high to suggest honesty.

"Why, what are the chances."

Logan nodded, not believing a word she said.

"So, you didn't know that Faith had painting lessons with him before she and her sisters moved to Scotland?"

"I knew she had circle of friends in the art world in London, but I could hardly tell you their names," Belle said, her chin rising.

"I see."

Believing that to be the end of it, Logan turned to wait for Faith. But after a pregnant pause, Belle spoke once more.

"I don't think you do," Belle said. He glanced over his shoulder.

"Excuse me?"

"I don't think you do see. Because if any of those friends were to write to me, saying, oh something along the line of how they had a painting that would ruin my darling Faith, unless a certain amount of money was offered to compensate them, I would be most upset, you understand."

Logan watched the old woman with fascination as she stood up and walked around her desk.

"Is that what happened?"

"Of course not," she said, smiling too brightly. "But if it had, I might have had to do something about it, you understand."

Logan considered her confession. That anyone would try and blackmail Faith made his stomach turn; evidently, Lady Belle had felt similarly. She had played the game to save her niece from humiliation, and Logan couldn't fault her for that. But why she had chosen him to be her instrument in safeguarding the painting baffled him.

"But why me?" he asked after a moment.

"You love art, do you not, Mr. Harris?"

"Yes, but Faith and I—"

"You and Faith remind me of another couple that never got their chance to try for something lasting and real." Belle's stare turned wistful.

Logan nearly asked her who she was referring to when

Faith's footsteps sounded behind him.

"What the devil do you... I mean, Mr. Harris," Faith said upon seeing her aunt. Coming fully into the room, he turned to see her. She wore a simple, blue-floral-pattern gown and a stare they could freeze fire. "Hello."

"I'll just leave you two alone," Belle said, moving toward the door.

"Ah, Aunt Belle, you really needn't leave," Faith said, turning to follow her.

"Yes, she does," Logan said firmly.

Faith whipped her head around to face Logan as her aunt closed the door behind her.

"What do you—"

She stopped abruptly; her eyes focused on the ground. He waited for her to finish her sentence, but she didn't. Instead, she bent forward slightly, completely distracted. Confused, Logan looked down as well and saw nothing. Except... Was that a puddle beneath his foot?

She came over to him at once. She touched his leg forcefully and painfully, startling him. "What happened to your leg?"

"Damn it." He cursed under his breath as she stood up. "It must have been that second shot."

"Shot?" she repeated, her tone anxious. "What shot?"

"It seems someone is trying to kill me."

Chapter Sixteen

I NSTANTLY, FAITH TURNED into a nurse. After calling for a maid and sending for Grace, she practically pushed Logan onto the settee in her aunt's study she crouched down and began rolling up his pant leg, ignoring his resistance.

"There's no need to do that."

"Hush," she said, shooing his hands away just as the maid returned with a bowl of hot water and torn linens. "Don't move."

"Well, don't press on it like that."

The sight of blood dripping from his calf sent a chill through her. Who would want to shoot at him? Everyone within a hundred miles adored Logan Harris. In fact, that had been one of the most annoying things about him when she'd first arrived in the Highlands last year. Everyone seemed to fawn over him wherever he went. Whether it was because he was handsome or a war hero, she did not know.

"A fine thing to have happened to you," she muttered to herself as she began to clean the wound.

"It's not my fault someone took aim at me."

"Isn't it? You must have done something to anger someone."

"A fine quality, blaming me for being shot at," he sneered sarcastically.

Faith knew she was wrong to do so, but she couldn't help but slide back into her old argumentative ways. It was like Logan had said during her stay at Harris House. Anger was an easier emotion to feel and express than fear.

"Could it have been an accident? Perhaps you walked into the path of a hunter stalking prey."

"I was on the road. No one in these parts would be so foolish as to stalk an animal so close to a fairway."

"Not even early in the morning, when they had reason to believe the rest of the world was still asleep?" She shook her head as she dipped the crimson-soaked linen into the warm bowl of water. She squeezed it out and continued to wash away the blood.

He leaned forward, causing her to stop her nursing as she looked up into his hazel eyes.

"I wouldn't have been out so early if you hadn't fled from my home like some sort of spooked rabbit." His words were heated and for a moment she thought she saw fear in his eyes. "If the shooting was an accident, then I'm only grateful that it was me who was injured and not you."

His worry for her, even when she was completely fine, echoed in her heart like a hammer striking a horseshoe. Perhaps it was her fault. Oh, why had she fallen asleep so quickly last night? She should have stayed awake, crawled out of his warm, tender arms, and destroyed the painting once and for all. Then he wouldn't have felt the need to chase after her—and wouldn't have ended up on the road, in a bullet's path. But she hadn't been able to bring herself to destroy the portrait any more than she'd been able to resist the urge to fall asleep next to him.

Going to Harris House had been a wasted venture. Though she would cherish the memory of their experience for the rest of her life, she feared the consequences that might come of it. All the more so since she had lost her lucky amber during her rush out that morning. She might not fully believe in the idea of the stone being lucky, but it had been comforting to have something to hold on to. Now that comfort was gone.

And now, Logan was bleeding in her aunt's study, distracting her once more from what she wanted to say.

"What's all this now?" Grace asked as she entered the room,

her eyes widening at the sight before her. "Oh dear. Mr. Harris, you're bleeding."

"He's been shot," Faith said, standing up as she motioned her hands toward his leg. "Fix him, will you?"

"I suppose I should try, shouldn't I?" Grace said, seemingly bemused by Faith's reaction.

A maid hurriedly moved Aunt Belle's chair over, and Grace sat to inspect Logan's leg.

"It's nothing," he said, his tone annoyed. "I barely even realized it before Faith noticed it."

"That's to be expected," Grace said calmly as Faith peered over her sister's shoulder. "Adrenaline can cause muscle extension and a temporary loss of feeling pain." Grace leaned closer to inspect it. "Yes. You wouldn't have noticed, particularly if you were on the run."

"How did you know that?"

"Graham told us," Hope said from the doorway, causing everyone to look in her direction. "He came to see me just before he left for Glencoe."

"Great," Logan said sarcastically, but Faith was suddenly panicky.

"What do you mean, you were on the run?" she asked. "Who was shooting at you?"

"I don't know."

"You must know," she insisted.

"I don't."

"But you must have seen something."

"I just said—"

"Um, pardon me," Grace said, lifting a hand. "I'm afraid I'm going to need to interrupt this squabble. Una?" she said, calling to the maid.

"Yes, my lady?"

"Would you fetch me my sutures? They're in a brown leather bag I have on top of my desk in my room."

"Of course, my lady."

Faith's heart sank at her sister's words.

"Sutures? He needs stiches?"

"Oh, just a few," Grace said, gently cleaning the wound as Faith glanced down.

A crab apple-sized bloody indent showed just at the swell of his calf. It was blistering around the edges, and Faith wince upon seeing it. Logan cleared his throat, bringing her attention to him.

"It's all right," he said quietly.

"Of course, it is," Grace said, seeming unaware of the tender back and forth playing out over her head. "It's a clean wound. No bullet lodged in here. We'll just have it cleaned and tied up as soon as possible."

"Does he…" She began before redirecting herself to Logan. "Do you need anything?"

"A dram of whiskey?"

"Oh no," Grace said. "Alcohol increases bleeding. I won't have you drinking for at least a week."

"A week?" he said, looking down at Grace. "You don't actually believe that, do you?"

"It's true, Mr. Harris. I certainly do not care if you believe it or not. As my patient, I strictly forbid it."

"God save any man who becomes your patient," he muttered as Una returned with Grace's leather bag.

"Faith, dear, come over here," Hope said, standing behind a chair.

Faith glanced at her elder sister and noted the death clutch her fingers had on the chair she stood behind. In fact, her whole face was quite pale.

"What's wrong?" Faith asked, going to her sister.

Hope released the chair and gripped Faith's hand in an almost painful grasp.

"We should leave. There will be blood, no doubt," she said faintly. "Let Grace tend to it."

"But I can help," Faith argued.

Grace turned around and gave them both a concerned look.

"Faith, can you escort Hope back to her room, please? I don't want her to faint and I've my hands full at the moment."

"Faint? Hope has seen blood before," Faith said somewhat stubbornly. "She tended to Graham last year when he was shot."

"Yes, but in her current condition, I believe the sight of blood will make her sick. Now will you please remove her?"

Grace's words fell on Faith slowly as she looked at Hope and then back at Grace.

"Her condition?"

"Oh, please keep it quiet," Hope said, her breathless tone suddenly worrying Faith. "If Graham… If Graham finds out, I'll… I'll…"

"Take her away *now*, Faith," Grace ordered.

With a shared look of confusion with Logan, Faith turned and guided her sister out of the room. Within moments of leaving, Hope seemed to feel better, and by the time they reached her rooms, she had even gained some color back in her cheeks.

Faith was sure to handle her with care as she brought her into the room, where Hope sat on the edge of her bed before looking up sheepishly.

"I'm sorry I did not tell you sooner," she said quickly before Faith could ask a question. "But I've been trying to keep it secret, you see. If Graham were to discover it, I'm afraid he would become unbearably overprotective."

"Why did you tell Grace then?" Faith said, unable to keep a slight hurt out of her voice.

Hope shook her head.

"My dear, you try keeping a medical condition away from that girl. Besides, she was the one who informed me, actually," she said. "I thought I had a head cold."

Faith smiled then, unable to stop herself. Of course Grace had guessed. It would be foolish to assume they could purposely keep a medical secret from her. She squeezed Hope's hand.

"A baby. I can't even imagine," she said softly. "Does Aunt Belle know?"

"I didn't tell her, but that woman has a knack for knowing everything about everyone at all times," Hope said.

"When will you tell Graham?"

"Soon, most likely. It will become obvious to everyone before long."

"Oh, Hope," Faith said, feeling suddenly emotional. "I'm so happy for you."

Hope smiled warmly at her sister.

"I guess you can understand now why I was so against you leaving for London. I didn't want you to be away from me during this time." She looked down. "But I guess that was rather selfish of me, wasn't it?"

"Selfish? Goodness, no, Hope. Had I known, I never would have even suggested it."

Hope perked up.

"So, you won't be going to London?"

Faith's smile became strained as she thought about her question. She had more reasons to stay than go, but the biggest reason to leave was sitting downstairs in Aunt Belle's office.

It wasn't that she didn't like him. In fact, the opposite was true. She found that she had come to enjoy their back and forth. It was ridiculous, but the constant, simmering heat between them had become something she looked forward to. But then he had proposed and ruined everything. It was purely out of obligation, and she couldn't bear it.

"You should rest," she said, avoiding the question. "I really should be helping Grace. I'll have Una bring you some tea."

"Thank you," Hope said as she lay on her bed.

Faith returned to the study just as Grace cleaned her hands with a damp cloth.

"Well, then, Mr. Harris. I'm afraid your pant leg is ruined. As talented as I am with sutures, I'm a sight worse with embroidery." She said, smiling at her little jest as she stood up. "But you should heal up just fine. I'd keep off the leg as much as you can for a day or two—and as I said, no drinking any spirits for at least a week. If the wound becomes red or raised, send for either myself or Dr. Barkley."

Logan peered down at his torn pant leg.

"Thank you, doctor," he said, causing a blush to stain Grace's cheeks.

"Oh, well, yes," she stuttered before turning to Faith. "I'll leave him in your capable hands then. If you'll excuse me."

Faith was left alone with Logan, who appeared unaffected by his injury. In fact, he looked almost bored, as he stared at the opposite wall. Turning her head to follow his eyes, she saw that he was gazing at her grandmother's portrait.

"Who is that?" he asked, nodding at the painting. "She looks familiar, but not all at once."

"My grandmother, the late Lady Alice Sharpe," Faith answered. "She was Aunt Belle's sister."

"That's it," he said, more to himself then to her. "She's been painted rather sternly. Not quite as smiling as Lady Belle."

"Well, she was rather stern."

"Is it a true likeness?"

"I believe so."

He glanced at Faith.

"Is it yours?" he asked, which unfortunately caused Faith's cheeks to warm. His brow lifted. "It is, isn't it?"

"How did my sister do at stitching you up? You certainly seem well," she said, coming forward as she ignored his question. "Was it painful?"

"No doubt you wish it would have been." He peered back at the painting. "It's a good portrait."

"How would you know?" she asked, her tone tinted with humor. "You never met her."

"Why should that matter? I never met Elizabeth I, and yet I have a portrait in my gallery that looks just like her." Faith frowned. "I think you tend to be hard on yourself when it comes to your artwork."

"I don't... That's not..." She tried to ignore his observation.

"But you are. Take for example this portrait. You were able to convey her character through it, weren't you? The colors are smooth, and the shading is particularly impressive." He glanced at her. "I think I would commission you to paint my portrait, if you weren't leaving for London."

Faith hated that she should be so pleased with his observation as well as his flattery, but the reminder of London gave her pause. Unsure how to accept his praise, she turned the subject back to his wound.

"Are you sure you're not in any pain?"

"I'm sure. I'm quite used to cuts and scrapes, you know."

"Are you?"

"Yes," he said with a nod. "I suffered a number of injuries aboard the *Medusa*, though nothing serious."

"Was the *Medusa* your ship during the war?" she asked, coming to sit next to him.

"Yes."

"Jeanne told me her husband was lost on that ship," Faith said slowly, unsure why she even mentioned it. Surely it was a sensitive topic, but then she was curious. "I can't imagine that it was easy for you."

He gave her a cautious look before speaking.

"We were told it was a liberation mission. That the sitting government was a tyrannical one, and we were saving the people from despotism—but the truth was we weren't even supposed to be there. We were used by the East India Company to further their business interests. But I was a soldier with a job to do.

"Duncan had been ill for nearly a week before we were attacked. We were ambushed from both sides of the river without warning. A stockade was set ablaze, smoking choked out the space between the riverbanks. We were desperate to get out of there, but before we could escape, Burmese soldiers began to board the ship.

"I had been a part of several skirmishes at that point, but this was different. The unrelenting heat, the lack of visibility, and impending dread made it feel like we fought for hours. Before I knew it, the ship had been freed, and we could withdraw. Nearly every man made it that day…except Duncan. He had only just returned to duty from the sickroom below decks, and he was struck right at the start of the ambush, causing him to fall overboard. His body was never found."

Faith stared at him, suddenly understanding why he refused to use his title.

"And you think because Duncan was lost, you don't deserve your knighthood?"

"I don't," he said plainly.

Faith heartily disagreed, but Logan's countenance told her now wasn't the time to argue. Instead, she changed the subject.

"Why are you here, Logan?"

He gazed up at her, his unfairly handsome face making her heart flutter as he did so.

"I came, because you and I have unfinished business."

"We do not."

"We do," he said, shifting slightly. "Why are you so determined to say no to me?"

She looked down at her hands as they folded together in her lap.

"I don't understand why we must make such a drastic, life-altering decision when if I hadn't been…" She shook her head, unsure how to word it. "All I mean to say is, you needn't feel required to offer."

"My feelings on the matter are not relevant. It's what needs to happen."

"That's where you are wrong," she said, standing. "I'm not going to be anyone's burden, Logan. I've no desire to be connected to you for the rest of our lives simply because we made the mistake of—"

"Mistake?" he scoffed as he stood, wincing only slightly. "There was no mistake, you stubborn fool. I want to marry you."

She shivered at his words, embarrassed that she was so satisfied to hear them. But she didn't want to be pleased by his words. She wanted to be free of him for good. It seemed that the only way she could be was to tell him the truth.

"You may not still feel that way after hearing my confession." His gaze turned dark, but she continued when he didn't speak. "I only came to Harris House... because I wanted to destroy *Odalisque Reclined*."

Faith didn't dare look up at him as the room filled with silence. She knew how bad it sounded; what an absolute, conniving person it made her to say it out loud. She decided that this was it and that she would confess all her sins now.

"When I sent you that note, to meet me at the Lismore Hunting Lodge? I knew Hope and Graham ventured there weekly at that precise time. I wanted us to be nearly caught, to prove that Harris House was the only place we could truly have an affair, but you wouldn't budge. So, then I invited you to Loch Fyne, knowing Grace needed to gather medicinal herbs for Dr. Barkley. I invited myself on her outing, knowing that we would be caught and hoping that the experience would prove that Harris House was the only place we could be together, solely to gain access to that painting." Faith paused and squeezed her eyes shut. "You see, Logan? I'm not someone you should want to marry."

A long pause followed. Faith anticipated a loud shouting match, but he spoke quietly after what felt like days.

"Was everything a lie?"

Her head snapped up, and she saw the bitter pain in his face.

"No," she said desperately. "I do have feelings for you, but I've deceived you—and all for..." She shook her head. "You don't know what it's like, to have a painting that displays every bit of your insecurities. It displays a time in life when I was at my most vulnerable. I was so sure of myself when it was painted, so glaringly unaware of the mistakes I was making. I've only myself to blame for the broken heart I had at the end, but I could not simply move on, the way other people do after heartbreak. No, there is a massive shrine to my idiocy—"

Instantly, she was in the strong bands of Logan's arms as he squeezed.

"You're not an idiot, Faith," he said softly, savagely. "You just…"

She nodded as a tear fell down her cheek. She knew she had wounded him. She had lied and hurt him because she had been lied to and hurt, and it wasn't fair.

To her surprise, Logan let out a strangled breath and released her. Turning, he walked out of the room, leaving her alone.

Convinced that she had finally ruined her chances with him, Faith turned and followed him out, watching as he headed to the front door without a single look back. She stared at the door for a long time after it closed behind him, wondering how long the ache in her heart might last this time.

Chapter Seventeen

A SEARCH PARTY to find the shooter had been organized by Graham and the McTavishes, but no one in the search party could find hide nor hair of him. It would seem that a ghost had shot Logan, if not for the stitches in his calf that proved otherwise. Much to his displeasure, he promptly passed out upon his return to Harris House later that same day and did not take part in the search party.

His father and Arabella were shocked to hear about the shooting when they returned from Glasgow the following day. Arabella, in particular, was emotional about the entire thing. She even insisted on inspecting his injury but promptly turned away after just a glimpse of it.

His father had remained quiet. Guessing that the man didn't know what to say, Logan concluded that his father wasn't particularly interested until later that night when Logan found him in the family parlor.

Arabella had long since gone off to bed, but their father was seemingly wide awake, pacing before the marble fireplace. Logan hadn't seen him walk like that in ages. While Arabella had said that their visit to Dr. Hall had been successful, he doubted that his father could have made such a quick recovery.

When the old man noticed he was no longer alone, he paused and looked up at Logan. The two stared at one another for a moment before his father broke the silence.

"You are well?" he asked, his voice shaken.

Logan frowned, unnerved by his tone.

"Of course. I have suffered far worse than this." He kicked out his leg. "It's barely a scratch, really."

His father shook his head and focused on the floor before him. Logan assumed their meeting was concluded when his father spoke again.

"You know, I worried about you in Burma," he confessed, startling Logan. "Every day, I prayed for your safe return."

"I know, Father."

"No, I don't think you do," the old man said. "Every day when the mail came, I was petrified to open it. I always made sure to leave before it was delivered so that on the off chance that there was word of your death, I could live a few more hours believing that you were alive."

Logan stared, almost dumbstruck. Why was he confessing all this now? Unsure how to answer, Logan came to sit partially on the arm of the sofa that faced the fireplace.

"I didn't know that."

"Of course you didn't. I never told you."

"What I mean to say is, Arabella never told me that."

"She didn't know either. Or at least, if she suspected it, she never betrayed my confidence," he said, looking into the fire. "She is the spitting image of her mother, you know. But at the same time, she is nothing like her."

Logan shifted uncomfortably. They hadn't broached the topic of Logan's mother in years. If he had been feeling combative, he might have disparaged her, but his father seemed thoughtful at the moment, and Logan wanted to see where their conversation might lead.

"I remember Mother's face," Logan said. "Arabella's cheeks are rounder."

"Your mother's were the same, in her youth."

"Arabella smiles easily."

"Your mother did once."

"Arabella's here," Logan said, startling his father into looking directly at him. Shame slammed into him, and he cleared his throat. "But I suppose Mother was once."

"No," his father said suddenly, surprising Logan. "Your mother was never here, even when she was. She was always longing for London. I might have kept her, had I gone with her."

Logan frowned.

"I never realized that was an option."

"It wasn't, really. There was no job in the city of London for a man of my abilities. Or even if there was, I didn't belong in England, so far away from family and friends. I told her so over and over but she couldn't comprehend it. She had been disowned by her family, you know, for running away with me, but she was convinced her uncle would pay our way, if we asked. Only I couldn't bear to live on an allowance. I was too proud—and my pride lost her," he said, glancing at Logan. "She wanted so much to raise you both in London, you know."

Logan stared at his father, unsure how to continue.

"Did she… did she try to take us when she left?" he asked. It was a question he had always wondered.

His father exhaled slowly.

"No. When she informed me that she was leaving, I begged her to stay. I tried everything—even, as shameful as it is, to use you and your sister as collateral. I told her if she left, I'd never share either of you." His brow creased as emotion flooded his expression. "I didn't mean it. I was only trying to hurt her. But then she left and I never saw her again."

Logan watched his father, unsure how to respond. How was he supposed to handle all this information? And why was his father telling all this now after all these years?

"Did you ever try to contact her?" he asked.

"Yes. Dozens of times, but she never responded."

Logan nodded absently.

"Why are you telling me all this?"

His father's eyes met his.

"I know you think I'm ready to die. That I've moped about

this house for too long, wallowing in my own self-pity. And perhaps I have. But to learn that you were shot at, seemingly on purpose, after I thought I had been freed from the fear of you being killed on the battlefield, well…" He shook his head, seemingly uncertain. He took a deep breath and continued. "You've come through so many battles, scratched and bruised, yet you never seem willing to give up."

Logan felt the back of his neck warm up. He hated praise, which nearly always felt insincere to him… but coming from one's father, it seemed entirely different.

"I just wanted you to know that the day you came home from Burma was the greatest day of my life."

Logan's entire body stiffened, not used to the expressive words from this man who had ignored life for so long. His throat constricted as he tried to respond.

"Thank you," he said pitifully, but his father only smiled.

"Arabella tells me that you've given up on me. It's all right. I don't blame you. I've not given either of you any reason to believe in me. But I think, I'd like to try and live a little bit longer, if only to see if I can."

Logan nodded, rife with emotion. He was suddenly eternally grateful for being shot if it meant his father now wanted to live.

"All this, because I was shot at?" he asked, unbelieving.

"Well, that and your sister told me while we were in Glasgow that if I insisted on dying a pitiful death, she'd toss me into Loch Fyne."

Logan let out a startled laugh.

"She did not."

"She did. Evidently, our sweet Arabella has a temper."

"If she does, I've never seen it," Logan said. "And she must have the longest fuse known to man."

"Well, it seems it's solely reserved for her father," the old man said with a chuckle. He shook his head. "Now, may I ask you something?"

"By all means."

"Why is there a portrait of Miss Sharpe in your room?"

Logan's entire being stalled, as if he had just been caught doing something wicked. His eyes met his father's. The older man was giving him an unreadable look.

"How do you know about that?" he asked numbly.

"One of the servants mentioned it to me, not long after it arrived. I believe it came to light during Miss Sharpe's illness, while you were away. It seems the sheet that you've been covering it with had slipped and before they could recover it, it was noted that the piece looked rather like Miss Sharpe."

"So, one of the servants thought she looked like the model in the painting. That is their opinion. Art is subjective and there are only so many ways the Lord can arrange two eyes, a nose and mouth," Logan said, his tone defensive.

"I see," his father said, which for some reason, irritated Logan.

What did he possibly see? Nothing, to be sure, yet Logan wished to hear his opinion on the matter for the first time in a long time. But in the same breath, he wouldn't betray Faith's confidence.

What was he to do?

"Well, it has been a trying day. I think I'll try to get some rest tonight," his father said, moving around Logan. "You should try and sleep too."

Logan nodded as his father patted his shoulder. Then, abruptly, he turned and spoke.

"Would you have forgiven her anything?" he asked. His father turned back, a questioning look on his face. "Mother, I mean. If she deceived to you, would you have forgiven her?"

"I would," he said slowly. "Even now, I think I might forgive her after all these years."

"Because you love her?"

A gentle, near heartbreaking silence followed before his father nodded his head.

"Yes. Because I love her," his said. Glancing up, he gave Logan a small smile. "Goodnight."

"Goodnight," Logan said as his father moved passed him.

For a long time, Logan didn't move as he absorbed his father's confession. Even now, after all these years, the old man was still willing to forgive his wife everything. Logan couldn't decide whether he was a romantic or a fool. Deciding on neither, he exited the room and climbed the stairs toward his bedchamber.

Upon entering his room, he saw the painting, shrouded in a sheet as it usually was. Stalking toward one of the chairs, he began unbuttoning his vest when his foot landed on some object.

Stepping back, Logan looked down to see a near-black stone laying on the ground. A piece of debris tracked in on his boots, perhaps? He almost ignored it, but then he noticed that it was almost perfectly round.

Reaching his hand down, he picked it up. The light of the fire caught on it, causing a honey glow to shine in his hands. Instantly, his body froze.

No. It couldn't be.

A small hole had been carved in the middle, perfect for stringing it on a length of leather. It was impossible. How in the world had his piece of amber, lost with Duncan in a river in Burma, found its way back here?

Picking up his head, he looked around the room, almost expecting Duncan to appear. But he was alone. As he inspected the stone once more, he noted a series of scratches and even a little chunk missing. Perhaps this wasn't his stone.

But a part of Logan seemed so sure about it, that he kept it on his nightstand all night.

When morning came, Logan tucked the piece of amber into the pocket of his vest and wrapped up Faith's painting with brown paper from the kitchens where Jaco had been sleeping. The dog stretched and followed Logan to his room, where Logan tied the paper around the painting with twine. He ensured it was doubly secure, even though it would only have the short journey to Lismore Hall.

He'd intended to give it to her since she'd first asked him to destroy it. While it was a masterpiece, he knew it could never be truly his. It should belong to no one but her. And if she chose to destroy it once it was in her possession, that was her right.

He wrote a quick note, and upon daybreak, he and the dog found Evans.

"I want it delivered to Miss Faith Sharpe first thing this morning," he said. "No one is to see it and you are not to leave until it is in Miss Sharpe's care. Do you understand?"

"Yes sir," the butler said as they exited the front door.

Several servants had been instructed to carry the heavy work of art into the carriage. Logan had instructed four servants to help bring it to Lismore.

"Will you be coming, sir?" a footman asked. "I brought your horse around."

"No, I don't think so," he said.

Logan noted that Evans was staring off into the distance, apparently distracted. He called out to him.

"Oi, Evans," he said as the butler turned. "Do you mind?"

"I'm sorry, sir, it's just... There's a man on a small horse over there," he lifted his index finger to the tree line. "Watching us."

Logan approached the butler, staring in the direction he was pointing at. There, sat on the Connemara pony Sweetness, was a man wrapped in a black overcoat and battered hat. He was too far away to make out his face, but Logan felt the sick tickling of instinct in his stomach. He knew this man, somehow.

The grave warning of Jaco's growl reverberated throughout the small group. The man on the horse turned abruptly, hurrying away up the path that led around the northern route of Loch Fyne. Jaco started barking, jumping back and forth between the runaway and Logan as if waiting for his response. Instinctively, Logan turned and jumped on his own horse.

"Deliver the painting to Lismore Hall at once," he said before taking off, with Jaco close behind.

"But, sir!" Evans called after him, yet Logan was already

halfway across the field.

Whoever this man in black was, Logan knew that this was the man who had shot him. As the sting in his calf throbbed, Logan increased his speed. The forest-carved path weaved in and around pine trees as the ground turned steep. The Connemara was too small a horse to outrun him, and he was hot on the trail, coming up toward an open field beneath the mountain.

The assailant turned back momentarily before steering his steed to the right, heading for the old, abandoned stone crofter's house—the perfect place for a crook to hide.

All too quickly, the man jumped off his horse and ran around back. Sweetness took off briefly before circling back, unsure where to go. Logan was quick to jump off his own horse. Stalking toward the back side of the cottage, he'd just stepped through the doorless walkway when the cocking of a gun echoed around him.

Logan froze as his eyes adjusted to the dark room. It was empty, save a few knocked-over chairs and a broken table with a stack of stones used for one leg. In the corner near the hearth were some rags, possibly being used as a bed? But who would choose to live in such a place?

"By the grace of God and Her Majesty," a dark, eerily familiar voice sounded behind him. "Sir Logan Harris."

Cold dread slithered down Logan's spine at the sound of that voice. It was impossible. Outrageous, even. Only in his dreams had he heard that voice.

It was the voice of the dead.

Taking a deep breath, he lifted his hands, aware that a gun was most definitely pointed at him. Turning as slowly as possible, Logan tried to ignore the erratic thumping of his own heart. His eyes landed on a disheveled mess of a man. His red hair had been cut unevenly as if done with a dull blade. His clothes were filthy and torn, and upon closer inspection, weren't black at all, only covered in dirt and grim. A white scar cut up across his left eye, down his cheek, but as the man sneered at Logan, he saw the man he once knew.

"Duncan?"

"Didn't expect to see me again, did you?" the raspy voice spoke, chilling Logan.

Jaco's growling drifted in from one of the broken windows. With a single, smooth motion of his arm and a dead stare, Duncan turned the pistol out of the house and pulled the trigger.

A piercing boom echoed throughout the tiny space, and Logan instinctively covered his ears, but not before the faint whimpering of a dog caught his attention. Turning on the shooter, he nearly attacked, but then he saw that he'd missed his opening, for the gun was once more pointed directly at him.

"Now," Duncan began, leaning back against the stone wall, "I have several things I want cleared up before I shoot you dead."

Chapter Eighteen

F AITH DRESSED SLOWLY that morning, still as despondent as she had been when Logan left without a word two days prior. She knew it was her own fault, that Logan was probably appalled with her and her plot. It was just as well, though, she concluded as she headed to breakfast. It had become too easy to believe that Logan was the type of man who might actually care about how she felt. He had come dangerously close to her heart, but he had proven that he could not love her beyond her faults, so it was best now to put the entire thing behind them.

If only she could.

Downhearted, she went to the dining room, where her entire family was gathered for breakfast. Aunt Belle and Hope discussed fabrics, and Grace was reading a book, as per usual. Graham was in the corner, frowning heavily as he examined something with their head groom, Daughtry.

"Concerning indeed," Graham murmured as Faith walked by to make herself a plate from the breakfast buffet.

Though there were at least a dozen dishes to choose from, from strawberry tarts to poached eggs, bacon, sausages, puddings, and the like, Faith felt she could only manage toast. Taking two slices, she brought her plate to the table, where both her sisters and aunt looked up. Noting the spartan food choices, they peered at her with concern.

"Faith?" Hope said.

"Hmm?"

"Are you feeling well?"

"Yes," she said in a monotone voice as she scraped a bit of butter against the bread.

Though she didn't look up to see, Faith sensed her aunt and sisters were sharing a concerned look. But it didn't matter as Graham spoke to the room before anyone could press her further.

"Thank you, Daughtry," he said as the head groom left. He turned to address the family. "I've some unfortunate news for everyone, but I don't want anyone to panic."

Of course, at the word "panic," everyone turned, anxious to hear what he had to say.

"What is it? What's happened?" Aunt Belle asked.

"There's been a theft from the stables," he said, his gaze flickering to Faith. "Sweetness was stolen last night."

"Stolen?" Hope said. "Are you sure? Couldn't it have simply run off?"

"No," Graham said, shaking his head. "The harness and bridle had been cut and an empty bottle of scotch was found near the grooms' room."

Faith frowned while Belle let out a laugh.

"Someone pickled the grooms before robbing them?" she asked. "They might have earned that horse."

"Belle," Graham said, his tone one of warning, but the old woman rolled her eyes.

"Was Sweetness the only one who was taken?" Grace asked.

"It would seem so—for now, at least. I'm going out with Daughtry to try and track her."

"Is that safe?" Hope asked, standing up.

It was sweet to see how concerned she was for Graham. Where most men might tell their spouses that there was nothing to worry about, Graham was always the sort to be honest.

"Possibly not, but we can't have horse thieves running about the Highlands, can we?"

"But what if it's the same man who shot at Mr. Harris?" Hope asked, reaching him.

"I assure you, love, that if someone is willing to shoot me dead for a Connemara, they wouldn't make it far."

"Be that as it may, a stray bullet can find anyone by chance."

Graham moved his hand to the back of Hope's head and pulled her toward him, giving her a comforting kiss on the forehead.

"Worry not, my love. If there's any pressing danger, we'll manage it."

"But—"

"Hope," he said, his tone gentle in its command, and Hope snapped her mouth shut. "Thank you."

She didn't answer as he left the room, seemingly more put out than usual. When she retook her seat around the table, Faith leaned toward her.

"You haven't told him then, have you?"

Hope glanced between her sisters and aunt as they all patiently awaited her answer.

"No, not exactly." All three ladies sighed and leaned back into their chairs, making Hope sit up defensively. "It's not that easy."

"Why not?" Aunt Belle asked. Evidently, she knew Hope's secret too. "I'll give you that men aren't the most attentive sort, but any talk of a baby should make them focus."

"Graham is plenty attentive, thank you very much," Hope said, quick to defend her husband. "It's just that I don't know how he will feel about it."

"Well, I'm sure he will feel happy about it," Grace said, looking around the table. "It's nature, isn't it? The goal of all males, in any species, is to reproduce. I believe he will be plenty pleased by this news."

"Yes Grace, compare him to giraffe or an egret," Faith said sarcastically, eyeing Grace.

"I didn't mean it like that," Grace scowled.

"He's going to be thrilled, my dear," Aunt Belle said, giving Faith a lightly chastising gaze. "Absolutely thrilled."

"Yes," Hope said, unsure. "I hope so."

Faith took a bite of her toast, grateful to have any sort of distraction from her own worries. It seemed everyone was just about to return to their meals when Andrews, who was standing next to the doorway, turned. With a nod, he took a step forward.

"Mrs. Jeanne Carlyle," he said as Jeanne entered the room.

Dressed in a cream-and-brown gingham riding habit with a matching tam-o'-shanter, Jeanne smiled broadly as she came swooping into the room.

"Good morning, my friends," she said as everyone turned to look at her. "What's this? So much gloom for so early in the morning. I hope there is nothing in the tea that's turned your stomachs?"

"Of course not," Belle said, waving a bejeweled hand at an empty chair. "Please. Join us."

"I've already had my breakfast," she said, turning to Faith. "Are you ready?"

"Oh dear, were we set for lessons today?"

"Yes. Don't tell me you forgot."

"Not exactly, but I'm afraid lessons won't be possible today," Faith said, picking up her teacup. "Sweetness has been stolen."

Jeanne's smile fell away.

"A horse thief? In these parts?" she asked, unbelieving. "That's preposterous."

"It's true," Hope said. "And Graham and several of our grooms have gone to try and track him. Much to my dismay."

Jeanne looked back and forth between Hope and Aunt Belle.

"Do you think the man who shot at Mr. Harris just two days ago is the same one who stole the horse?"

"Well, it certainly wasn't a faodail," Faith said, more to herself than anyone, as she sipped her tea.

It was a throwaway comment. She had grown to enjoy the Gaelic terminology, and she seized the excuse to use the newest word she'd learned. But when she cast her eyes on Jeanne, her cheeks had turned ghostly white, and she was staring at Faith with eyes as round as saucers.

"What did you say?" she breathed, her tone barely above a whisper.

Faith gave her a curious look as she gently set her teacup down.

"Did I not use that correctly? I thought I did," she said, noting her sisters' confused stares. "It means lucky find, doesn't it? I meant that Sweetness wasn't just found, was she?"

"Where did you learn that term?" Jeanne asked, taking a trepid step toward Faith.

Faith looked back at Jeanne, puzzled at the intensity in her voice. She noted that the others were watching their exchange with interest.

"Mr. Harris taught it to me," she said honestly. "Just the other day."

Jeanne blinked once, then twice before her shoulders dropped. She shook her head and inhaled slowly.

"Oh. Of course," she said. "Of course."

"Well, not exactly," Grace said, leaning forward. "We heard that voice by the loch, didn't we?"

Faith nodded at her sister.

"Yes, that's true. I only asked Mr. Harris what it meant later—"

"What voice?" Jeanne asked suddenly, coming fully up to Faith before crouching before her. "What voice called that out to you?"

The urgency in Jeanne's eyes gave Faith an unsettling feeling as Jeanne gripped Faith's hand on her lap. She squeezed it.

"There was this… this voice," Faith said, shaking her head and looking back at Grace for assistance. "A man's voice. Grace and I heard it when we went to the loch one morning to pick herbs. And…"

"And what?" Jeanne asked desperately.

"And I heard it other times, as well—during Aunt Belle's birthday party and once when I was out walking alone," Faith said. "It sounded like someone was calling out to me, but I wasn't sure what he was saying. It wasn't a word I had ever heard before. Fortunately, when I spoke it to Mr. Harris, he explained what it meant—though he said it can also be used as a term of endearment. I guess it's comparable to darling, or sweetheart, or—"

"My love," Jeanne whispered, her eyes glazed over with some forgotten memory.

Almost instantly, she stood up, releasing the death grip she had on Faith's hand.

"I have to go. If you all will excuse me," she said, turning on her heel, nearly knocking into Evans, the butler from Harris House.

Evans? Faith stood up just as Jeanne tore out of the house.

"What the devil was that all about?" Aunt Belle asked, but Faith's focus was on the butler.

"Evans?" she said, coming toward him. "What are you doing here?"

The man bowed.

"My lady, we bring you a gift from Sir Logan," he said, waving his hand behind him. Three strapping young servants brought a large, rectangular package wrapped in brown paper and twine.

Faith's heart beat erratically as they placed the piece on the ground before her. Had he sent the painting to her? Or was it something else?

No, she thought, coming toward it. *This could not be anything else.* Her shaky hands reached out as she moved the tips of her fingers over the rough paper. He had given her the painting. He had given her *Odalisque Reclined*.

She could barely believe it. He had been so adamant about keeping it. He had even made her consider not ruining it simply because it truly was a masterpiece, regardless of the subject matter. The artist in her didn't wish to hurt it, but her pride wouldn't let go of her. It had been the most critical thing in the world to her, and now that it was finally hers, she felt only slightly relieved.

For now, the thing that mattered most to her wasn't here.

"This is a most puzzling morning," Aunt Belle said as a chair moved noisily against the flagstone floor somewhere behind Faith. "What is it?"

"It's nothing," Faith nearly croaked, spreading her arms wide to shield them from it.

After a moment of silence, Belle spoke.

"A most puzzling morning indeed. Andrews? See to it that this package is brought up to my niece's room, at once."

Andrews nodded to his mistress and directed the other servants to carry the piece out of the dining room. Faith looked at her aunt, who seemed to know what was beneath the paper.

"It was very generous of Mr. Harris to, er, gift you, one of his paintings," she said firmly, her eyes flickering to the others.

In an instant, Faith knew what to do.

"Yes, well, he is a great collector," she said diffidently. "I am most appreciative of his kindness."

"Oh, is it the horse painting?" Grace asked before turning to Hope. "There was a dreadful horse painting in Harris House that is apparently very valuable to artistic folk. I didn't like it much, but then I don't know about these things."

"Is that so?" Hope said, turning to Faith. "How kind of Mr. Harris."

"Yes, and I should like to inspect it at once. If you'll excuse me," she said, leaving the dining room in haste.

Faith followed Evans, Andrews, and the footmen up the staircase as they carefully carried the painting to her room, which overlooked a swan pond that Aunt Belle had installed years prior. Once they set the work of art up against the far wall, Faith thanked them as they began to file out, resuming some previous discussion.

"...Shall we alert Mr. MacKinnon about Sir Logan going after that curious character, then, Evans?" a footman asked over his shoulder to the butler.

"Yes, immediately," he answered, giving Faith one last nod. "Good day, my lady."

"Oh, um, Mr. MacKinnon is out, I'm afraid," she said as the butler and footmen paused. "He went out this morning to trail a thief."

"A thief, my lady?"

"Yes. My horse, Sweetness, was taken during the night."

The butler's dark eyes widened slightly.

"Is that so?" he asked before turning to the footmen. "We have to return to Harris House at once."

A pebble of worry settled in Faith's stomach as she looked at all their faces. Something was wrong.

"What's the matter?"

But before Evans could open his mouth, a muffled barking could be heard from outside. Turning, Faith hurried into her bedroom and looked out the window.

Along the stone block edging of the swan pond, Jaco was barking and jumping erratically back and forth, scaring the pair of swans clear across to the other side. She swiveled around to look at Evans and waited, staring at him expectantly.

"My lady, a man appeared this morning, on the edge of Harris House lawn. He was dressed in black and appeared to be riding your Connemara."

Faith's brow scrunched.

"A man dressed in black riding Sweetness? Are you certain?"

"Yes. Sir Logan took off after him."

Her eyes widened.

"Did anyone follow him?"

"No, my lady."

"Why?"

"He ordered that we were deliver this to you first and foremost. But we will begin our search now, my lady." He dipped his head and disappeared out of her bedroom.

Faith watched them leave before returning to watch Jaco jump and bark almost frantically. With one last look at the wrapped painting, Faith gathered up her skirts and rushed down the hallway to her sister Hope's room, which had a staircase leading from its balcony down into the walled garden. Faith rushed across the room, through the French doors, and down the stone stairway, before running through the garden to the gate.

"Jaco!" she said in a loud whisper.

The dog instantly stopped his barking and jumping. He cocked his head in her direction and, upon seeing her, came rushing over. Faith was kneeling immediately, petting, and rubbing the dog's fur.

"There's a good boy," she cooed, scratching his head. "Good boy. Where did you come from?"

She scratched behind his ear, and he whimpered suddenly, dropping his front paws from her lap. Concerned, Faith pulled her hand back and noticed a slight red on her fingers. Was that blood?

Peering down at Jaco, she moved her hand gently over his head. One ear was in excellent condition, but the other had the most minor of curves cut into his flesh.

"Oh, my good boy, what happened to you?" she asked.

Faith heard the footmen's carriage pull away as a sinking dread settled in her heart. Was Logan injured? Looking behind her, she knew she could get through the forest and to Loch Fyne in minutes. Turning back to the dog, she made a decision. It might be reckless, but then she didn't much care at that moment. Graham wasn't home, and she refused to endanger either of her sisters. If she alerted anyone else to her plan, such as a servant or groom, they might try to convince her to stay put, so she decided it would be best to go alone.

"Where's Logan, boy?" she asked, and the dog's head perked up. "Where is he? Can you lead me to him?"

Jaco barked once, then again before taking off around the garden's stone wall toward a grove of pine trees that edged the loch's eastern shore.

Faith gathered her skirts into her hands without looking back and took off running after him.

Chapter Nineteen

LOGAN STARED ACROSS the small, dirty cottage at a man he had long believed dead. Never in his life would he have guessed that Duncan Carlyle was alive. Even as he stared at this shadow of a man, thin and gaunt faced, a part of Logan was sure that his eyes were playing tricks on him. How could he be here? And why was he so hell-bent on killing him?

Well, that at least was to be expected. Logan had abandoned him in the jungle, and now, apparently, he was back to exact his revenge. Guilt had been Logan's constant companion these years since his return from Burma. But now Duncan was back, and everything in the world seemed to flip onto its side.

Logan stared into the bloodshot eyes of a man he had once considered a dear friend, and curiosity got the better of him.

"How are you here, Duncan?" Logan asked. "What happened to you?"

A bitter sound escaped the man's chest. He spat on the floor but kept his unnerving, cool glare on Logan.

"I'm guessing you never thought you'd see me again.

"No. I thought you were dead."

"Well, sorry to ruin your day," he said, clicking the gun back. "But some fools just can't stay dead."

Logan shook his head, not sure what he meant.

"Duncan, I never wanted you to die. If you knew what hell I've been through since that day—"

"What hell *you've* been through?" Duncan shouted, cutting

Logan off. "I should love for you to know one day of *my* hell."

Logan nodded, aware that he had no right to compare their experiences.

"Then tell me, Duncan. What happened?"

"Well, I was shot, wasn't I? But I think you remember that, don't you?" he asked, his tone acrimonious.

"I do," Logan said slowly. "You had come up from below deck. You had been sick."

"I was still sick," he barked. "Sick as the devil on ice. My head… throbbed," he said, his eyes shifting as the memory came over him. "And I couldn't see, couldn't think. I was on death's doorstep, I was. Then, by the grace of God, I was shot. And you know what? I was grateful. Grateful to finally have a release from the pain and the damn drumbeat in my mind."

Duncan's free hand reached the side of his head, and he pressed it into his temple as if still experiencing the pain. Logan's eyes shifted around the room, searching for anything he could throw at the man to knock the gun out of Duncan's hand, but only a few chairs and torn blankets lay scattered about—none close enough for him to reach.

"I was so sure of death, that when I awoke, I was convinced I was in hell. The heat was unbearable. It was as if someone had tossed me into a fire. I later learned that my fever had returned, due to an infection this time. Supposedly, I was bedridden for six or so months."

"You don't know how long it was?"

"I was a prisoner," he snapped. "No one told me anything. They only kept me alive as collateral, but a poor Highlander doesn't pay much ransom. When the war finally ended, they kicked me out of the town without anything. It took me weeks of walking through the jungle to find a port and then another month or so to work for passage to Australia."

"Australia?" Logan said. "Why?"

"Because passage to Britian was too expensive and I was weak. I couldn't work as fast as I had before the fever and I had to sleep along the wooden boxes and crates that lined the docks. By the time I reached Australia, I was flea-infested and half my former size."

That was true. Duncan had always been a mountain of a man, but he was now rail thin, with sunken cheeks and dark circles around his eyes.

"But why didn't you inform someone of your rank and troop? As a prisoner of war, surely the British government would have found you passage home."

Duncan laughed.

"Is that what you think? When has anyone ever cared about a half-dead solider months after an unpopular war has ended? Even if I did retain any of my former clothes or items, do you think I was the only poor bastard, wailing on the docks about my woes? No one cared. And worse, if you complained, you could get passed over for work. So, I kept my head down and fought and stole and begged for work until I could reach Australia."

Logan's stomach turned at the thought of Duncan, battered and filthy, living on the streets in a foreign land, knowing that no one was searching for him because everyone believed him dead. Logan felt as if he should have known, should have handled it somehow. But he pressed forward.

"How long were you in Australia?"

"Two whole years," he said, his eyes drifting momentarily. "It was hotter than sin there. Worse than the jungles. At least in the jungle, there was water in the air. Australia was dry, and it was relentless. For two years, I dug ditches. It was the only work I could get that paid steadily, and every penny went into my ticket home. I didn't even have enough to post a letter home. All I wanted was to be home again."

The wistfulness of Duncan's voice turned suddenly savage as he refocused on Logan.

"And then I returned to find that you had betrayed me."

Logan was sure Duncan's hatred of him was valid for leaving him in the jungle, but he frowned at his accusation. How had he betrayed him here, at home?

"Do you mean the knighthood?" Logan asked, shaking his head. "You have to believe me; I did not want it."

"No, not the bloody knighthood," Duncan snapped. "I mean Jeanne."

Logan stared at him.

"Jeanne?"

"Yes, my Jeanne," he said, his rage barely contained as he shook his head. "I knew I was damaged. Broken. Scarred," he said, gesturing to his face. "I knew I was coming home a pathetic imposter of who I had once been, but she is still my wife and I had hoped…" The emotion in Duncan's voice seemed to break, and he brought the gun up to his head and began hitting himself in the forehead with it. Pity flooded Logan's chest, and he stepped toward Duncan, but the gun was quickly turned back on him. "Stay there!" he barked, now shaking.

"Duncan, I don't know how you came to this conclusion, but Jeanne and I have never—"

"Don't lie to me!" he shouted. "I saw it with my own eyes, Logan! My own damned eyes."

Logan couldn't help but feel aggravated that he should be accused of something so ridiculous. Duncan knew perfectly well that Logan had never fancied Jeanne, not even before the war. He took another step forward, the gun be damned.

"Then perhaps you lost your sight in Burma as well as your sense," he yelled back. "Because I've not laid a finger on Jeanne, ever."

"I saw the two of you together, multiple times. You, all preening and pathetic and my Jeanne wrapped in the cloak I gave to her before we left."

"What are you talking about? What cloak?" Logan said before it dawned on him.

Faith's cloak. *Jeanne's* cloak.

He recalled the Carlyle plaid that trimmed the cloak Faith had borrowed time and time again so that she wouldn't be recognized by anyone seeing her from afar. With Jeanne being a widow and so heartbroken about her husband's passing, neither Logan nor Faith considered that anyone would look twice if they saw Jeanne roaming the countryside.

But someone had seen, and it had been her own husband.

Realizing the mess he had made, Logan lifted his hands as the distant sound of horse hooves vibrated through the dirt floor.

"Duncan, I swear to you, that wasn't Jeanne."

"You lying son of a bitch!" he said, backing up to peer out of the window. Someone was close.

"It wasn't Jeanne, I swear to it," Logan insisted.

"Stop lying to me!" he shouted as a form appeared in the doorway next to Logan.

Windswept, copper-colored hair was the first thing Logan saw. Jeanne stepped into the house, her eyes on him before something close to a choking sound came from Duncan. She turned her head and made an equally unsettling noise before freezing.

A wash of pain, longing, and disbelief passed over Jeanne and Duncan's faces as Logan glanced between the two. He felt almost rude for being in their presence during such a tumultuous reunion.

"Oh God," Jeanne whispered, shaking her head. "The devil's come to trick me."

Duncan's eyes were intent on her. Jeanne took a step forward, but Duncan raised the gun higher, keeping her away. She stopped immediately.

"Stay back," Duncan said, his voice distraught and cracking.

"Stay back?" she repeated breathlessly. "Faodail, me?"

"Aye," Duncan said, seething. "You."

Logan spotted a half-burnt log sticking out of the fireplace. It might be enough to distract Duncan before he wrestled him to the ground. He looked back at Jeanne, who had tears in her eyes.

"Do you not recognize me?" she said, her hands reaching before pulling back. "It's Jeanne."

"I know you… And I know it wasn't your fault," Duncan said, glaring back at Logan. "He's a predator, he is. No doubt he would have shot me himself eventually just to have you."

She tilted her head, her brow creased as tears rolled down her cheeks.

"What are you talking about?"

"You've been laying with this one," Duncan said, pointing the gun at Logan for emphasis. "I know you have—there's no use denying it."

Jeanne's eyes went wide.

"Excuse me?"

"I've been watching it for weeks," he snapped all his attention on Jeanne. "You can't tell me otherwise. I've seen it with my own two eyes."

Logan felt their precarious position become more dangerous. Jeanne's breathing became short. Then, she scowled as her cheeks turned as red as her hair, and she took yet another step forward.

"Duncan Carlyle, what the devil is the matter with you?" she spoke hotly. "You dare accuse me of being unfaithful? Of lying? When you've been home for weeks without telling me? Without coming to me or your family? And now you're holding me and your best friend at gun point?"

"I…" The question seemed to stump him, as if he couldn't quite connect the practicality of her words to the present situation. "I thought you might…" Duncan rubbed the butt of the gun against his temple, an expression of agony on his face. It was obvious that he was unwell.

"Thought I might what, Duncan?" Jeanne asked.

"That you might not like what I've become," he said, looking at her. "I've done things… Terrible things, Jeanne."

For a moment, the old Duncan was staring back at them. Jeanne had always been the only person ever who could scold Duncan into shame.

But that had been years ago. Duncan shook his head, unwilling to be spoken to this way. He lifted the gun a fraction, and

Jeanne's advance stalled.

"But I know what I saw!" he shouted, his pained tone echoing throughout the small cottage.

Logan knew that Duncan was unsettled, but Jeanne was visibly aggravated. She seemed unaware of how dangerous a man with a gun could be.

"I've not touched any man since you left, you daft fool," she hissed, though she didn't advance. "And may the devil take me if I'm lying."

"It's true, Duncan. Jeanne wasn't the one wearing that cloak."

"Cloak?" she repeated. "What... You mean, my cloak? I haven't seen it in weeks. I thought I lost it."

"That's not true," Duncan said, more to himself than to them. Both hands came up to the sides of his head, and he started hitting himself again. "You're both lying."

"My friend, you are not well," Logan said with his hand outstretched, coming forward. "Put down the gun and let us take care of you."

"If I put it down, you'll just kill me," he said, his eyes closing in obvious pain. "This blasted banging..."

"I should kill you for pointing that at me," Jeanne said hotly.

"Jeanne, *please*," Logan pleaded.

"What?" she said, frustrated. "He'd do better to turn it on himself, because when I get a hold of him, I—"

"You are not making this any easier!" Logan shouted, and Jeanne's mouth snapped shut.

Edgy about the situation at hand, conflicted over what to do next, Logan was momentarily distracted when he heard a low growl nearby.

Jaco?

In the next instant, two figures appeared in the doorway, one tall and the other short. The shorter one charged through the door and leaped up, attacking Duncan, who fell backward as the gun went off. Everyone ducked as the bullet when through the thatched roof. Duncan yelled out in pain as Jaco's jaw latched onto his arm. Logan had to physically pull the dog off Duncan.

In seconds, Logan had the gun in his possession. He jammed it into his coat pocket as a miserable and bleeding Duncan clasped his arm to his chest. Logan thought to tie his injury up, but Jeanne had thrown herself onto Duncan.

"You daft, stupid, foolish man!" she said as she peppered his dirty face with kisses. "Oh, I could kill you!" she said as her hands touched his face, holding him tenderly. "I love you and only you, you miserable idiot!"

"Jeanne," he said, wincing. "I've missed you so."

Logan turned his back on them to give them some privacy. He did not envy Duncan's position, as Jeanne would likely prove a terrible nursemaid, but at the very least, Duncan was finally back where he belonged.

Lifting his gaze, he saw Faith standing in the doorway, looking frightened at all she had witnessed. Sheer elation filled him at the sight of her, followed by terror that she should have come to a scene of such danger. Grabbing her wrist, he pulled her out of the house and into the clearing behind the cottage.

"What the blasted hell do you think you're doing here?" he snapped as he twirled her around to face him. "Have you any idea how much danger you just walked into?"

Faith, surprisingly, was at a loss for words. She only stared at him and then back at the cottage.

"What..." she began. "What in the world..."

But Logan's blood was pumping furiously as the adrenaline began to subside. His anger and panic at the situation caused him to react without thinking.

"What could have possibly possessed you to come out here?"

Faith blinked, then frowned as she stared up at him.

"I was worried," she answered honestly, nodding over his shoulder. "Jaco was bleeding and agitated, I thought something happened to you."

"You didn't think to call on Graham? Or someone else?"

"He wasn't around," she said defensively. "So I came myself."

"Of all the foolhardy things you've done," he said, shaking his head in exasperation. "You might have been hurt."

"He was pointing the gun at you, not me."

"It could as well have been you."

"But it wasn't."

"It could have been!"

"Well, I don't see what the point of it all is now."

"No, you wouldn't," he continued. "Because you don't seem to realize that if something happened to you, anything at all, that would be it for me. I wouldn't know what to do."

Faith's eyes widened at his confession.

"Excuse me?"

"I," he thundered before his voice dropped. "Damn it. I…"

Faith's hand rose to the center of his chest. His skin tingled beneath her warm palm, and he tried to push past his insecurities.

"You what?" she asked gently after a moment.

Logan looked into her green eyes, the same that had aggravated him, aroused him, annoyed him, and excited him. His hand came up to her cheek.

"I love you," he said gruffly, feeling more exposed than ever.

To his pleasure, the tips of Faith's mouth curved up, and she took a small step forward, leaning against his solid frame.

"You do?" she asked, her tone amused.

"Yes, although I should probably have my head examined, like Duncan in there—"

Without warning, she reached her hands up, grabbed either side of his face, and pulled him into a desperate kiss.

Suddenly, everything that had once been so important in his life ceased to matter. His nightmares, his anxieties, his mother's abandonment, hell, and even his art collection paled compared to his desire for Faith. She was the most important person in his entire world, and he wasn't sure how he would convince her to marry him, but he would try.

The rumbling of horse hooves galloping toward them barely distracted Logan long enough to pull away from Faith as Graham and several grooms thundered across the open field to where they stood. Jeanne and Duncan came out of the house at that moment, with Duncan wrapped in a hole-filled blanket and Jeanne pressing a dirty rag to his forearm. His other arm was wrapped tightly around her shoulders.

"Logan!" Graham said as he and the others came to a halt. "And Faith? What are you doing here?" He glanced around from on top of his horse, and when his gaze landed on Duncan, his mouth fell open. "Duncan Carlyle? It can't be."

"It is," Jeanne said lovingly, looking up at her husband with a tear-stained face. "He's finally come home."

Graham looked back at Logan, who shook his head.

"Our horse thief and shooter," he said before quickly adding, "but he is not well. He needs a doctor. Whatever damage he's caused, I will take care of restitution personally."

"Well, the horse is clearly right over there," Graham nodded. "Besides shooting you and cutting a few leather straps, I don't think he's wanted for much of anything."

"Good," Logan said, tightening his own arm around Faith. "Then let's bring him to Harris House. And call a doctor."

Graham gave him a nod and swung off his horse. He helped Duncan to Jeanne's steed, and once the both of them were on its back, he instructed his grooms to take Sweetness home.

"Faith," he said after everything had been settled. He eyed her and Logan with interest. "I think you should come home too."

She nodded and started to draw away, but Logan pulled her into a kiss before she left his arms. Faith gasped but then melted against him until he broke off, settling her away from him. He glanced at Graham who was frowning.

"Logan," his friend said with warning.

"I'll see her back."

"Now, wait just one moment—"

"Please, Graham?" Faith pleaded, sinking back into Logan's arms. "Please?"

Her brother-in-law was visibly annoyed, but after a long pause, Graham smirked and shook his head.

"An Englishwoman then, Logan?" he said with a friendly taunt.

Logan gazed back at Faith and smiled.

"Aye," he said. "An Englishwoman, indeed."

Chapter Twenty

O NCE LOGAN DEPOSITED Faith at her family home, he left to return home to see to Duncan. Faith knew the responsibility Logan felt for his friend, so while she wasn't particularly pleased to be left behind, she understood that he needed to be there for Jeanne's husband.

"I'll send word later tonight," he said, kissing her hand after she climbed off his horse.

Jaco seemed perfectly content to stay behind as his master left. Hope, Grace, and Aunt Belle all watched in stunned silence from the doorway as Logan rode off. Turning to face them, she saw a flood of questions just waiting to be tossed at her. Immediately upon entering Lismore Hall, they began interrogating her.

"What in the world was that about?" Grace asked.

"Where's Graham?" Hope asked. "And why did Mr. Harris kiss your hand? I thought you loathed one another."

"What is that dog doing here?" Aunt Belle asked, eyeing the animal as it trotted in behind them, cutting in front of the matriarch.

Faith led them into the parlor and explained at length what had happened. She told them that Duncan was alive and had mistakenly believed that Logan and Jeanne had been secretly meeting. When they began to ask why he had thought that, Faith tried to avoid the explanation. Thankfully, Aunt Belle ordered a break in the story so that they could take tea.

Unfortunately, Grace couldn't hear the rest of the story as a messenger arrived from Harris House. She opened the letter and read it immediately, her brow bunching together as she did so.

"What is it?" Hope asked, standing up.

"Is something wrong?" Faith asked.

"It seems Dr. Barkley is feeling unwell and is unable to attend Mr. Carlyle. Dr. Hall has requested my presence to attend."

"For a dog bite?" Faith asked, confused.

"No," Grace said, looking up. "There seems to be another issue besides the bite." She looked around. "I must go at once."

"Of course, dear, of course," Aunt Belle said as Grace hurried out of the room. She turned to Faith and Hope. "Now what are we to do?"

For the rest of the day, all three busied themselves with nonsense. Hope took to her sewing, while Belle sat at her desk, working. Faith however, couldn't bear to sit quietly in her aunt's office and decided to retire to her room, where she was able to bandage Jaco's ear up. The big dog whined the entire time and fell asleep on her bed afterwards.

Once she finished with that, she went to the desk that sat before the window. Her hand moved gently over several paint brushes, as well as the unfinished canvas that stood on the easel next to her desk. Deciding that there was nothing better to do, she sat and worked on the landscape painting of the loch that she had begun weeks ago.

For several hours, Faith painted as she tried to sort out everything that happened. Logan loved her and to her surprise, she found that she loved him too. She regretted not telling him so.

When no news came by suppertime, Faith decided to put away her paints and crawl into bed. She soon drifted to sleep.

When Faith opened her eyes the next morning, she saw Grace enter her room. Jaco, who had followed her to her room last night, began to growl.

"Jaco, stop," Faith muttered into her pillow.

"Good morning," Grace said, her eyes puffy from sleep. "It's time to wake up. Things are happening."

"What things?" Faith asked before sitting up quickly. Jaco, sleeping on the bed behind her curled legs, stood up, stretched, and then jumped down. "Grace. You're back."

Her sister smiled.

"Will you get dressed?" she asked.

"What happened? What took you so long?"

"I'll not repeat myself again," she said warily. "Come along. The family is in the parlor."

With Una's help, Faith dressed in a daffodil-colored morning gown. Una seemed to take her time brushing and styling her hair. After what seemed like ages, Faith was finally set free, and she hurried to the parlor, followed faithfully by Jaco.

Upon entering the room, Faith saw her sisters, Aunt Belle, Graham, and Logan, waiting for her. Logan stood the furthest away, leaning against Aunt Belle's desk as the others spoke. Jaco hurried over to him and was rewarded with a scratch behind the ears. Faith found it hard to keep her eyes off him. There was a buzz in the air. Feeling uncomfortably like she was the last to know something, she slowed.

"Ah, Faith, coming here, my dear," Aunt Belle said, patting the spot next to her on the sofa where she sat. "Grace has some news."

Faith's brow lifted quizzically as she sat next to her aunt.

"News? What news?" she asked.

"Well," Grace said, stepping toward the middle of the group. "Everyone here knows that I've been trying to garner entrance into any medical school that might take a woman. Unfortunately, I've not been accepted." She smiled brightly as Faith looked around, noting that the others seemed just as confused. "But none of that matters, as I've been recommended by Dr. Barkley to shadow Dr. Hall in Glasgow as his assistant."

Faith's chin dropped as Hope came forward. Both sisters crowded Grace.

"Oh, darling, that's wonderful," Faith said, gripping her hand tightly. "Dr. Hall has permitted this?"

"In a roundabout way," Grace said, her eyes dropping a fraction. "Dr. Barkley informed Dr. Hall that he is to mentor me over the next six months, during my time in Glasgow."

"And what power does Dr. Barkley have over Dr. Hall to command him this way?"

"It would seem as though old Miss Fletcher is actually Dr. Hall's aunt and she has quite a lot of influence on him," Grace said, a proud smile coming to her lips. "Supposedly, he is the one who keeps her in such stylish gowns. And for whatever reason, she has insisted, quite ardently, that her nephew grant me a six-month commitment."

"How fortune for you, indeed, my dear," Belle said, her silver eyes twinkling with delight and possibly mischief.

"It is. And I will offer my thanks to Miss Fletcher and Dr. Barkley at once for using their powers to coerce Dr. Hall into agreement."

"But are you certain you wish to do this?" Hope asked, concerned. "A professional life for a lady is… Well, it's not done often."

"No, it isn't. And it can be very difficult," Aunt Belle said as she peered back down at her. Then, she winked. "But I believe if there was anyone ready for such an adventure, it would be our Grace."

Grace smiled.

"Thank you, Aunt Belle."

"But who will go with you?" Hope asked, still worried.

"Well," Grace said, nodding toward Logan. "Mr. Harris had the suggestion that his sister, Arabella might accompany me, if," she said, turning back to Aunt Belle, "we have a chaperone. That way I can work with Dr. Hall and Arabella can enjoy the social side of the city." Her expression turned pleading. "Would you be able to chaperone us, Aunt Belle?"

The old woman stood up and clapped her hands together loudly.

"Why, what a brilliant idea, indeed!" she said, giving Grace a kiss on the cheek. "I would love too. Oh. Except," she turned to Faith, "I've a prior commitment."

Faith stared at her aunt and then at Logan. Heading to London had been the idea, but since she had concocted that plan, everything had changed. Gazing over at Logan, Faith suddenly felt as if all eyes were on them.

"If I could," he started, reaching for Faith's hands as he came forward. "I was hoping that I might convince you to stay in Scotland for just a little while longer."

"Just a little while?"

Logan smiled.

"If I say forever, will you hold it against me?"

Faith giggled, ashamed that her eyes felt suddenly wet. She turned to face her aunt.

"I..." she started before shaking her head. "Aunt Belle? Would you mind terribly if we don't go to London?"

Belle gave her a gentle smile.

"Of course not, dear," she said before turning to Hope. "And now I believe it's your turn to share some news?"

Hope swallowed visibly, gave everyone a short nod, and turned to Graham.

"Well, since everyone is sharing. I... um, we, actually..." Hope stumbled through her words as Graham's hand came to rest on her arm.

"What is it?"

"We..." Hope said, her cheeks turning bright red. "We are... Expecting."

Graham frowned ever so slightly as if he didn't understand.

"Expecting?" he repeated. "Expecting what?"

"You know," she said.

For a fraction of a moment, it seemed he *didn't* know, but then Graham's entire face changed.

"Are you..." Graham started, but in the next instant, his arms were wrapped tightly around Hope as he twirled her around.

Just as quickly, he put her down and gingerly touched her

stomach. It might have been inappropriate in front of everyone, but as it was just family, neither Graham nor Hope seemed to mind.

"Are you alright? Can I do anything?" he asked, almost frantic. "Do you feel well?"

"Yes, yes," Hope said, laughing.

As everyone congratulated Graham, Logan pulled at Faith's hand, and they stole away to the corner of the room. Logan spoke softly to not have the others hear.

"I was hoping that you might have a different answer to my previous question," he said, rubbing Faith's knuckles with his fingers.

"Previous question?" she asked, tilting her head.

"Yes," he said, smirking. "I'm sure you remember."

"Would you mind refreshing my memory?"

"Minx," he said. "Very well. Would you marry me, Faith?" She opened her mouth to answer, but he immediately spoke over her. "And not because we've been together. Not because of any reason other than the fact that I love you."

Faith's smile spread across her face.

"Yes. Yes, I would like that very much."

"God, Faith… Come, let's ask Belle for her blessing," he said, but as soon as they turned toward the others, they noticed that Belle already had a steady eye on them.

"If the best laid plans of mice and men all go awry, it's because no one ever let a woman take charge of a situation," Aunt Belle said smugly.

"What does that mean?"

"Only that the world would be a far more organized place if women were in control," she said, smirking. "Who else could facilitate two relationships within a year, all on her own?"

"Wait," Hope said. "You certainly meddled in my and Graham's lives, but I don't think you can take credit for Faith and Mr. Harris."

"Can't I?" Belle said. "I'm very well connected, my dears.

Wealthy and determined. I promised your grandmother that I would marry you three off, and marry you off I shall."

"But that's impossible," Faith said slowly. "Unless the painting…"

"The painting was the easy part," Aunt Belle said with a wink.

Faith's eyes widened as she stared at her aunt.

"But there isn't any possibly way that you…" Faith said, her face falling. "Unless you somehow knew…" She turned to look at Logan. "Did you—"

But he was shaking his head, holding his hands up.

"I didn't know."

Faith whipped around to her aunt.

"Aunt Belle, how on earth can you claim to have orchestrated all this? It's impossible."

"If there is one thing I've learned in all my years, it's that nothing is truly impossible," she said with a wink. "Besides, I would do anything for my girls."

"Still, there's no possible way—"

To stop another quarrel, Logan pulled Faith into his arms and kissed her firmly in front of everyone. Faith's ire began to melt away and she wrapped her arms around Logan's shoulders. Jaco barked happily at them as they broke their kiss, smiling and laughing down at him and then at everyone else. Yes. This was where she belonged.

Faintly, Faith heard Belle speak.

"Who says fairytales don't exist?"

Through Jaco's barking, Faith barely registered Grace's response.

"I don't know about fairytales," Grace answered. "But matchmaking two out of three of your nieces is quite successful. Unfortunately, I think your talents will fall short for me, as I have no intention of ever marrying anyone."

And just as Faith's kiss with Logan ended, she heard Aunt Belle quietly retorted, "Oh, but my dear, you're next."

The End

About the Author

Matilda Madison lives in the Pocono mountains of Pennsylvania. A history lover, she finds immense joy in knowing useless facts, exploring the woods around her home, and drinking copious amounts of tea. When she's not writing, she can be found researching obscured periods for her books, refurbishing old furniture, and baking.

Catch up with me anytime on my socials.
Website – www.matildamadison.com
Instagram – matildamadisonbooks
TikTok – @matildamadison